The Flower COTTAGE

A Novel

— MARY FLYNN —

Author site: *www.MaryFlynnWrites.com*

Cover art by Michael Butler
Michael by Design, Graphic Design Services,
www.TorqueCreativeLLC.com

ISBN 978-1-7328380-6-2

DEDICATION

For my cousin Theresa Kunkel

"*Non est ad astra mollis e terris via*"

"*There is no easy way
from the earth to the stars*"

— Seneca

OTHER BOOKS BY MARY FLYNN

—•—

— FICTION —

Margaret Ferry

Wishbones and Other Short Stories

— POETRY —

As One Delighted

— NON-FICTION —

Disney's "Secret Sauce"

The Little-Known Factor Behind...
The Business Wordl's Most Legendary Leadership

— CHILDREN'S —

Reggie & Rocky

The Ring-tailed Raccoons

Reggie & Rocky

The Naughty Raccoons

— MIDDLE GRADE —

Mrs. Peppel's Pillows

OTHER PUBLISHED WORKS

—•—

The Saturday Evening Post Anthology of
Great American Short Fiction

14th Annual Writer's Digest
Short Short Story Competition Collection

Acknowledgements

I would like to acknowledge the individuals who both influenced the creation of this story and contributed greatly to the tone and texture of the tale. Jack Yerk, whose hotdog stand became a center of our young teenage lives in the early mid-fifties; Mr. Piro, whose fabulous apple orchard served as a guiding landmark in our daily wanderings through the Long Island woods; the book vendor at The Nassau Farmers Market, whose fifteen-cent Perry Mason novels captivated us on many a lazy afternoon in our hiding place under the trees; my Aunt Tessie, who fed us the best tuna fish sandwiches I've ever had along with great summer night suppers; as always, my editor Marsha Butler at Butler Ink, and my graphic arts designer, Mike Butler at Torque Creative graphic design, for his fabulous covers and layouts; and most of all to my cousin Theresa, with whom I spent many of the best summer adventures of my life and without whom I would never have happened upon the flower cottage.

Chapter One

Long Island, New York, 1953

ABIGAIL SWEET WATCHED the cortege make its way to the exit of the cemetery like a long, black curl drifting amid the flanks of sycamores. The last of the mourners but hardly the last of the mourning, she thought, turning her gaze back to the gravesite that she and Ben had picked out only a few years earlier. Now, here they were—one of them anyway—and much too soon. Oh, Ben. Ben. She wanted to cry out, but remained silent. Not even a tear. Everything was different and she was too outside of herself to make sense of it.

"Breathe. Breathe with me. Breathe." Over and over, she thought of those last words whispered in desperation until words and breath were exhausted. How quickly a life can be over. How easily a marriage of twenty-seven years can come to an end. The doctors were kind; she knew they had done all that was possible. And then the altar with its veil of smoky incense drifting above the casket. Now this.

Funny, the things you remember from the darkest moments—the water stain on a ceiling tile, the clack of someone's hurried footsteps in a hospital corridor. Amid the worst of it, the light-hearted chatter at the nurses' station outside the ICU, the sober muttering among police and staff dealing with a wounded robbery suspect. Ordinary things don't stop just because an ordinary life is about to.

The thoughts that tumble recklessly through the mind—regrettable things, disappointments, unfulfilled dreams and plans. Maybe it's best that way. It balances the blissful memories of love and joy and beauty that make it impossible to withstand the devastation.

Oh, Ben, my darling, there was still so much we wanted to do together. She was thinking of that beautiful hawk near the river trail where the magenta phlox appeared ghost-like in the early morning fog. All his magnificent photographs she had turned into paintings. And then the book they would never be able to finish. They had put their hearts into it, labor of love that it was. She felt guilty—he had always been the cheerleader with endless support and encouragement. Always so modest with his special gift for helping young aspiring hopefuls find their way. *Oh, how I wish I had done as much.* Having lost all sense of time, she sat staring off. *Is any of it still possible?*

Abigail Sweet watched the afternoon shadows peel away the sunlight from the freshly mounded grave and pondered the finalities of death, wondered about this far-from-ordinary existence taking shape before her eyes.

Chapter Two

One Year Later

"PLEASE TELL ME this isn't happening, Edward." Kate got to her feet, waiting for an answer from the man who until a moment ago had been her boss.

Professor Edward Darian leaned forward, hands clasped in front of him on his desk. He didn't look up. "I wish I could, Kate. I really do, and I'm so sorry. This is all about budgets and funding not at all about anything to do with your performance. You've been among our top professors. But there were expenses we had to curb, and although it often doesn't seem to make sense, you know it's true that faculty is typically the first place they look for cuts."

"They? What do you mean 'they'? You're on the Board, Edward. You couldn't speak up for me? Didn't my performance count for anything? Our friendship? At least, that's what I thought it was."

"Of course, it was. It is," he said.

"You would think the awards I've received over the years testify to my excellence as an instructor. The dozens of grants I've been awarded on behalf of the school." She felt as though she'd been run through with a long dull knife, leaving a hole from which her energy, heart and spirit were gushing out like a punctured water balloon. She was, after all, suddenly and inexplicably out of work. Out of work. Sole provider with a mortgage and now an ugly black smudge on her previously pristine curriculum vitae. She sat back down to face him across the desk. "Edward, I'm a year away from tenure."

"I know, Kate. I know. But my hands are tied."

"Did you even say anything on my behalf, for all my hard work, my loyalty?"

"The Board was…is…very sorry about it, but adamant. I'm just one voice."

They sat in silence for a long, tense moment. Then. "What about the others?" she asked, her tone as flat as her ego. "How did they take it? Being terminated, I mean?"

"Others?" Darian moved in his chair. "Oh…you know… no one is ever happy when something like this occurs."

"Was Lonny…as shocked as I am?"

"Lonny?" He had lost eye contact again, rolling a rubber band back and forth around his thumb and index finger. "Well…"

Kate narrowed her eyes. "Wasn't Lonny Kagan let go?"

Darian rose and went to the window, making a sweeping gesture to the vista of rolling hills and stately turn-of-the-century buildings. "The cuts were, you know, across the entire campus. Lonny wasn't in the mix at this time."

"Not in the mix?" Kate got to her feet and went behind Darian's desk to where he was standing. "Lonny Kagan, who's been here a little over a year and hasn't gotten through a single semester without a crisis? Assistant Professor Kagan who would have already been thrown out on his ear from any other institution for his improprieties? That Professor Kagan?"

Darian lifted his shoulders in a slow begging shrug, still without looking at her, and said nothing.

"Who then?"

He hesitated, cleared his throat and almost inaudibly said, "One from Grounds. The Polish woman in the cafeteria."

"Are you kidding me?" She pressed her lips tight together, and nodded. She felt her nostrils flare. "I see."

He turned to her. "I'm not sure you do, Kate. You are one of the finest professors Milston College has ever had. Awards, yes. Grants, yes. The highest student satisfaction rating. But the fact is that…well, for one thing you've been slow to publish, and…"

"Slow to publish? Tell me you're not serious. Who was it who did all the research and crafted that article for you on Max Perkins and Marjorie Kinnan Rawlings? And the one on Hemingway and Scott Fitzgerald? For which, if I may be so bold as to mention, you received the Fittingham award." She covered her face with both hands, as if to shut out the moment. "How can you do this to me, Edward?"

"You must know, Kate, how endlessly appreciative I am of all your efforts here. Truly. But all that aside…"

"Oh, yes," she said, stepping close to look him in the

eye, "let's definitely push all of that aside—my efforts and achievements. Yes, just push them aside. Push me aside." She felt her throat thicken.

"What I'm trying to say is…and I know this is hard to hear…but the fact is you're a bit low key."

She folded her arms and didn't respond.

Darian extended his arm to point toward the door. "Lonny is out there. He's managed to get himself on the program at conferences. He does a little talk here and there. He has a local media presence, such as it is. But he's on the right track. It's what the school needs."

"Oh, and don't forget the uncle on the board."

"Kate, you know how it is. Everywhere Lonny goes he's got Milston's name on his lips, telling Milston's story. He's good for enrollment and donor money."

"All these years, Edward, when you told me what a terrific job I was doing, never once did you ever mention a media presence. Not once. Was that because it would take time away from my writing your precious papers, my creating your literary presence?" She headed toward the door, then turned. "*Hmm*, maybe I should just go out the window along with your principles."

"Kate. Wait." Darian came around the desk. "Wait. Please know how much we all admire the work you've done here over these last four years. How well liked and respected you are. This was, to say the least, a very difficult decision." He picked up a white business envelope from his desk and handed it to her. "There's two months' severance, and one heck of a letter of recommendation. Why not treat this as if you were taking the summer off to scout a new position for the fall semester?"

He said it in such an off-handed manner that, at first, she could only stare, drilling him with her eyes. Shiny black hair threaded with silver, prominent brow. She had always thought of him as a decent looking man. Odd that the word *decent* should come to mind. There was a definite shift in her perception of him now. How different people can appear when you hone in on the survival tactics that ultimately belie their integrity.

She and Darien had always enjoyed a respectably close and comfortable relationship that included many a long talk about life and learning over lunch at the local diner. Nothing more to it than that. They were trusted colleagues sharing their insights and opinions about the school's needs and shortcomings with openness and honesty. Had she been taken in? Had she been too honest? Who is this man, after all, that she had shared her French fries with? "Try this chicken salad; it's the best," he might say. "Are you going to eat that pickle?" How easy it is to be cozy or lofty when there's nothing at stake.

On occasion and off the record, they had discussed Lonny. He was a risk. Darian had acknowledged it. She could have gone on about him now—young, incapable Lonny, whose chief asset was his charm in getting someone to bail him out of his crises and save his neck. That and his mother's brother, Jonathan Rorimer, who served on Milston's board. More than once, Lonny had entered the women's dorm at night, and most recently was told by the Polish woman in her typically diplomatic manner to please not come into the cafeteria after hours to remove snacks and beverages on his way to a party. The woman had been kind enough not to report him, but she was given a warning when Lonny had a note put in her file suggesting that she was the one pilfering food. Kate had defended her. Even school officials knew it to be a lie. Interesting that she, too, had just been terminated. They all knew what Lonny Kagan was. No need for Kate to badmouth him. Nor did she wish to. It wasn't her way.

"Kate, losing you is hard for all of us, for the school."

"Expect things to get harder, Edward. You've still got Lonny Kagan on your hands." Without uttering another word, she left.

IT took the conductor, aware of her daily commute, to inform her that she was already two stops past her usual station. It wasn't until she finally returned home that she cried as she hadn't cried in years. There had been many days of tears when her grandfather passed away months earlier. That wonderful man who had helped raise her. His passing at 89 had not been a devastating shock, but a sad and lonely loss, a prayerful end of a special life that had spiraled into erratic behavior and perilous falls. Today was different. So completely unexpected. No solid ground underfoot. *How on earth could this have happened?*

It was the end of the day. Not late enough for bed, but she went to bed all the same, removing only her jacket and shoes before slipping despairingly under the covers.

Chapter Three

SHE FELT EVEN worse in the morning when the shocking replay on wakening settled into a slow toxic drip of anguish and fear. Light of day brought moments when Kate slumped half-dazed on the sofa, and moments when she was at once furious and bereft. A half-eaten bowl of breakfast cereal sat on the kitchen table until she moved it a few hours later to the counter by the sink without emptying it. She made toast and left it to get cold in the toaster. She poured juice and took only a sip. The scent of coffee turned acrid from the percolator simmering too long on the burner.

A little after noon, the phone rang, startling her. She gathered herself quickly. It could be Edward telling her the school had made a terrible mistake. Maybe he'd gone back to the board and got them to reconsider. It was definitely possible. Wasn't it?

"Everything okay?

It was not Edward Darien. Kate's heart sank. "Oh…Ellen. I…I'm…why do you ask?"

"Well, for one thing, you're at home on a weekday. I was out walking Tony and saw that your front door light is still on and your newspaper is still on the stoop."

"I'm fine."

"You sound nasal. Are you all right?"

"I…I…" The flood of tears returned. This was the first she had spoken to anyone since her conversation with Edward, and she couldn't hold back.

"Hey, what's going on?"

"I can't…talk…right now."

"I'll be right over."

Good friends are just that—good. They come to your side to comfort you. They sit there handing you tissues as the tears dribble unrelentingly down your puffy red face and you begin to believe this may be the big one, the one that finally does you in.

Ellen's brownstone next to Kate's made it easy to be at her friend's front door in a matter of moments, and for the next hour she listened to the halting and sniffled account of Kate's firing. Ellen fixed Lipton's chicken noodle soup and read Professor Darian's letter of recommendation. "I think your boss is absolutely right—they really must admire and respect you. This is no ordinary letter. Look: *a stellar presence, exceptional competency and scholarship*. Who talks like that? You don't find those words on any template. They mean it. I'm going to take it to the office tomorrow to make a mimeograph copy. Make sure you keep the original in tip-top shape; don't slobber all over it."

In the days that followed, Ellen Castle, forty-two, seven years divorced with no children, brought comfort in the form of bagels and coffee, grilled cheese sandwiches and chocolate ice from Lombardi's, their favorite Italian bakery, all the time insisting Kate keep reading her letter of recommendation out loud at least twice a day. Kate had no will and no words to resist. On the day she was fired, somewhere between Milston College up in Westchester County and her home in Carol Gardens, Brooklyn, a little over an hour's train ride away, her voice had faded along with her promising career.

She had been a good instructor and a good writer. She had worked hard for Milston, for her students, for her profession, always believing she was giving her best for a noble institution, now recognizing she had given blind trust to the boss who ultimately betrayed her. In the beginning, Kate had covered for Lonny, chalking it up to ignorance of school policy and so on. But over time, the offenses became more unsettling—Lonny Kagan wasn't "learning." In truth, he appeared to have no respect at all for the school's policies. Evidently, no homage to right vs. wrong, no doubt confident that his uncle could get him out of any unsavory situation. Wrong is wrong, Kate had thought, naïve. No matter how Edward Darian might deny it, it was clear to Kate that this last time around, the time when Kate spoke up in Mrs. Stanek's behalf, Lonny Kagan had successfully campaigned for Kate's removal along with Mrs. Stanek's. In any case, all she had to show for her years of hard work was a severance package and a high-blown letter of recommendation. The school she had been loyal to had shut the door in her face. The only thing she felt motivated to do was crawl back into bed.

She kept the TV on low volume, wanting the distraction but unable to focus. A half-read novel was buried in a pile of Kleenex as unopened mail piled up on a side table. At one point, she came across the folder for a project she had been involved in for Milston and threw it across the room with such force that she nearly knocked over one of her lamps. Projects and homecomings and spring flings and Milston's beautiful winter carnival—all gone now. Her students. Her bright and wonderful students whose hopes and plans she had invested in so deeply. Gone. She hung her head in her hands and sobbed endlessly. And she prayed, pleaded really, completely unable to come to grips with what appeared to her as incredibly unfair and uncalled for. No matter how beautifully worded a letter of recommendation is, wouldn't another school…a good school…still wonder about the "real reason" a professor was terminated? Fired? A year before tenure?

She stopped answering the telephone after what must have been a few dozen calls, having been hopeful each time that it was Edward calling to ask if she would please forgive them and accept her job back. But the calls had been from faculty well-wishers, friends, and students stunned by the college's decision. She wanted no more of it.

The doorbell had rung on a few occasions. Again, she had straightened up and in a fleeting moment of optimism hurried over to peek through the curtains in case it was someone from the school coming to rectify things or perhaps the mailman with a special delivery letter that would rescind her termination. But it was only the boy up the street likely collecting for some kind of school drive, and Mr. Wallace, the Fuller Brush man in his fine brown suit. As she watched him retreat up the street towards his car, it was as if she could see her hopes carried off in that sturdy leather case, amid the whisk brooms, dustcloths and mop heads. There would be no redemption. It was hopeless. First her grandfather, now her career. And she couldn't overlook her break-up with David. Her life was in free fall.

After a week, things shifted, at least for Ellen. "I want you to know," she said, speaking over the squeaky wheel of the clothesline pulley, "I feel very bad that you lost your job. I honestly do. You have every right to be upset and disappointed and angry and confused, probably afraid too, considering that all this has happened not so very long after losing your grandfather…and I don't even want to mention you-know-who."

"Why do I feel there's a *but* coming?"

"*But…* it's been over a week, Kate Gannon. And it's really okay until now that you haven't done much with your hair. I'm curious to know, is there a bird living in there? I know you must have washed your face once because you had one of those little noodles stuck near your lip and it's gone."

"I didn't have anything stuck any place," Kate protested, running her fingers across her mouth.

"Well, I think it's about time you start shaping up." She began folding towels.

Kate leaned her elbow on the kitchen table, her right hand propping up her chin. "How can I? I'm just no good for anything right now."

"My point exactly. Remaining in this stupefied state of melancholy makes you no good for anything. I agree. So, time to make a change. A week is long enough. And, actually, it's been a bit longer than that. Either way…we're going to have to agree that it's enough."

"I'll decide what's enough. I'm miserable. And what would you know about losing a job…a career? You've got your own business. Who can fire you?"

"First of all, stop saying you've lost your career. Milston is just one little college. One. And as for me, hey, the marketplace can fire me. Owning your own business isn't always a dream job and real estate is no walk in the park." The tea kettle whistled and Ellen reached over to turn off the burner.

"But at least when you're the one in charge you would see it coming, whatever it is. You might have a chance to…to do something…to maybe head it off. Prepare yourself. Not be blown off your feet like…like…" She made a limp swipe at the air. "…that." She wiped her nose with a tissue. "It's such betrayal, Ellen. That's what makes it hurt so bad."

Ellen turned and leaned against the kitchen counter facing Kate and dunking a teabag in and out of a cup of hot water. "Know what I think?"

"I'm afraid to even guess."

"I think it might be the times in life when we are most shocked that we are most ready for a change."

Ellen's words of encouragement were sometimes achingly intrusive as wisdom often is. Kate turned to look at her with tired eyes. "Please tell me you're not going into your 'everything happens for a reason' routine. I'm just not up to it."

"I believe this whole thing is a perfect example of …"

"No, don't say it." Kate got up from the kitchen chair and shuffled toward the living room. "I don't want to hear it."

"Providence," Ellen called out after her. "It must be time for you to move on to something better."

"I didn't need something better. I liked what I had."

"Did you really like it?"

"Please."

"Seriously, Kate. Milston proved that they don't deserve your talent and energy. Edward Darian was an opportunist passing himself off as a trusted colleague. There are other schools that will honor your contribution. And I know you'll find the right one. Think of it as a destiny thing. It's time to find the job you truly love."

A long moment passed as Kate stood at the window, her back to Ellen. "I have learned that neither jobs…nor people… necessarily work out just because love is in the equation."

"Okay, that's it." Ellen threw on her silk neck scarf and collected her purse. "Tomorrow morning we're going to breakfast. Nine o'clock. Be outside…dressed. And I don't mean those bag lady pajamas and slippers you've been living in. I want to see you upright, scrubbed and combed. That includes lipstick and mascara." Before Kate could mumble her disagreement, Ellen went out the door and closed it solidly behind her. "Nine o'clock," she shouted from outside.

Chapter Four

Springtime was Kate's favorite season, but on this May morning, as she and Ellen walked the few blocks up to Court Street, it might just as well have been the depth of winter. Kate moped along, blind to the bright yellow forsythia boughs threading the wrought iron fences outside the brownstones or the window boxes filled with lavender and orange crocuses. Oblivious also to the chattering of the birds and the sweet smell of the season itself.

Here and there, when a neighbor waved, Ellen responded with her typical cheerfulness, while Kate gave a sullen, halting nod. She had come out on time as Ellen had instructed: scrubbed and fresh as a kindergartener off to her first day of school. She wouldn't admit that it actually felt good to be out of her scruffy house clothes and into skirt and lightweight sweater. She'd cinched her hair at the back with a broad bone clip and finished things off with her tiny single-pearl earrings. When they reached the avenue, Kate turned her head toward the curb to avoid eye contact with the storeowners she knew so well.

"Just smile a little," Ellen coached. "You've been holed up in the house for so long, you're blinking in the sunlight like a prisoner of war."

"I just don't think I'm ready for all this yet."

"Sure you are. You look nice. I'd forgotten how shiny auburn hair can be when you wash off a week's worth of dust and cracker crumbs."

"Don't be annoying. I'm here. Do I have to look like I'm enjoying it?"

"Then, just pretend. And the best way to do that is to quit acting like you're entering a leper colony. These people are friends and neighbors."

Lenny's Luncheonette, a cozy, if time-worn, eatery with a tin ceiling dating back very nearly to the end of the previous century, never ceased to flare the nostrils with the aromas of bacon, fresh brewed coffee and pancakes. Along with a scattering of small tables, the counter had enough stools to accommodate fourteen diners, old-timers and newcomers alike, along with a steady flow of businessmen grabbing coffee and the morning paper before rushing off to catch the subway to Manhattan.

Kate and Ellen seated themselves at one of the tables along the side wall, as an elderly couple they knew only as regulars, smiled and said goodbye on the way out. As usual, the place was abuzz with chatter about taxes, baseball, politics and neighborhood gossip. Here and there, a few laughed at a joke they'd heard on the Sid Caesar show the previous Saturday night, punctuated by a loud voice or two raised in benign disagreement about this and that.

Gloria, the big-boned waitress who'd worked there for as long as anyone could remember, arrived with coffee, wearing her usual brown gingham apron with a filmy embroidered handkerchief flourished in the pocket of her lapel. "What's it today, Ladies?" She took a quick look over her shoulder. "We're out of cheese Danish; just cherry left."

"Thanks, Gloria," Ellen said, then placed her breakfast order of one poached egg and a waffle.

"Just toast today," Kate said in a gloomy tone as she poured cream into her coffee. She didn't look up.

"By the way, Hon," Gloria whispered, "I'm sorry to hear about…you know…the job. You're gonna be okay." She winked at Kate and walked away.

Kate put her cup down and glared at Ellen. "You told her? I can't believe it. Why are you telling anyone? It's nobody's business but mine."

"Get a grip. It's all about goodwill. I figured it would be easier on you if some people knew in advance and didn't ask why you look like your cat died."

"I don't have a cat. And what do you mean some people?" Kate glanced about as if to identify others who looked as if they knew something. "Who else have you told?"

Lenny arrived at their table with a sympathetic smile and a small plate holding two French crullers. He put an arm around Kate's shoulder. "Something sweet for a bitter time. You're gonna be okay, kid."

Kate had to struggle to get out the words "Thank you," and

after Lenny left, she fixed Ellen with a hard stare. "Sometimes you are no friend. And if I wasn't afraid it would create even more of a stir, I would leave right now. You were not like this when I lost my grandfather. Why are you this way now that I've lost my job? I'm up against it and I'm miserable not knowing what to do or where to turn. Can you not see that? What's happened to you?"

Ellen tidied her napkin and stirred her coffee. "Your grandfather's passing was a genuine loss and you had no control over it."

"Oh, so, my job was not a genuine loss? Are you crazy?" Kate looked about, fearful that she had spoken too loudly.

"I know about the long hours you put in at Milston. The missed vacations. Writing award-winning articles your boss took credit for, the same guy who said 'adios' without batting an eye. You deserve better and I think the timing of all this agrees with what I'm telling you."

"What does any of that have to do with you telling the whole neighborhood?"

"First of all, it wasn't the whole neighborhood." Ellen leaned in. "These people care about you, Kate, which happens to be a good thing to keep in mind after the way Mr. Betrayer and his cronies treated you."

"Okay, okay. I get it." Kate put her fork down and pushed a wisp of hair off her cheek. "I know Milston wasn't ideal. But I was good at my job. I had a future there."

"You *thought* you had a future there. But that's neither

here nor there at the moment. Maybe it's time you find your dream job at another college that will love and appreciate having a star like you on their faculty."

"Why do people put so much stock in dreams? My grandfather's dream was to play third base for the Brooklyn Dodgers. He became a typesetter."

"Did he like being a typesetter?"

Kate turned away, not wanting to go where Ellen was leading her.

"Well?"

"Yes, he loved his work."

"So, my point is he found another dream."

Gloria arrived with their breakfast plates, then leaned down closer to Kate. "See that fella at the end of the counter. The one with the gray sweater. He lost his job two years ago and I talked with that other customer that comes in Saturday mornings…you know, the one who usually leaves his little dog tied outside in the shade near the bench while he's having breakfast? He works in school supplies. Travels all over the place. Well, I talked with him and he hired that fella there in the sweater." She looked about. "Problem is, I have no idea who to talk to about a professor job. If I find out, I will let you know immediately." She straightened up, put her hand slowly to her head and smoothed the wave of her blond page boy. "You're a nice person and I'll do whatever I can for you."

"Tell me you're not touched," Ellen said after Gloria walked away. "Tell me."

The look of exasperation on Kate's face gave way to one of amiable resignation. "I give up."

Once outside the restaurant, Kate turned to her friend. "I'm sorry, Ellen. I know you're trying to help me. I've just been so sideways and out of sorts. Although you haven't exactly made it easy. Still…"

"I'm sorry too. I've been pushing you. I was just afraid that…well…it doesn't matter what I'm afraid of. I need to keep my mouth shut sometimes."

"I know you always have the best intentions. You know me too well. I needed a swift kick. Getting out today has been good for me—I'm feeling better." She took a deep breath and gave a slow look up and down the street. The shadows of the large-leafed sycamores danced across the sidewalk blunting the heat of the near midday sun. "Would you mind if I go for a walk by myself for a while?"

Ellen put her arms around Kate. "Call me later if you feel like talking or maybe even a movie. Imagine, Saturday night and neither one of us has anything better to do. And…if you want to ignore me for a couple of days, that's okay too. You may need time alone right now…but in a good way?"

"Right." Kate smiled. "In a good way. I promise."

As they headed off in separate directions, Ellen called back. "By the way…" Kate turned. "That sweater needs a scarf."

It was the first time Kate heard herself laugh in over a week. "Yes, and if I hadn't left my little white gloves on the subway, I'd have worn those too."

Three blocks along on the corner playground she sat on one of the swings and moved lazily forward and back, her feet barely leaving the ground. She felt grateful that she hadn't lost her job in the dead of winter with its day-long steel gray skies that turn to early darkness, and the blizzards that could have snowed her in for days.

She'd been missing her students, certain ones more than others. Steven Falcone, with his droll sense of humor about his quest to replicate Shakespeare. Pretty awful, but he would improve with time because he was smart and his head was in the right place. He would go far; she had no doubt. Josie Kunkel, the greatest talent of the lot when it came to essays, and always eager to help others. So many young, growing, active minds that she had become so invested in. But in the end, they were people, after all. Dolores McMasters, hoping to finish out the school year before her required surgery to repair two disks in her back. Victor Cardinale, struggling to focus since the loss of his father in a construction accident. She felt, in a way, like a hen who'd lost track of her brood. Kate would have to remember the advice she always gave Victor: "Your dad would want you to move forward, be the best you can be, and keep your heart open so that joy, peace and love can find a home there again." At this time, wouldn't Kate's grandfather wish the same for her?

She drew in the milky-sweet scent of fresh mown grass, as a fly buzzed about and a darning needle swept above the boxwood hedge. She was surprised by a momentary awareness of freedom. Maybe it was time to get down to the business of moving on to something better. She could come to believe it. All she had to do was suspend her sense of dread about the uncertainty that lay before her like an uncharted prairie with nothing but emptiness all the way to the horizon. *No.* She stopped herself. Even in her current state she knew better than to spoil this beautiful day, this beautiful moment with dark thoughts.

What was it that had pulled her up after her grandfather died? Even in her grief, she had come to the conclusion that the right thing had happened. He had gone to a better place. That's what everyone said including Doctor Pardi and Father Craven who said the funeral Mass. She believed it too, and that belief had given her serenity. So, what about now? Had she been needing, in some way, to go to a better place? Find a different dream, as Ellen had suggested? She took a deep breath. For right now, right this minute, there was no better place than a swing in a park on a warm afternoon with all the scents and sounds and wonders of spring. Maybe when she got home, she would write an essay or a poem about it. *Hmm.* She hadn't thought of doing that in a long time—it made her think that old habits never die, but in truth, she'd been well out of that habit for quite a long time.

Some small tingle of confidence and relief told her that this could be enough for now. She was beginning to reason that there was no desperate need to hurry. Milston, in fact, had been very generous with severance. That, along with her unemployment benefits and money she had set aside for emergencies, would more than satisfy the necessities. She would be okay for a while. She began to entertain the notion that she had time. And with that, she began to consider things.

Chapter Five

"I THINK YOU'RE the perfect candidate, Professor Gannon, and my client does too. You present very well." Miss Lester sat across from Kate in the Park Avenue office of the agency that touted its reputation as the leading university recruiter. "I can set up the interview this afternoon and you can be on a plane to Ohio first thing in the morning." The woman gave a slow wink and nodded her head with deliberation. "Truly a premier opportunity. Wear a dark suit and your hair pulled back. It will help give you a more, shall we say, mature look. They may be surprised by your youth. You've done well in academia for a twenty-eight-year old."

"Ohio," Kate said flatly.

In the weeks that followed, Kate applied only to schools that she could reach by train or bus from Brooklyn—Fordham, Hunter College and City College of New York, her top choices. She wrote two articles for *Faculty and Campus Magazine* and attended a university club meeting in Manhattan where she mingled with some of the elites of higher education, grateful that no one was there from Milston. Two of them offered to keep her in mind when something came up. She spent a good portion of her days making phone calls, filling out applications, and writing letters to accompany her curriculum vitae.

And something else. For the first time in two years she took down the Nikon camera from the shelf in her bedroom closet. When she was ten, her grandfather gave her a Brownie camera for Christmas. She had carried it everywhere, using up rolls of film by the dozen until her grandfather had to admonish her over the considerable expense of developing so many photos. His mandate forced her to become selective, to nurture an eye for things that were unusual, people's expressions, the way that shadows fell across buildings and bridges, the eerie look of the trees in Prospect Park when the fog set in, the view of the ocean from the top of the Wonder Wheel at Coney Island. The play of light, and how it created different dimensions of color. The scribble of leaves against a storm sky. Where was all that now? Her photos, her writing? Where was her poetry? *Dear Grandpa.* When had she let the things she had felt such passion for slip away? Was it possible to get them back?

As usual, it was Ellen's idea. "Let's take a vacation."

"I'm not sure I can do that right now, Ellen."

"Just a week. After all, it is summer, and you've been working hard at finding a job. A break will do you good, so why not? One week away won't matter. You would have taken a vacation anyway if you were still at Milston." The logic appealed to Kate; a week's get-away would be nice. They once had been to the Bahamas together and Ellen was mostly a fun travel companion, except when she became domineering by wanting to manage every detail of the trip.

"I think you're right," Kate said. "Let's do it."

For the next few days, every time the doorbell rang, it was Ellen showing up with more vacation brochures. They had already looked at Miami Beach, San Juan and train travel to the Adirondacks. "I've found the perfect place," she said, rushing to the kitchen table. "Look. Eastover Resort in Lenox, Mass. You remember Becky. She and her friend, Margie, go for a week every summer. I don't know why I didn't think of it before. There's horseback riding, hiking and canoeing, everything. And at night, Red Robinson's orchestra plays till the wee hours."

Kate agreed it sounded wonderful—the Berkshires. A beautiful place, lots of activities, fun. The woodsy mountains, her favorite. Why not?

But then one morning, Kate happened to spot a tiny ad in the classified section of the *New York Daily News*. She'd nearly missed it: *For rent, summer only, cozy bungalow, rural L.I., Serenity in Nature.* She wasn't sure why, but she felt compelled to call. The rental belonged to an abbey in the obscure Long Island hamlet of Spiritu, a place Kate had never heard of, about eighty miles from Brooklyn. Even as she dialed the phone, she wasn't sure why she felt such a tingle of interest.

The handful of little summer bungalows scattered about the area was a source of income for the abbey, she was told, and they were usually booked solid for the season. But one of the renters had backed out at the last minute because of a family emergency. The abbey usually preferred rentals longer than a week, but they would make an exception for such an unexpected, last-minute opening.

Although intrigued, Kate resisted at first. What on earth would they do in a little bungalow in the country? But, clearly, it must be a nice place with things to do because all the rentals were taken. Kate felt that it was definitely worth exploring.

Ellen wanted no part of it. "Are you kidding? The whole idea was to have fun, lots of activities, dance, meet people, and not be by ourselves like hermits. I don't understand you. Count me out."

Kate had considered and reconsidered, unsure of just how much serenity she would be able to withstand. But she had a telephone conversation with Father Elway, the Abbot, whose kind manner along with the pastoral images he created in her mind swayed her.

"Oh, it's quite a lovely place, Spiritu is," Father Elway had said. "That's where our abbey is, of course, along with all the bungalows. And if you go in the opposite direction," exaggerating the word "opposite" as if on the phone she might not have gotten that he meant the *other* way, "you will come to Old Country Road, which, although it is a dirt road, has a somewhat reliable bus that arrives at that corner once an hour on the hour until eight in the evening. It can take you into Hicksville, a lovely little town with a rich and wonderful history. That's actually where the train station is, if you decide to come out on the Long Island Railroad."

"I don't know why this far-away place has piqued my interest, Father. My friend and I were planning to go to a resort in the mountains."

"This might be one of those moments we are called to for whatever reason—but called, nonetheless. Please keep in mind, Miss Gannon, we're not completely without amenities. Hicksville has a movie theater and an ice cream shop, along with some other little stores that carry this and that. Also, a wonderful Catholic church, St. Ignatius of Loyola. Very nearly a hundred years old. Civil War era. And even that's not as old as Hicksville itself. Our hope, of course, is that you will enjoy the serenity of nature, but there's a lot of both out here."

"That must be the appeal, Father. I haven't enjoyed much serenity lately, but I've always loved nature."

He chuckled. "That's good, then. And, oh, let's not forget the Nassau Farmer's Market. You can get lost there looking at everything from the butcher's fine roasts to candies, toys, lawn chairs and bric-a-brac to hats and used books. You name it it's there, Miss Gannon. The books are my favorite. You can buy a Perry Mason mystery for fifteen cents."

Ellen was still not impressed. "I said no and I mean it. I don't care how many conversations you have with a monk, or whatever he is. You expect me to trade a mountain resort for a Farmer's Market and a bus ride to see a movie? You're bats, my friend."

"Would it be so bad to give it a try, Ellen? It might be interesting, don't you think? A kind of adventure. Something different."

"Different definitely. And interesting maybe to someone who spent the better part of their life living in a cell. I can't believe you're serious."

"Even I have to agree that it does seem a bit odd, but I have a kind of feeling about it. Would you just agree to give it some thought?"

"Okay. Sure. No. That's all the thought I'm giving it. Have a nice time."

KATE arrived at the Hicksville station on a Monday, still feeling guilty over the change of plans with Ellen, a change that she herself was challenged to understand. Truth be known, Kate didn't mind not having Ellen along. Something about this whole thing struck Kate as adventuresome. A place to discover. A time to explore. Ellen really had no interest in those things. So, Kate couldn't blame her for being upset. But she did settle down when Kate assured her that they could do something another time, maybe even before the end of summer.

The train trip took more than two hours, counting the transfer at Jamaica Station. Then another half-hour car ride from the Hicksville station to Hummingbird Lane, the narrow country road on which her rental house was located. She had taken one large and one smaller brown leather valise along with a small square train case.

Father Garrett met her in what he referred to as the town and country, a wood-sided station wagon. He was a lean, cheerful man of about fifty and, as he told it, the only priest at the Abbey of the Fathers of Serenity who had a driver's license.

"Do you drive, Miss Gannon?"

"Oh, please, call me Kate, if that's all right, Father. And, yes, I have a license, but no car. There's very little need for one in Brooklyn—we take trains and buses everywhere. I'm not sure I can even recall the last time I drove. It's been a few years."

"Well, the town and country will be available to you just the same. Once you get behind the wheel, I think it will be like riding a bike again, as they say."

"This car?" Kate turned around in her seat to face him. "You would let me borrow this station wagon?"

"Of course, why would we not, barring any special need of ours at the moment, but those needs are rare. After all, you may want to explore beyond the bus route, although you may find that strolling the lanes and side roads right here in Spiritu is also quite fulfilling. Whatever else you do, you will definitely wish to see the garden at the abbey. And perhaps visit often." He gave her a somber look. "Only one word of caution, Miss Gannon—when you are out and about on foot, please be certain to know the way back to your bungalow. This is a rural area where most of the houses, including the house numbers, are obscured by trees or shrubs of one kind or another. Our little lanes can look very much alike. And… the woods are quite deep."

"Ah, '*the woods are lovely, dark and deep, but I have promises to keep…*' Frost. Sometimes I can't resist," she said.

He laughed. "Frost was quite an enigma, wasn't he, Miss Gannon? Some say he was pondering suicide when he wrote that, although, on the bright side, it is considered a perfect poem."

Not being able to find her way back to the house had never crossed her mind. The very thought of getting lost here gave her a jolt, and that little suicide footnote darkened the moment even more. But he was right, of course, and she was glad he had warned her.

"You like poetry, Father?"

"Very much. The good ones, anyway. And who can decide what's good, except oneself." He laughed. "But Frost happens to be very good to my way of thinking. Some see him as simplistic, but he was splendid at creating the most powerful imagery with the smallest and most ordinary words. No more than two or three syllables."

"Are you a teacher, Father?"

"Was. I taught some courses at Marymount many years ago." He threw out his index finger. "Oh, something else, before I forget. Mrs. Wick, our housekeeper, has left a picnic meal for you in the kitchen, along with some staples in the refrigerator to get you started…milk, eggs, butter and bread. Some cheese and things. Knowing Mrs. Wick, likely a few sweets, as well."

Kate was so taken with her introduction to the place that besides a sincere "Thank you," her only response was silence, as they wended lazily farther and farther into the countryside. She was enthralled by the kindness she'd been shown and the beauty that enveloped them. She could smell the cabbage fields and the sweetness of the loam, grass and hay along with the occasional waft of horse scent, the buzz of things and the warmth of fresh humid air against her face. How on earth had she actually come to be here?

One thing was certain, Ellen would never have taken to Spiritu, and although Kate felt guilty about not going to the Berkshires, the fact that this opportunity had popped up so unexpectedly intrigued her and somehow made it feel right. Besides, she and Ellen had not actually made any plans. For all Kate knew, Ellen might have shown up with yet another suggestion. In any case, Kate would be back home in a week— maybe they'd still get to the Berkshires after all. For now, Kate was an explorer, open to possibility, although the more she saw of the rural countryside, the more she wondered exactly what possibilities this remote little hamlet could offer.

Edward Darien had crossed her mind very little these past few weeks. This bit of time away might be just the thing to finally quell the image of herself as a failure. It was a word she'd come to label herself with in the weeks that followed her dismissal from Milston. Not that she thought herself a failure as an instructor, she knew better than that, but a failure at knowing how to protect herself within the system. Lonny Kagan knew the tricks. How terrible that tricks might be required. If that were actually true, she would wonder how to ever fit in again, since she would have no part of it.

Not understanding fully how things had happened left her with the terrible notion that, having trusted her boss and peers so completely and been so betrayed, how could she ever again be certain of her standing in any job. She knew that whatever position she chose, she would put her heart and soul into it, but she also knew that no job could guarantee permanency. How could she ever again trust the character or motives of the people in charge…or the people who influenced them? Accolades and awards and high-performance evaluations could no longer signal to her the comfort of feeling secure with school officials when her dedication and hard work had ended so badly, so unexpectedly at Milston. Could she ever be sure that there wouldn't be another Edward Darien, another Lonny Kagan, another board whose self-interest would prove fatal to her position?

"Oh, I'm sorry, Father. Did you say something?"

"Only that we're getting very close now. You might want your first look at your new little neighborhood. The house is right up ahead. Our lanes are narrow. They're named after birds, trees or flowers. This is Hummingbird. There are other names like Sparrow, Starling, Oriole, Blossom, Iris…and so on. Some are very small lanes, just the length of, let's say, two properties…and not necessarily belonging to the abbey. Other lanes will be longer, curving this way and that. So, always take note."

"I will. Thank you, Father."

"Here we are," he said, slowing the car.

"How sweet," she said, seeing no house at all, only the dense overhang of maples and elms. There were no sidewalks, merely arched tendrils of various bushes and shrubs flanking the narrow road with its well-worn asphalt pavement. Then, there it was, a moss green bungalow with a low peaked roof and a porch enclosed by a white-wood railing. There were two tall, white-framed windows, one on either side of the front door. The yard was well maintained with trimmed bushes and freshly mowed grass. A sprawling maple shaded the front walk and half the lawn. Although there was no other house that she could see, she immediately felt safe and at home. "Oh, this is very nice, Father."

Father Garrett stopped along the grassy edge and removed Kate's luggage, then led the way up the flagstone walk to the front door.

"It's wonderful," she said, hearing the thunk of the wood plank steps. Father Garrett placed her luggage just inside the door, but he himself did not enter. "Oh, please, Father. You're welcome to come in."

"I'm afraid not, Miss Gannon." He dipped his head a bit self-consciously. "It's a rule. We must choose never to put ourselves in situations that could ever possibly be considered...well... inappropriate."

"Oh, I'm sorry. I didn't realize..."

"But...if you want to go about checking light switches and so on, I'll wait right here to be sure everything is in working order and to your liking."

It was a pristine space whose charm instantly captivated her. A cozy setting with deep, comfortable looking arm chairs done up in country floral chintz, as was the bedroom with its polished maple furniture. The windows in the small dining area to the left were trimmed with white crisscross sheers and the kitchen at the back had crisp yellow gingham curtains. The chrome and white of the appliances gleamed, and the polished wood floors were covered here and there with colorful hooked rugs. A small Sylvania television set sat in one corner of the living room, and in the middle of the kitchen table a wooden lattice picnic basket. Kate peeked out the back door to see a small but private yard surrounded by a neatly trimmed boxwood hedge. A large apple tree, positioned at the center of the yard, cast a welcoming shade onto two deep green Adirondack chairs.

"The television sometimes has a lot of snow," Father Garrett said. "Fiddling with those rabbit ears might help. Sometimes the reception isn't very good. And if a tube should go out, we can always take it up to Hughie's pharmacy for a replacement. I can help with that, or anything else you might need, Miss…Kate. And if all else fails, that radio in the corner plays clear as can be. You'll be able to get your favorite shows, even Martin Block's 'Make-Believe Ballroom' …well, sometimes anyway."

Kate put her hands together, prayer-like. "Everything is perfect, Father. Thank you. Thank you."

"You're welcome," he said, turning to leave, then stopped and leaned in, pointing to one corner of the living room. "Oh, and the telephone is on that little table just there. All the numbers you need are written on a pad beside it. There's a Mr. and Mrs. Walters in one of our rentals on Oriole, not very far from here. I've given you their number and mentioned you to them, as well. Always good to know of someone nearby. By the way, the abbey is only a fifteen-minute walk." He chuckled. "Of course, you wouldn't want to do that at night. Did I mention that there are also no streetlights?"

By now it was four o'clock with plenty of summer daylight left. Kate gave the house a more thorough walk-through once Father Garrett had driven off, then hurried to unpack her bags, eager to get out into what remained of the afternoon. But first, the picnic lunch; she was famished.

As she sat by herself at the tidy little Formica-top kitchen table relishing one of Mrs. Wick's fried chicken legs, she was bemused by the scenario—a little house rented from an abbey of benevolent priests in a tiny hamlet she'd never heard of. Was this some kind of a fairy tale? Was she Alice, about to go down the rabbit hole? She laughed, wondering, as she sometimes did, about her choices. At this moment, she couldn't imagine regretting that she had not gone along with Ellen's Berkshire Mountains idea, although she was sure it would have been lovely. Still, here she was, no plans, no activities, utterly alone and enchanted. She had packed her camera. Bright and early the next morning she would go exploring. Eat your heart out, Edward Darien.

When she was done eating, Kate gave the bungalow another walk-through, pleased with the number of windows that allowed the sunlight to fill nearly every corner. She did a quick little bounce on the edge of the bed. Mmm. Comfy. Good sleeping, for sure.

Chapter Six

WHAT KATE HADN'T counted on was that long first night, when the sense of being all alone in a remote and completely unfamiliar place becomes weighty. The constant chirping of crickets joined with the katydids in an endless insect chorus played against the otherwise black silence of the surrounding woods. Those wondrous natural elements, so inviting by day, took on their true primordial form by night. Were they, whoever *they* were, the ones she swore she heard scratching at the window screens, giving an occasional thump against the front door, pattering across the attic, trying to get in? Toward midnight, even Edward Darien would have been a welcome companion as she sat still dressed and wide awake at one end of the couch with all the lights on in the house, afraid to close her eyes. It was summer, after all, and the place was too warm, but she didn't dare open a window. Nor would she run the fan for fear that the noise would prevent her from hearing an intruder in another part of the house.

What had she done? Suddenly this was impossible and scary. Crazy. Divine by day, a nightmare after dark. In Brooklyn, there were signs of life all around, all the time, day or night—a passing car, a voice or two nearby or within a few blocks, a siren, a truck bounding over a pothole, the creak of a neighbor's gate, the ding of the trolley bell on the avenue. Everyday sounds. Even the occasional airplane headed in or out of Idlewild. You blocked them out, but they resided somewhere in you like oxygen.

Two in the morning and she was still sitting up, fanning herself with the latest issue of Redbook Magazine, hot and exhausted. She would have liked to believe that she was being totally unreasonable. But she couldn't quell her fears. Whatever had made her choose such a place, such an out-of-the-way, lonely place? She was up for anything in daylight. She could climb and hike and be pretty much at ease roughing it anywhere. But nighttime was different. She remembered going on a class camping trip to Bear Mountain when she was nine, the only one in the group who had to sleep in the back seat of the teacher's car while everyone slept in tents under the stars.

She had tried the television—snow; the only two channels available had signed off at midnight with the National Anthem. She had played the radio on low, but most of the local stations had lost their signal and after a time there was nothing but static. *What was that noise? A bear? A fox? An intruder?*

Eventually, exhaustion overtook her and she drifted in and out until she fell into deep sleep. The next time she opened her eyes, it was daybreak and she nearly cried with gratitude and relief. She got up, walked wearily through the house, giving it the once-over to assure herself that no door or window had been breached, then lay back down on the sofa and slept until a knock at the door woke her with a jolt.

She jumped up, tipping over the lamp on the side table. "Who…who is it?" she called out. She felt as if she'd been drugged. Head sloggy. Completely disoriented.

"It's Father Garrett. Are you okay, Miss Gannon? I thought I'd stop by to see how everything is. I've brought the newspaper."

The light coming through the window was much brighter now. What the heck time was it? She was frantic, still wearing yesterday's clothing and yesterday's make-up, strands of hair spiking in every direction, like a doll the dog got hold of. Her face hadn't even been washed. What would he think of her? How could she possibly open the door? He would see her for what she really was, a complete loon. "Oh. Yes. Yes. Good morning, Father." She caught sight of the clock. "Oh, look," she tried, with feigned cheerfulness, "it's nearly noon already. I…don't know where the morning went. It really did fly by. I'll be there in a minute." As she hurried to straighten herself, her foot got tangled up in a cord, knocking the telephone to the floor.

"Miss Gannon?"

"It's okay. Okay, Father." She was breathless now, struggling to untangle herself and recover. "I'm fine…yes… everything is fine. I'll…I'll be there in a minute. Just give me a minute."

"No need, Miss Gannon, as long as you're all right. I've got to be on my way. Just wanted to leave you the morning paper. It'll be right here outside the door. Call if you need me for anything…anything at all. I pray you will have a lovely, blessed day."

She heard him walking down the path. "Oh, yes, Father. Lovely. Thank you," she called out, slinking behind the door. "You, too. And many thanks for…for the newspaper." Thank God he didn't wait for her to open the door. She made her way to the kitchen to put on a pot of coffee, opened the blinds and caught sight of her reflection in the window. She gasped. She was a mess all right, with no clue as to how she would possibly conquer her evenings in this place. No matter what pleasures the countryside afforded her by day, the scary prospect of nightfall would hover like a shroud all through the daylight hours.

She got into the shower and washed her hair, letting the water beat down on her. A fresh start would make everything better. And she was right, enjoying eggs, toast and coffee at the small square redwood table on the front porch as she skimmed the paper that Father Garrett had thoughtfully left. *Thank you, too, Dear Mrs. Wick.* It was nearly two in the afternoon. She felt invigorated and past ready to get out and explore. First thing tomorrow, she would walk over to see the abbey and meet Father Elway.

The second night was nearly as harrowing as the night before, with Father Garrett, bless him, jolting her awake near noon the next day. "Just here with your paper, Miss Gannon. I pray all is going well for you. Should you need any help, please do call. You have friends here." Friends, she hoped, that would not think her a crazy loon, but how could they not.

But things settled themselves and she strolled the nearby lanes, using the directions that Father Garrett had given her for the twenty-minute walk to the abbey, the humid air pleasantly thick and fragrant. Dew glistened on the leaves and the woods ticked with the patter of droplets amid the primal, pungent scents of loam and musty vegetation.

When the abbey first came into view, set back as it was against the woods and across a small pond at the end of a long, winding gravel drive, it lay before her like a picture postcard from another country, maybe another century, she thought. A long, low stone and timber structure under a deeply pitched roof with thick wooden shingles and multiple peaks. The narrow, mullioned windows, arched alcoves and doorways gave it the look of vintage European architecture, appearing at once historic, charming and sacrosanct. She could imagine it on a remote English hillside at a time when a mead and mutton supper was the meal of choice and the monks busied themselves with painstaking cursives of Bible translations. She had no intention of entering, mainly because she hadn't yet had the opportunity to pick up a little something as a thank-you for Mrs. Wick. But she was glad she had found the place. She assumed they had a chapel and hoped to spend some time there during her stay in Spiritu.

After dark, she ran the fan and opened a front window a few inches, securing it with a short, broken-off branch that would prevent it from being opened further. Although she still slept on the couch, she felt less anxious, allowing for a peaceful and much needed sleep no longer violated now that Father Garrett was leaving the paper on the porch without knocking.

Even with little rest those first few days, she was out of the bungalow with her camera to enjoy and capture the beauty and charm of the place. She had walked the lengthy distance up to Old Country Road to scout the bus stop and explore a bit of what was outside of Spiritu's little domain. She discovered a small bench in the shade of a maple where she sat enjoying a coke and a foot-long from Jack Yerk's hot dog stand, all with the delightful sense of time being suspended.

"Are you happy, my Kate?" her grandfather used to ask. "Are you happy?"

Why had he asked? She had always reassured him that she was doing what she loved—teaching at Milston—although his question had forced her to ponder her situation. She loved seeing her students' faces, especially when they'd accomplished something they could be proud of. She loved imparting what she knew to others. She loved to watch them learn and, in turn, to learn from them. She loved Milston itself. It was, after all, more a revered institution than a mere school. It had history and tradition. In her everyday reality, it had even more—it was brick and mortar, a place to go to each day, reliable and steady, a second home, she had foolishly thought. In any case, had she been truly happy with the idea of it all? Did she love Milston more for Milston's sake than her own? Was that too selfish a thought? She was fairly compensated for her efforts—wages and benefits, accolades, awards, however little they ultimately counted in securing her tenure? What was it that her grandfather had sensed? He had known her better than anyone. Had he picked up on some sign of discontent that she had not been aware of within herself? What would he have wanted for her? What would he have suggested to remedy such a state of affairs? What would he think of all this now? Of Spiritu?

In the late afternoon hours, she retreated to the porch to sit with her cup of tea and a lined pad, trying to tame the scribble of random musings about birds and quiet and wild blackberries and peace into lines of poetry. She relished the silence of the surrounding woods and something else she couldn't quite identify—a pang of…what was it…longing? Or was it belonging? An idea of something beyond herself, not yet defined. Whatever was taking hold in her, she felt sure that something important or odd or powerful was happening…or about to.

Chapter Seven

Matt Reagan eyed the library's wide entry and ran his fingers through his hair. "This is a bigger job than you might think, Leo." He stood back, pointing at the heavily timbered structure overhead. "That archway is a load-bearing wall. On top of which, there's stone behind it. I'll do it if you say so, but I'm just not sure this is a project you want to undertake."

Father Leo Elway put his hand to his chin, pondering the unwelcome news, and sighed. "*Hmm*, hadn't anticipated that."

Matt folded up the measuring stick and tossed it into his tool box. "Tell me, Father, what is it exactly that you're trying to accomplish. Let's see what our choices are."

"Well, we've talked about it here—the priests, that is. Even our dear Mrs. Wick has had a say. We have all agreed that it would be a good idea to begin opening up the abbey for visits…you know…other than after Mass…with some special kinds of programs or talks that people might like. Community things. Bring people together." He hesitated, looking down at his shoes. "And, of course, raise money to keep things here on an even keel."

"I see."

"It would be reasonable for you to think that the rentals make a big difference. Well, in fact, they do. But there's always upkeep. Our expenses have gone up. We haven't raised the price of the rentals in over fifteen years."

"Well, wouldn't that be a good thing to consider, Leo. Fifteen years has been a pretty fair run for all the regulars."

"I know you're right, Matthew, but I guess I don't want to disturb the peace, so to speak."

"I know what you mean, Leo. Maybe you're right. Maybe this whole community idea will do the trick. The abbey is beautiful." He gestured to the surroundings. "It's historic, spiritual. The garden out back." He nodded. "Let's just see how to get this plan of yours done."

They had met some years earlier when Matt first started going to Spiritu for a summer break. Although now and then seeming a bit hapless, Father Elway was a compassionate and open-minded man with a sense of humor and purpose. He made no secret of the fact that he admired the man twenty years his junior— "a straightforward troubleshooter with a caring spirit as big as his talent for getting things done," was how he had first introduced Matthew Reagan to fellow priests.

"We naturally thought of the library," Father Elway went on, "since it's a large room and we could open it up to the reception area out there. Make a bigger space for people to gather." He rubbed the back of his neck. "Not such a good plan, after all, I guess."

For a long moment they were silent, Father pacing with his hands crossed behind his back, Matt assessing the doorway and the area beyond, where the front entry was located.

"What about going the other way, Leo?" Matt pointed across the spacious reception area.

"Our utility room?"

"You bet. There are no main electrical lines or water sources in there. Those are all in the mud room near the barn. Your utility room is really a storage area. A pretty good sized one at that. And…" he turned to look squarely at Father Elway, "Mrs. Wick's huge pantry is right beside it. We could take that too, and once we do the breakdowns and join it with the reception space, you'll have all the room you'll ever need."

Father Elway, at first appearing heartened by the idea, darkened at the prospect of tampering with Mrs. Wick's space. "Oh, I don't know," he said, shaking his head.

"We can relocate the pantry to the office next to it. It's not really an office anyway. It's more of a catch-all, isn't it? And it's still within easy reach of the kitchen. It even has a window, which should make Mrs. Wick happy." He waited. "It's about time, Leo, that we make good use of a lot of the wasted space around here."

Father Elway took a deep breath and scratched his chin. "Let's go look, I guess, but listen here, my good friend." He turned to Matt. "You're the one who will have to tell her; I'll make sure I'm at prayers when you do."

The reception area, lit by a row of mullioned windows with its view to the woods beyond, was a large rectangle of ornate paneled walls and a coffered ceiling trimmed out in dark timbers. An antique Kayseri rug filled the center of the parquet floor, on which were set two upholstered sofas with lamp tables. A handful of ornate, high-backed chairs were positioned here and there around the sides of the room.

As they made their way across to the utility room, Father Garrett came through the front door.

"How are things going for you today, John?" Father Elway asked.

"I'm on my way to check on Miss Gannon again." He sighed and raised his eyebrows.

"Is there a problem?"

"She's not getting on very well, I'm afraid."

"Oh, dear." Father Elway rubbed his chin. "Is she ill?"

"I don't know what the problem is exactly. All I know is that when I drop off the paper for her, she just mumbles on through the door. She sounds quite a bit…I don't know… incoherent… stumbling about knocking things over. I can't imagine."

"Oh," Matt said, "You suppose there might be something wrong? Is she elderly?"

"On the contrary. She's a lovely young woman."

"Do you think she's in need of some medical attention? Has she been out and about?"

"Well," said Father Garrett, thoughtful, "when I go back in

the afternoon, I see some little things on the porch table that indicate she'd likely been out there. I saw a pair of sneakers set outside the front door earlier today."

"Hmm. Good idea to keep checking on her," Father Elway said.

"Do you suppose it's possible...I mean it doesn't seem so to look at her...we know looks can be deceiving," Father Garrett said, "but could she have been...perhaps...drinking? Before noon?"

"Oh, dear," Father Elway said. "Hadn't even thought of that. I hope not."

"If she is a drinker," Matt said, shaking his head, "she's picked the perfect place for it. Remote. Doesn't know anyone and she doesn't have to be anywhere, so there's no one to fuss about it?"

"As long as she doesn't create any disturbances or cause any harm to herself or to others," Father Garrett said. "We'll have to monitor this as best we can. We certainly want to help where help is needed, but we also must consider our other renters along with our reputation."

"Keep an eye out for now, John." Father Elway said. "She's bound to come over here to the abbey. We should be able to judge if there's an issue of some kind. If she is in some kind of distress, she may want to talk to someone about it at some point. In the meantime, let's pray she doesn't do any harm to herself."

Father Garrett nodded. "You're right, Leo. Maybe we can

find a way to help her while she's here." He looked to Matt. "Too bad. Such a lovely young woman."

Chapter Eight

OAK HAMMOCK WAS a pastoral lane, and Kate's vision was most definitely that of an old-fashioned country summer. Now, instead of fearing the night, Kate very nearly welcomed "the noisy silence" after dark and what were perhaps only the imagined scratchings, thumps and patter. All had finally come to feel right in this new little world as she donned her Keds and headed out with her camera for a brisk walk before breakfast, well rested and eager to explore. Each day, she had waved to a passerby or two in another lane, and they had waved back. She found herself enjoying the slightly distant friendliness. She likened it, in a way, to her several days without speaking when she attended a Franciscan silent retreat in Massachusetts right after she graduated college. She could handle a few days of silence—good for the soul, she thought.

Silence gives you time to reflect. She thought about David, and not in any way that would make her feel regret about having broken it off. It was natural that he might come to mind in this setting. She had always liked the woods; he preferred the ocean. So, when he had broached the subject of one day having a honeymoon, a possibility that had never seemed truly comfortable for Kate, his ideal was Myrtle Beach. She would have chosen the Adirondacks. She liked cozy, quiet restaurants but somehow they always ended up in a place where they could hardly hear each other speak. She could not have cared less about getting attention…except, of course, for a job well done in her work; he craved to be noticed. He gravitated toward crowded places and parties where they would stroll in half an hour late.

Over the course of the year that they dated, he had managed to occasionally redeem himself by his expressions of respect and concern for her grandfather. Yet, when she had needed him most in those sad and trying last weeks of her grandfather's life, David had reason upon reason to make himself scarce. That had been the final straw, and now in this far-off country hamlet that fed both her passion and her peace, she once again thanked God for saving her from a life with David, however aware she was that at nearly thirty she had not one prospect of marriage in sight.

Still, there was no quelling the joy she felt on the daily trek that took her in and out of narrow tree-canopied lanes and paths where she oriented herself by singling out a certain bungalow or a distinctive cluster of flowering bushes that were sure to point her way back to the rental. She had already gone through two rolls of film.

One morning, she met an elderly gentleman who greeted her with a smile and a tip of his cap as he walked by with a brisk gait and a stout little bulldog. "Dobbin is his name," the gentleman paused to reply in answer to Kate's question. Later on, she encountered two teenage girls out for a walk on a day's visit to their grandmother. They were polite but said little and giggled as they continued along. Such sweet and ordinary little moments but, surprisingly, they held great attraction for her. How could one week possibly be enough? She had mentioned that to Ellen in their telephone call, but her dear friend, concerned and dismayed, had neither understanding nor acceptance of Kate's decision to extend her time there.

"How can you think of staying another week? What are you, a hermit?"

"I don't know what it is, Ellen. There's just something about this place and I want more of it. I feel as if…as if I'm waiting for something."

"Well, excuse me for reminding you, but you don't get a job by hanging around waiting for it. You're supposed to be looking for one."

ALTHOUGH she wasn't yet able to tell a warbler from a grebe, she had begun to recognize some of the birds from the book she'd purchased at Scribner's before leaving Brooklyn. She had written something every day, a poem or a short passage she might later turn into an essay or an article. She mused that there might be a novel somewhere in all this—the thought of which danced within her. Is this what her grandfather had noticed was missing—the joy of some true passion?

The endless sensory qualities of Spiritu called her to it, as if sitting down to a lavish buffet before realizing you were hungry. She had, in fact, been starving. And although her students had brought her much enjoyment, pride and inspiration, she had to wonder why she had been willing to spend so much of her talent writing prize-winning articles for an unappreciative opportunist like Edward Darien. How blind can a person be?

Now, in this most pleasurable and unlikely of places, she was content to stroll at peace with the birds and squirrels, drinking in the wooded beauty that, for the most part, obscured the houses amid the trees.

On one of her morning strolls, a certain little cottage stopped her cold. It was nestled in so dazzling a profusion of flowers of every kind and color that it very nearly took her breath away. She stood for a long moment, gazing at the garden's extravagant beauty before even thinking of raising her camera.

Great mounds of blue and pink hydrangeas nearly enveloped the front of the house up to the windows, while sprawling tendrils of forsythia mingled with a wild array of rhododendron, clematis and delphinium along with varieties whose names she didn't know and some she had never seen before. The entrance off the road was just a short dirt path not wide enough for a vehicle and although difficult to make it out in the dense brush, it appeared to intersect at a right angle with a walkway that cut through the garden to the porch step, right up to the cornflower blue front door.

The two double hung windows on either side of the entry were neatly fitted with white shutters and window boxes, themselves rivaling the garden beds with geraniums, cosmos, dahlias and bachelor buttons. An astonishing bit of splendor in an already splendid setting. Kate snapped a few photos, hoping that the erratic light and shade playing off the canopy of maples and sycamores would allow her at least one good shot.

From the corner of her eye, she detected movement and turned to see an elderly couple walking along the road in her direction. Kate greeted them as they approached. "Good morning,"

"Good morning to you," the woman said, smiling. She wore a pink visor, the man a white ball cap. They stopped. "I don't believe I've seen you here before. Although we really never see anyone. Very secluded kind of place, Spiritu."

Kate laughed. "I know what you mean. This is my first time here and only because my cottage renter cancelled."

"Well, that's something." The man turned to the woman. "Don't recall any of the cottage rentals ever cancelling. Our neighbor back home tried to rent this summer and last, but there was nothing available, which seems to be the case every summer. I guess there has to be a first for everything." He touched his cap. "Nice to meet you anyway. I'm Tom Walters and this is my wife, Regina."

"Oh, Father Garrett mentioned you. I'm Kate Gannon. Nice to meet you."

"You're Kate Gannon." Regina Walters gave a nod of recognition. "Yes, Father Garrett gave us your phone number, and I believe he gave you ours."

"It was very thoughtful of him."

"We know Father Garrett well," the man said. "Mrs. Walters and I have been coming here for years. Gets us out of Queens for a while. And everyone at the abbey is wonderful."

"Is this your place?" Kate asked, turning in the direction of the flower cottage, but a shaft of sunlight through the trees made it impossible to see the house.

"Oh, my goodness," the woman said, shielding her eyes. "That sun is so bright already."

"No," the man said, pointing back behind them. "Ours is two lanes over on Oriole."

"Oops." The woman tapped her watch. "We've got to hurry, Tom. So sorry, but we're off to catch the bus."

"We'll all see each other again, Miss Gannon." Tom Walters touched his cap. "Call us for certain if there's anything at all that you need."

"Cheers," Kate called after them, then turned to take one last look at the cottage before moving on. The sun had moved behind the trees and the spectacle of the place was once again fully visible. "I'll be back tomorrow," she whispered.

The next day she was out of the bungalow by 7:00. The air

was light and filmy. She could almost feel it settling on her—like grace, she thought. Inspiring. And reminiscent—she had spent the summer days of her early years amid the hills and trees of Prospect Park, where the rustle of the maples was weighty and the earthy scents rich and sweet. Here it was again. Something to draw the images from her camera. Something to draw the poetry from her soul. She had missed it.

Milston was becoming more and more distant. Oddly enough, she hadn't thought much about home either. It was as if she had stepped into another realm, whatever that meant. It had occurred to her only fleetingly that at some point she might need a reality check—was she losing touch with the truth of her situation, her need to find a job? Nevertheless, she was going to take the bus into Hicksville. She would get a bite to eat at a restaurant there and rub elbows with the locals. She had stretched Mrs. Wick's provisions as far as she could along with an outing or two at Jack Yerk's, having had no desire to break the spell with something as mundane as grocery shopping. Now, out of necessity, she would call Father Garrett, hoping he would agree to her borrowing the town and country the next morning for a trip to the Nassau Farmer's Market.

"Yes, that will work out just fine, Miss Gannon. The car is yours…if you feel up to it. We won't need it back until five."

If she felt up to it? What an odd thing to say. In any case, her plans were set for the next morning by the time she boarded the bus to Hicksville.

Chapter Nine

THE TOWN OF Oyster Bay was vast and rural with beaches and hamlets, pricey homes and modest, and like most of Long Island, farms and barns dotting miles and miles of fertile acreage. Here and there, a scattering of small stores barely populated the main roads and now, as well, the area's first mall with more fashionable shops circling an open-air plaza. Kate, one of only three people on the bus, watched with interest from the bus window until the driver called out, "Broadway. Hicksville."

Not like the Broadway I've always known, Kate thought. As much as she loved the big city version, she was immediately taken with the charm of the place. On the day she had arrived, she had gotten right into the station wagon and had caught only a glimpse of her surroundings. The bus driver, a strong-looking, dark-haired man with a round face, must have sensed her attempt to get her bearings and pointed her in the direction of the heart of the village. "Everything you need is up there," he said. "Just remember, Broadway and Marie Street. You'll pick the bus up here later."

"Are you from the city?" she asked.

"Ten years ago, yeah. You?"

"Just here for a week or so," she said. "I'm from Brooklyn. I was surprised to hear a city accent this far out on the Island."

"There's lots of us. We all left the city. It's changing. You staying in one of those abbey rentals? Maybe I'll pick you up again." He caught himself. "I don't mean pick you up pick you up. I mean…you know…like this…on the bus." He put out his left hand showing his wedding band. "I'm married, so no worries, right?" They laughed.

"No worries." And she headed down Broadway toward the movie theater, eager to take in everything as she went. The Five and Dime caught her eye—always a fun place to spend some time and pick up this or that, none of which she would likely have a real need for. Long Island National Bank—that might come in handy, especially now that she was hoping to stay longer. A woman passed her on the sidewalk and smiled; a man went by and gave a polite, if abrupt, nod. *You'll find the people here the same*, the poet Edwin Markham said. Or was it Ibsen? Oh, well.

She snapped some photos outside The Sweet Shoppe, an enticing place with its name written in gold and black on the window and the smell of malt spilling through its double doors. The interior was fitted out in sparkling chrome and mint green Formica with a long counter where Kate took a seat. A tall, thin man wearing a white apron wrapped around his waist handed her a menu. She glanced at the wall clock and leaned closer to the counter.

"Is it too early for me to get a hamburger and a coke

before nine in the morning?" She was practically whispering, a little self-conscious about her request. As appreciative as she'd been of Mrs. Wick's hospitality, the fried chicken was long gone and she was over toast, cheese and eggs.

"I'll serve you meatloaf and gravy if that's what you're hungry for?" He didn't smile when he said it, but Kate could tell from the warmth of his eyes that he'd said it with good humor. The name George was stitched in navy blue on the pocket of his white shirt.

"Thank you, George. I'll save the meatloaf for another morning."

George looked back over his shoulder as he slapped the patty onto the griddle. "You're new here. Come on the bus?"

"Yes to both. I'm staying in Spiritu in one of the abbey rentals. This is my first time in town."

"You'll like fries with that, right?"

"Right."

"It's good around here," he said. "The shops are nice. You saw the movie house." He gestured with the spatula. "That little bakery next door is the best around. Don't miss out." A few customers came in and George greeted them by name.

A woman who'd been seated at a small table by the window came up to the counter and took a seat on one of the stools near Kate. "I heard you say you're staying in Spiritu. How do you like it, if you don't mind me asking?"

Kate turned to see a woman who appeared to be an attractive fifty or so, upscale casual in pale blue trousers and a crisp white shirt tucked in at the waist, small pearl earrings and hair done up at the back in a French twist, a very different look from Kate's pedal pushers and cotton pullover shirt. "I'm really enjoying it out there. It's an interesting place. Lots of nature and quiet."

"I don't know about the interesting part, but I've heard about the rest." The woman pulled over an ashtray to flick her cigarette. "You're not bored? You're the first person I've met from there. My husband couldn't make it out this year; too much going on at work—we've rented here for about ten years, usually pretty close to town. We feel it's more to our liking. A bit more activity."

Kate chuckled. "I can understand why Spiritu wouldn't be for everyone. But I'm curious—just what is it you've heard that makes you think you wouldn't like it?"

The woman shrugged. "Too quiet. Isolated. I think people make up stories about it—you know, like fairy tales. What do you do for fun?"

Fairy tales? The word *fun* struck Kate, as well. She didn't know anything about the fairy tale part, but she hadn't thought of Spiritu in terms of fun, not in the typical sense, anyway. She felt she might have to be careful how she answered, so as not to appear odd. But did she really care? "It's the quiet and isolation that I'm enjoying. I write a bit. Take pictures. Morning walks."

The woman appeared amused. "Mmm. Exactly as I thought." She wrinkled her nose. "A great place for writers.

You're all happy, I guess, just spending your days thinking. Not much fun." She shrugged. "George, I'll take a coffee to go now."

'You got it, Ed."

Kate smiled. "Ed?"

"Edna Mallory."

"I'm Kate Gannon."

Edna Mallory took the coffee container and slipped off the stool. "Hope to see you again."

"Yes. Nice meeting you." Hmm…fairy tales, she thought.

Kate spent the next hour browsing the shops, including a small art gallery on Nicholai Street.

"Something in particular you're looking for?" the woman in the gallery asked.

"Just browsing, thanks." Generally speaking, the collection appealed to Kate…a mix of oils, water colors and lithographs—street scenes, English countrysides, still lifes and a few portraits, one or two splattered canvases in the style of Jackson Pollock, not a favorite of Kate's.

"That's a particularly fine one," the woman said, referring to a painting Kate had stopped in front of—a stream flowing through a misty woods. There's another over here. And others like it." Kate nodded and walked with her to the opposite wall to see *Bird Sanctuary*.

"That's an original watercolor, but we have the lithograph. It's half the price."

"They're lovely." Kate said.

"Are you an artist? A collector?"

"Oh, no," she laughed. "A former college professor." The word "former" came out so effortlessly that it took her a moment to realize she'd actually said it. The naturalness of it shocked her. When she thought about it later, it occurred to her that she had not even wondered whether there were any responses to her job applications. She had simply put it out of her mind and it gave her pause. What was she doing? She was too bound to the necessities of life—food and shelter—to become a blithe spirit. She was beginning to scare herself. "I just like taking pictures." She gestured to her camera. "Is there a place to get photos developed?"

"Hughie's. Right around the corner, toward Marie Street. It'll take a few days to get them back, so leave yourself time."

"I'm actually a little surprised to see a collection like this in such a small town," Kate said, gesturing to the expanse of wall space.

"Hicksville is really a kind of hub, highly accessible from the City. A popular commute. Actors, singers live here or at least have country homes. Sylvia Dee, the songwriter who wrote "Too Young" and "Chickory Chick," lives about three miles from here. Lots of others. Don't be surprised if you run into Dick Van Dyke at the movie theater with his kids."

"Wow." Kate continued to browse a while longer. Some of the artists rang a bell, but there were so many unknowns…to her, at least…who had done truly beautiful works.

She left the gallery, resolute about coming back into town

again. She would take more pictures and return to the gallery. She would have George make her a meatloaf sandwich at nine in the morning and maybe run into Edna Mallory—she seemed ok—without getting too close. In the afternoon, she would sit on the porch and sip lemonade. She would write. And, only slightly baffled by her cockeyed spontaneity, she would definitely stay another week...maybe two.

On the way back to the bus stop, she stopped at Englert's Bake Shop for a few pastries, and found that George had been right—she wouldn't have wanted to miss this gem.

"Could you please put a dozen of those chocolate rounds in a separate box? I'll take that cinnamon coffee ring too." Those would be for the abbey in the morning, a small thank you for Father Garrett and Mrs. Wick.

She hadn't waited on the corner very long before the bus came. A car horn sounded—Edna Mallory in a blue Chevy convertible. "Need a lift?"

Kate waved. "Oh, thanks. This is fine. Thanks again."

The bus door opened and there he was again, the friendly driver who'd brought her into town.

"Hey, it's you again. I see you've already made a friend. I'm Sal, by the way."

"I have something for you, Sal. I'm Kate." She held out one of the white bakery bags. "I hope you and your wife like apple turnovers."

He took the bag and after peeking inside with the smile of a little boy, set it down next to his lunch pail on the seat behind him. "You're too much."

"What an afternoon," she said, settling into her seat with a satisfied smile as two passengers headed toward the rear of the bus.

Sal closed the door and pulled away from the stop. "You like this place."

"I like this place. I like everything. A lot." Kate chuckled. "Only trouble today is that I got so caught up enjoying myself, I forgot to pick up a box of matches for the kerosene lamp. I don't know what I'd do if the bungalow lost power."

"Hey, I can help you with that. There's a book of matches right back there in my jacket pocket. I sometimes smoke a cigar when my shift is over. But take them. They're yours."

"That's so nice of you, Sal. Thanks." Kate reached over and found the matches. "Dusky's Tavern."

"Yeah, you probably walked right past it today. We had our bowling dinner there. They put out quite a spread."

And they chatted about this and that all the way back to Kate's stop.

Chapter Ten

Edward Darien looked across his desk at the man he had long ago considered a respected colleague. "You must be crazy to think I could ever go along with a scheme like that."

"It's not a scheme, Edward. Scheme sounds so…so…"

"Dirty and underhanded?"

"You're over-thinking this. It would be nothing more than a minor adjustment. A few notations in a ledger."

Darian stared at Jonathon Rorimer and said nothing.

"All I'm saying, Edward, is to just think about it. It is, ultimately, for the good of the school."

"The good of the school? When has that incompetent and now corrupt nephew of yours ever cared about the good of the school? I'm definitely not going to be a party to covering up for that felon."

Jonathon Rorimer got to his feet. "Careful, Edward."

"Not this time around, Jon. We're not talking about skimming snacks from the cafeteria pantry, which, by the way, was bad enough. Embezzlement is a whole different matter; it's criminal. And I won't be intimidated. I want Lonny's resignation on my desk by end of day, and…"

Rorimer narrowed his eyes. "Remember who you're

talking to."

Darien stood and leaned forward, his hands planted on his desk. "Oh, but I know exactly who I'm talking to. I'm talking to a man I'm ashamed to say I've let have his head too many times. A man who has elevated manipulation and mean-spiritedness to an art form. That's who I'm talking to."

"If you value your job here…or anywhere in academia… you'll watch what you say."

"Here's what I say. I say that the great Lonny Kagan will be gone from this school by end of day. If the money isn't returned to the school within twenty-four hours, your darling nephew will face jail time." Darian sat back down and leaned forward, resting his laced fingers before him on the desk. "And I say that you make sure this is made right or you yourself will be gone from Milston quicker than you can say Ryker's Island."

"I've heard all I'm going to hear."

"I agree." Darian gave him a wry smile. "The board will hear the rest."

"You wouldn't dare."

"Don't count on it, Jon, because I'll take it to the papers if I have to. You and that thief of a nephew of yours will look just fine in prison stripes sprawled across the front page of *The New York Daily News*. And I'm sure Kate Gannon would be happy to chime in with everything she knows first-hand about the great Lonny Kagan. We did a bad turn for Kate and that innocent cafeteria worker. I've never felt more ashamed.

But I promise—I will redeem myself."

"You forget, Darian, I can go to the board myself. They'll believe my story over yours."

"Oh, Jonathon, please—the board has always known exactly what you are. They know what Lonny is. They've now got missing funds to prove it. And you're both up to your ears in embezzlement. Let me put it this way…you're done."

"I've never embezzled a penny. How dare you."

"Ahh, but you can come in here, knowing full well that your nephew has, and ask me to cover for him, to lie, to help you…how did you put it…make a minor adjustment to the books. You must be crazy. And where, by the way, is the money? On what selfish excesses has Lonny Kagan squandered Milston's funds? Fifty thousand dollars is not what anyone would call 'petty cash.'" Darian picked up a pencil and tapped it on the desk. "What you have to decide, my friend, is whether or not you're interested in occupying the cell next to his."

Rorimer held Darian with a hard gaze, then stood and turned away, shoulders slumped. "Edward, I…I…where would I get that kind of money?" He slowly faced Darian. "Go easy on me."

"The way you went easy on Professor Gannon? The way you went easy on Mrs. Stanek?"

"Then at least give me more time?"

"I'll give you more time than we gave both of them. I'll give you twenty-four hours."

Rorimer stiffened, then stormed out, slamming the door behind him. Edward Darien took a moment to settle his thoughts, then picked up the phone.

ON Saturday morning, Kate set out early for her twenty-minute walk to the abbey, carrying Mrs. Wick's picnic basket that now contained the cake and pastries she had picked up at Englert's the day before. She was especially grateful for the use of the car for her trip to the Nassau Farmer's Market. When she arrived at the abbey, a stout and serious looking little woman in a white pinafore apron answered the bell and opened the heavy wooden plank door.

"Oh," Kate said, delighted, "you must be Mrs. Wick. I'm so glad to see you. I'm Kate Gannon." She held out the picnic basket. "You sent such wonderful food. You were a life saver. I've added some bakery sweets that I picked up in Hicksville. A very small thank you."

"This isn't a desert island," the woman said, her mouth fixed in a line as hard as her tone. "I'm sure you would have found a way to survive. No need for thanks."

Mrs. Wick's acerbic manner was not at all what Kate had expected and for the moment it left her speechless. But she never did have much patience with rudeness. "It wasn't my intention to bother anyone. You may decide to enjoy the pastries, or not. But maybe Father Garrett and the others will, if you wouldn't mind delivering them. He was kind enough to offer me the use of the station wagon." She emphasized the word "kind." "Is he here?"

"Kind. Hmm," the woman snorted, and took the basket. "Father Garrett is not here, and neither is the town and country. They are both on their way to the auto repair shop in Plainview." The woman's tone seemed to become more acerbic with each word. "So, it seems you have wasted your time." She turned and marched off. "I'll see that the priests get these."

Kate called after her. "What about Father Elway? Is he…?"

"Morning prayer," said the woman, without slowing her pace.

Kate took a few steps forward, calling after her. "Could you please let Father know I'd like to extend my stay for…" but Mrs. Wick had already disappeared through a doorway at the other end of the room.

Exasperated though she was, Kate lingered for a glance around the room. She had never been inside an abbey. She had intended to visit the abbey sooner to meet Father Elway, but the days had gotten away from her. Because the morning sun was not yet at its fullest, the room was heavily shadowed in the spill of amber light coming from the half dozen or so table lamps. Somehow, even with the heavy dark beams and ornate carvings, the place had a warmth to it, an assessment that perhaps reflected her opinion of Father Elway and Father Garrett. She had no intention of allowing Mrs. Wick's crusty disposition to spoil that.

A flash of color caught her eye from beyond the mullioned windows at the rear of the room. Kate walked over for a closer look and saw a lovely garden, nearly enveloped by trees. She turned to see if there was anyone to ask about going out there and when she saw no one, she shrugged and pushed open the heavy wooden door. Kate stood for a moment taking in the unexpected beauty of the place, then stepped out onto a stone path flanked by deep red azaleas and white peonies. She hesitated only a moment before following the curve of path to a low stone wall, beyond which stood a large wooden cross beneath a canopy of maples.

Kate took a deep breath and closed her eyes, drawing in both the sweetness and the silence. She allowed her emotions to settle down and her mind to drift into prayer, her first thoughts being gratitude for yet another lovely experience in Spiritu. She felt thankful for the people, the solace that allowed such long-deferred reflection on her life, the blessing of new and invigorating ideas, possibilities and, above all, a feeling of hope. Her senses were enlivened. Something was taking hold, something that she could not quite identify. She looked up at the cross. *What is this all about? What am I meant to do?*

In an instant, the tranquility was shattered by a burst of movement from the low boxwood hedge. Kate screeched and threw her arm up as a fiery red cardinal circled above her, flapping its wings, as if in a frenzy, before landing on the tip of the crossbeam. She stumbled backward, dropping to the ground, her purse scattering its contents. As she managed to collect herself, she heard someone hurrying along the stone path behind her.

"Are you all right?" A tall, dark-haired man in work clothes helped her to her feet. "I heard you scream."

"Oh, so sorry. I…I'm okay." She rubbed her backside and straightened her skirt. "Thank you." She nodded toward the cross. "That crazy little bird up there scared the life out of me."

"Here, let me help," said the man, bending down to help Kate retrieve the items that had spilled from her purse. "You sure you're okay."

"Does wounded pride count?" She pushed a curl of hair behind her ear, "I probably shouldn't have been back here in the first place."

"There's no reason for you not to be. It is beautiful, isn't it?"

She nodded and wagged her finger in the direction of the cardinal. "That is one feisty little bird."

"Maybe it's his way of making up for that one slightly clipped wing. He just showed up one day recently and he sure has let us know he's around." He handed her the purse. "I'm Matt Reagan, by the way. I do some work here at the abbey."

"Nice to meet you. I'm Kate Gannon. And thanks again for your help."

"You're welcome to stay," he said.

"I'd better get going. I think I've done enough to disrupt things. And who knows what else our little winged friend might have in store for me?"

He walked back inside the abbey with her. "I couldn't help over-hearing your conversation with Mrs. Wick. I'd be happy to give you a lift."

"Oh…no…that's okay. I can't impose. I…"

"It's no imposition. My truck is around the side. I believe you said you were headed to the Farmer's Market."

"Yes, Father Elway had told me about it. It's time I picked up some groceries, especially if I'm going to stay another week or so. But I wouldn't want to take you out of your way."

"Truth is, I'm headed in that direction for some parts that I need." He started rolling down the sleeves of his blue shirt and buttoning the cuffs. "Father Garrett can pick you up later after he gets back from the shop with the town and country."

"Well, then, I'd appreciate it. I was kind of counting on getting there today."

Chapter Eleven

SHE HAD NEVER ridden in a pick-up truck. He opened the door to the dark blue Chevrolet, and she stepped up onto the running board to climb in.

"Thanks again for the ride," she said, once he'd gotten in behind the wheel.

He headed around the pond to the gravel driveway. "My pleasure."

"I really appreciate it," was all she could think of saying, and they were both silent for the next few moments. He seems like a nice man, Kate thought. Strong yet gracious. Helpful. Confident. She could see why he would work for the abbey.

"Mrs. Wick is not usually that brusque," Matt said. "She had just found out her beloved pantry is being moved. She really is a kind person."

"Actually, I'm not usually that brusque either. She just caught me off guard and I kind of felt I was a bit under attack." She laughed.

"Understandable." He gave her a long glance. "What brings you to Spiritu? I'm always interested in knowing how people find the place. It's off the beaten path."

She didn't mind his curiosity. He had a polite manner and

after so much alone time, she appreciated the chance to have another conversation, as she'd had with Sal, the bus driver. "I saw an ad in the paper."

"No kidding? I've never known us to run an ad."

She found the word "us" interesting. "You've been here a long time?"

"A few years. It's a big change from the city, and I needed the change."

"I know what you mean. I'm from Brooklyn." She caught herself quickly. "Don't get me wrong. I love where I live, but you're right—the change is nice."

They said very little after that, but she was aware that he glanced over at her a few times and she wondered what he was thinking. He was the first one to speak. "You getting along okay here? Any…you know… problems or…concerns?"

"Uh, no. Everything is working out just fine," she said, a bit baffled by his questions, which sounded more like concerns. "In fact, I've decided to stay longer…if the cottage is available. I like it here. I like the quiet and the pace. Nature. Time to be alone and…I don't know…maybe anonymous for a little while. It's inspiring."

He nodded slowly. "Nature can be a great healer."

Once again, his comment struck her as curious and she wondered if she was getting some insight into his own motivations. Maybe he'd left a troubled life behind, but she would never ask. They finished their ride in silence and when they'd arrived, he came around and took her hand to help her out of the truck. "Have fun."

"Thanks again for giving me a ride, Matt."

"You going to be okay?"

Kate gestured to the sprawling building. "I'm looking forward to the adventure."

He tore a piece of paper from the pad he carried in the pocket of his shirt and scribbled a phone number. "Here," he said, handing it to Kate. "Just in case you need to call the abbey. Have fun."

The Nassau Farmer's Market was an enormous one-story structure, housing narrow aisles of goods and delectables as far as the eye could see. Kate stood at the entrance for a long moment attempting to orient herself in the crowded maze before setting off. She had nearly forgotten what she had come for as she wandered past stalls with aprons and housedresses hanging from curtain rods, overflowing book stands and vendors selling car wax, fly swatters and bird seed amid the aroma of sausage and peppers and fried zeppole. Halfway along, she stopped at one of the stalls. "Excuse me. Is there someone here who sells paper or office supplies?"

"That's Carl," the woman said, placing a folded quilt over a display rack. "Al," she called up the aisle. "Al, show her how to get to Carl's."

A heavy-set man holding a box of fishing lures pointed the way, and after side-stepping a vacuum cleaner demonstration and a few vendors selling dog beds, window fans and shower curtains, Kate arrived at a place jammed with sagging shelves of file folders, typing paper, steno pads and black and white speckled composition note books—her favorite. She purchased a few things to fill a small paper bag and headed to the food area, keeping an eye on the time—Father Garrett would be there by 3:00, which gave her time for some shopping as well as lunch.

She browsed a few more aisles before deciding on a slice of pizza and a Coke. As she made her way to a small table, a man in the crowded aisle turned quickly and bumped into her, spilling hot coffee onto the floor. Kate jumped back to avoid being burned and with a sweep of her hand knocked over a glass of beer at a nearby table, sending the spill everywhere. The man with the beer sprang to his feet, his trousers soaked.

"I'm so sorry," she said, frantic. "Oh, my goodness." She quickly set her food and shopping bags down to grab at whatever napkins she could to help sop up the mess on the table and floor.

"It happens," the man said, more accommodating than Kate would have expected. "It's always a bit of a madhouse here, but fun."

A few people offered napkins while others just gave a curious look before moving on, accustomed as they likely were to whatever mayhem occurred.

"Please, let me get you another," Kate said.

"Don't worry about it," he said with good humor, "my wife will probably be happier that it's on me instead of in me." They laughed. "I hope you didn't get much on you."

Kate brushed at her clothing. "Not much at all." She laughed, "It's washable anyway."

After eating, she headed over to the butcher, then on to some of the other grocery aisles. The bakery was hard to resist but she did—she still had a few sweets from Englert's back at the bungalow—she would remember it for her next visit. This was definitely a place she wanted to come back to.

By ten of three, she was waiting at the curb with a nearly full cart, but it wasn't Father Garrett who showed up. It was Matt Reagan.

"Me again," he said as he came around the back of the truck. "That old beast of a station wagon was more in need than they thought. Father Garrett sends apologies."

"Now I really am sorry, taking you out of your way a second time."

"Not at all." He pointed toward the far corner of the building. "I was just around back picking up a couple of gaskets at the auto center. When Father Garret called the abbey to give us the bad news, I figured I could come get you…and the gaskets."

She smiled. "Well then, I feel a little better about it."

"What have you got here?" He started lifting the bags out of her cart to put in the back of the truck. "Are you sure you're only planning to stay another week?"

"Oh well…I picked up some pads and paper. Also a few books. How can you go wrong with Earl Stanley Gardner and Emily Dickenson for a quarter?"

"Do you write?"

"A little, yes."

"And you made it to the butcher, I see."

"Yes. Very impressive. I couldn't resist a little bunch of Cornish hens. Can you imagine?" She laughed. "I ordinarily don't even eat Cornish hens, but I was just feeling adventurous." Kate handed him the last of the small bags and climbed into the truck.

"That's good," he said. "Spiritu is the kind of place that can inspire adventure, but sometimes it may not be the best idea for a person to stay too much to themselves."

They were headed back up the road and she was grateful to be out of the din. "That's quite a place back there."

"Yes, it is." He looked over at her. "Find any treasures? Anything special to eat…or drink? Besides the Cornish hens, I mean."

"Had a nice little lunch, but not without a bit of chaos to go with it. Crowds and spills and pushing." She chuckled. "Overall, I'd say it's a fun place. I enjoyed myself and people were pretty nice. I'm looking forward to going back." She looked over at him. "Maybe next time I'll be able to get there on my own."

They were silent for a few minutes before they both started speaking at once. "Oh, please, you go first," she said.

"After you, Miss Gannon."

"Call me Kate. Please." She looked down at her hands. "What was it about the city that made you…and your family…want to make such a big change? I hope you don't mind my asking?"

"Not at all." He glanced her way a few times before answering. "I think…." he looked over at her again. "I think that's a conversation best had over dinner. There's a great little Italian restaurant right off Wantagh Parkway. I could come by for you about seven."

She was so taken by surprise that she felt her heart jump. He was a very attractive man. She couldn't help noticing how his hazel eyes held the light. And no wedding band. Obviously, a thoughtful kind of a guy and pleasant company. But the idea of a date. It was so unexpected. She hadn't been on a date since David. "I don't know…I…"

"Sounds like a 'yes' to me. How about it?"

She liked his smile and the sound of his voice, and surely his connection with the abbey had to count for something, but she still didn't know anything about him. Not all married men wore wedding bands. "Maybe another time."

She was standing on the front step, watching him walk back to his truck after he'd carried in the last of her bags. She took a deep breath, momentarily contemplating the way he moved and the strength she could see in his shoulders. "By the way," he said, turning, "no family. Just me. Say yes."

"SHE'S pretty," he thought as he headed home along Old

Country Road. "Nice to be around." He couldn't stop thinking about what Father Garrett had said, and wondered why an attractive woman with such a pleasing personality would have a drinking problem. He hadn't wanted to believe it. Still, as early as mid-afternoon, he could smell the beer on her when she got into the truck. He hoped to learn more over dinner. But he would have to be careful. People who hide their drinking are also good at hiding the destructive lives they lead. He remembered a guy he worked with years back. No one had a clue that he was a Class A functioning alcoholic. Got all his work done on time, would help anyone. You'd bet money on how fit and stable he was. Until his wife left him. He even hid that for a while before his life really started coming apart. Ended up in AA, which was a good thing. But he eventually left the company and no one had seen him since. If Kate Gannon had any idea that people suspected she had a problem, she would more than likely leave Spiritu, and that would be a shame on many levels. He would have to be very careful not to let on, and not to get too involved.

Chapter Twelve

ANGIOLO'S HAD ALL the charm Kate could ask for in a cozy eatery—deep red walls, low light under a dark beamed ceiling, crisp white tablecloths on which were set small glass and pewter lanterns that cast an amber glow. The aromas of garlic and pasta and pizza coming from the brick ovens at the back permeated the square room. In the center, a fireplace. Kate felt caught by the Saturday evening ambience with its fill of subtle chatter.

"What a nice place." She glanced at Matt, who smiled back.

"I had a feeling you'd like it."

She liked his looks, freshly shaved and handsome in his navy sport coat. These were unexpected pleasures—a great little restaurant, attractive date. She didn't know why she felt slightly embarrassed by the word "date." Isn't that what it was? How awful, she thought, to be so unaccustomed to the practice of dating that she would have to actually reflect on its meaning, for heaven's sake. But that's what it was—a date. And she had every intention of enjoying it. A few days earlier, she could never have imagined that this was how she would spend her first Saturday night way out here on Long

Island where she had not known a soul. How quickly things can change, she thought, relishing the moment.

A short, dark-haired man hurried over and with a thick accent greeted Matt, shaking his hand. "Good to see you, my friend. And with such a lovely lady."

"Good to see you, Tony. This is Kate."

"Ah, Bella. So nice to have you in my restaurant." He gave a quick little bow, then turned back to Matt. "I have a perfect corner table for you, Mr. Matt. Come." Tony led the way, then offered to get them started with a glass of his best vintage. He put his fingers to his lips to feign a kiss. "A beautiful Tinta Negra 1950."

"I think I'll pass for tonight, Tony."

"No vino?" He laughed. "And how about the lovely lady?" He smiled at Kate, but Matt answered for her.

"Maybe not tonight," Matt said, turning to Kate as if for agreement.

"Oh, that's fine," Kate said, masking her surprise with a smile. "I'll have my usual, which is club soda with just a hint of Grenadine. Not too sweet."

"You are sweet enough," Tony said. "And for you, Mr. Matt?"

"Just black coffee, please, Tony."

The background music was mellow, what Kate liked to call supper club piano, the standards—Lester Lannon, Oscar Peterson. She felt like humming along.

"You look happy," Matt said. Tony had brought their

drinks. She took a sip.

"Mmm. I am. I probably shouldn't admit it, but I haven't been out to dinner in such a lovely place in a long time. Thank you for asking me."

"Well, as I mentioned earlier today, spending time in Spiritu can be a great experience as long as we don't let it turn us into a recluse."

"I wonder sometimes just what's wrong with being a recluse…for a little while anyway. Not that I want to become one, although my friend Ellen is afraid that I might. She thinks I'm being completely ridiculous. Her choice was much different."

"Different how? What happened? You told me you saw the ad, but what was it that made you choose Spiritu?"

Kate wasn't sure how much to tell a person she hardly knew. "I actually think Spiritu chose me. I…had a couple of major changes in my life, and the abbey's ad just happened to catch my eye at the right time."

He nodded his understanding, but didn't press her. "As Providence would have it," was all he said.

Over a meal of manicotti for her and veal piccata for him, he talked a little about himself.

"When you find yourself working sixteen, seventeen-hour days, you have to know that something's gotta give. My job…I was a building inspector…took me all over the city. I lived in Queens and I reached a point where between the work and the subway commute, I was getting three hours sleep. Even a thick-headed guy like me knows that can't go on."

"I can understand that." She picked thoughtfully at the edges of her food with her fork. "Why Spiritu?" She looked at him, recalling his comment from earlier in the day. "Remember, that was the question we needed a dinner to discuss."

"Yes. Well…sure." He smiled. "I had a friend whose family came out to the country every summer. He invited me for a weekend and while I was exploring, I came across a station wagon broken down on the side of the road." He stopped and looked directly at her with a smirk. She quickly picked up on it.

"Don't tell me…not…"

"Yes. That very station wagon and Father Garrett with it. He's a funny fellow, Father Garrett. A wonderful human being, but things sometimes seem to go a little sideways when he's involved. They laughed. "Anyway, I got the old wagon started, but since the battery seemed weak, I decided to follow along to be sure he would make it back to where he was going—the abbey. And that's when I got to meet Father Elway, a good man who happens to love fishing as much as I do. When he discovered that I could fix things too, he asked me to do some work. I had three-weeks-vacation every year. So, I started coming out to tinker with this and that and the friendship was forged." He looked away for a moment, thoughtful. "Plus, I found that I needed Spiritu. I liked the area and the people I'd met. I liked the change of pace. The peace. One day, I just decided I wanted this to be not just a place where I could visit, but my way of life. I still do." He took a sip of hot coffee. "So, now, I have my own contracting business and in addition to helping out at the abbey, I do home renovations in the wider Hicksville area, and right here too, along with small commercial work. I'll say what I said earlier—Spiritu is a good place to heal."

"Did you have something that needed healing?"

"Not exactly. Just the lifestyle thing." He hesitated. "With the schedule I'd kept all those years, no relationship ever lasted. Why would a woman put up with that?"

"You never married?"

He shook his head, then looked at her. "No, although I was engaged once. Years back. One of the things that didn't work out. And funny thing, since I've been out here, there's never been a real…I guess you'd say…opportunity. I've dated a little, but…" He set his cup down. "Hey, I'm supposed to be learning about you."

She looked down. "Supposed to? That sounds like an assignment."

"I…I didn't mean it the way it sounded. I mean…I'm curious."

She folded her napkin onto her lap. "My grandfather raised me. He died the end of last year. He'd been failing for a long time and I knew it was inevitable, but it was still a big loss for me. We were very close. He was my only family…

outside of a couple of cousins who live down on the Jersey shore, but I haven't seen them in years. Then." She paused. Was she saying too much? What man really wants to hear this? Still, he was eyeing her with such intense interest. "Then I had a break-up. It hadn't been serious and I wasn't at all heartbroken over it. I was relieved, in fact, to finally have the courage to do it. He was…well, let's just say we were mismatched." She drew a deep breath. "Then, more recently…" She laughed. "I'm talking way too much. Sorry."

"No, you're not." He leaned in. "Please. I'm interested."

"A couple of months ago I lost my job. I was a professor of Literature at Milston College." She gave him a sheepish look. "I was really good at my job. Is that too proud a thing to say?"

"Not at all. I would think you were better than good. A lot better."

"Nice of you to say." His eyes were probing, an invitation to let go. He was quite close now. There was a sense of intimacy that was unexpected. She felt comfortable that she could trust him. "Anyway, I never saw it coming. I moped and brooded for a while, angry and shocked by what I took as betrayal. Then I decided…with Ellen giving me a swift kick in the pants…that it was time to get a move on. Examine my life, you might say. That's when Spiritu happened to show up. And funny thing, my dear best friend, Ellen, isn't at all happy about it. She can't imagine why I'm attracted to a vacation experience like this."

He rubbed the side of his face. "I've always had the feeling that Spiritu never just happens to show up. And, well, she's got a point. Why vacation here of all places?"

Once again, in reflecting on her reason for coming to Spiritu, it took her a moment to consider it. "I…I guess maybe it's that I'm not thinking of it as a vacation." She looked up at him. "Odd, right?" She took a sip of her drink, feeling a little uneasy discussing something that, as yet, she herself hadn't quite figured out.

"Don't you get a little lonely here? You don't know anyone. There's not much going on except in Hicksville."

"I don't think I can answer that yet…even for myself."

"Still…" he said, placing his hand over hers, "sounds like you've been through a lot. I'm sorry." Then, as if to catch himself, he drew his hand away. "Besides your friend Ellen, was there no one else to turn to?"

"No one close enough. I live in a friendly neighborhood, but just because the neighbors are friendly, doesn't mean they can be friends, if you know what I mean. I'm sure that's why my job counted for so much. You get into a routine with the same people and, in my case, students too. They become a focus in your life. Things revolve around them and the work you do. You learn who the ones are that you can best relate to and trust—at least you think you learn."

Tony came by rolling a trolley with desserts. "The best cheesecake outside of Brooklyn."

"That sounds too good to pass up," Kate said. "And a cup of decaf coffee, please."

"I'll pass, Tony, but I will have more coffee." Tony placed a slice of cheesecake on a plate and set it before Kate, then left. Matt turned to Kate. "Okay, you like Italian food and cheesecake. Let's see what else? Oh, yes, Cornish hens. But only for the adventure." They laughed. "We didn't order wine. So, is club soda always your preference?"

"I'm not much of a drinker." She put her fork down. "This cheesecake is delicious. Tony was right. Awfully rich, though. If I finish it, I'll never get to sleep tonight."

They sat quietly for a moment. For Kate it was afterglow—the food, the music, the setting. The company. She liked his openness…and so much more.

"So, Kate Gannon, what are the plans or ideas rolling around in that pretty head of yours?"

She felt herself blush. "I've put in applications at other schools. Had a few interviews. Ellen is keeping an eye on my mailbox. But for now, I just want to stay here a while longer, take more pictures. Do more writing. You saw that I bought pads and paper today. A little of this and a little of that to get my creative juices flowing again. It feels good. Milston nearly swallowed me whole. Even the articles I wrote that won awards had my director's name on them. My friend, my trusted colleague. Imagine." She looked down. "I feel like such a fool."

"We've all been foolish about one thing or another at one time or another. You wouldn't be the first person to give a lot more than you got. What's important now is to take the time to find the right path."

"Have you always been so philosophical, or is that something that has brushed off from Father Elway?"

"A little of both, I guess." He paused. "I attended Bronx High School of Science. Did two years in the navy. It was the end of the war and I never left Floyd Bennett Field, but later I went to MIT on the G.I. Bill and came out with a degree in engineering. I think I've always had an engineer's mind… this goes here, that fits there. I'm closing in on thirty-five and I feel as though I'm just beginning to learn things. Father Elway has definitely helped with that. He's serene and caring."

"I like that."

"I'm curious." He paused. "You're obviously a very talented writer. But you're only looking at the college market for a job. Do you prefer teaching over writing?"

"No. Actually, one of the things I've come to terms with just since arriving in Spiritu, is that I don't. My true passions are writing and photography, but most of all writing. Still, it's very difficult for someone like me with no publishing credits to my name to break into the industry as a full-time writer or editor. Believe me, I tried it. This is New York, after all—fast paced, high powered. I'm a little too old to intern, although I did intern when I was younger, at Conde Nast. All through my college summers, as a matter of fact. A good company, but I had expectations that never came to pass. I'd probably have done better with a small publishing house in another state. Or…maybe I give in too quickly, but a person needs to make a living and the fact is I can't afford to sit home and spend my days making up stories and poems. If I could, Matt, the truth is that I would write novels. It's a long, isolating kind of work, but I don't mind being alone or isolated. Hence, Spiritu."

He nodded. "I get it. I had to spend three summers hauling two-by-fours and pallets of bricks before anyone gave me a chance at something I was actually trained for. I used whatever time I could during those early years to learn from people I thought were the best. I was never really passionate about engineering, but it gave me some leverage in the beginning."

"I know what you mean," she said, taking a sip of water. "After graduating from college, I got a job at a big publishing house in the city, delivering photo slides to the art department for the magazines. When I finally got a chance to contribute an article, short as it was…but a good one…my editor got the byline. I don't mind the concept of "paying my dues," but don't you think that at some point the bill should be 'paid in full'?" Anyway…I got a lucky break…I met a person who knew a person and the next thing I knew someone was offering me a job at a college, and a good college at that. I guess in some way I felt redeemed. Off I went."

They were quiet on the way home. Kate felt serene. It was good to talk with someone who appeared to understand and share the same kind of feelings about things. For so long, Ellen had been her only confidant, but as much as she loved Ellen, sometimes her brash tactics unnerved her. Matt made her feel comfortable talking about herself, a practice she was not accustomed to. Fortunately, she had never felt that comfortable relating to Edward Darien on too personal a level. It must have been some sixth sense that kept her from telling him too much about herself. She hoped she hadn't said too much tonight.

They pulled up outside her bungalow. The truck windows had been rolled down, so they could already hear the insect choir and smell the musky fragrance of the woods. "Takes some getting used to, this kind of noise," she said amiably. "Not a lot of it in Brooklyn. We specialize mostly in car horns and sirens."

"Oh, I remember that well." He nodded, smiling. "I want to go back to something you said earlier, about feeling comfortable being alone and isolated." It was dark, but she could see what appeared to be a look of concern in his eyes. "Being alone and isolated are not always healthy. It may lead to…I don't know…maybe bad habits."

She couldn't help chuckling. "It's actually kind of nice to have somebody besides my bossy friend, Ellen, worry about me. You're very kind." She reached over and touched his arm. "Thank you for worrying about me, even if there's no need to."

He went around to open her door. "I've really enjoyed this, Kate." The night was balmy and dark as ink. This was her first time out after sundown since she'd arrived in Spiritu. As he guided her out of the truck, she slid down and raised her face in the darkness to breathe in the night air. She could feel him standing close. She felt safe with him. Safe and…did she dare think it? Her thoughts were mere whispers in her head. She wanted him to kiss her…but she knew she wouldn't allow it. What would he think?

"Tomorrow's Sunday," he said, in a whisper. "I'd be happy to pick you up for church in the morning, if you like. The abbey has only one Mass and it's at 9:00. After that I'm taking Father Elway fishing over at Captree. What do you think?"

"If it's no trouble, I'd be grateful, Matt. And thanks again for a wonderful evening,"

He finally let go of her hand. She hadn't even realized he'd been holding it…it felt so natural. Strong, comforting. Then he walked her to the door, his hand under her elbow and gave her a long last look. "See you in the morning."

HE had come that close to kissing her. What would she have thought of him? He looked at the clock: three a.m. She was beautiful. Smart. Independent, yet vulnerable. And she was smooth— that whole bit about the club soda told with such innocence. What was he to believe? She'd taken some tough blows. Loss. Grief. Getting the rug pulled out from under her at the school. That would drive anyone to drink. He hadn't planned on getting involved, just to offer a little guidance, find out what was going on. Now, here he was, in up to his neck, and the only thing he knew for sure was that he couldn't get her out of his mind.

No sleeping on the couch tonight, she thought, changing dreamily for bed. She slid under the covers and put Matt's business card on the pillow beside her, enchanted. He had shared so openly about himself. And he listened to her, interested, she was sure of it. No faking it. Genuine. So different from David. How odd to suddenly feel so safe and okay with everything just because she knew this wonderful man was out there somewhere. Less than twenty-four hours before, she'd never even seen him, known his name, heard his voice. Now, just like that, everything could so easily be about *him*. She could fall, really fall. Maybe it was just a girlish fantasy. But there was definitely something between them. It was palpable. She was sure he must have felt it too. She turned over, then turned again. How could she be sure of anything anymore? Maybe she was imagining a certain chemistry between them the same way she had imagined that she'd had trusted colleagues and job security at Milston. She looked at the clock: three a.m. She couldn't wait for him to pick her up for church.

Chapter Thirteen

ON SUNDAY MORNING, Ellen sat in Kate's kitchen, drumming her fingers on the Formica table top. She could kill that woman. What was wrong with her? Not a care in the world that there might be a response from one of the colleges she'd applied to. As a matter of fact, there were four, just sitting there for three days unopened. And who knew if there had been phone calls, schools trying to connect with her to set up interviews or make job offers. She went back into the living room to call Kate again, but for the fiftieth time in two days all she could do was let the phone ring off the hook in case her dear friend was anywhere nearby to be found. She wasn't.

Maybe she should worry that something had happened to Kate, roaming the Long Island countryside. She had said there weren't even paved roads; it was clear that she had entered some kind of la-la land. Ellen picked up the unopened envelopes—Hofstra, Hunter College, Fordham, CCNY. She set the envelopes down and picked them up again. She knew Kate wouldn't mind if she opened them. How else do you find out if it's anything important? Ellen got to her feet and paced around the kitchen table, furious. Whatever bug had bitten her misguided friend, it sure looked as if Ellen cared about this whole thing more than Kate did.

She opened a drawer, took out a steak knife and, one by one, slit open the envelopes, reading each of the letters: *We would be happy to speak with you about…; Your credentials would certainly add a great deal here at…; We can definitely fit you in for an interview during the next week or two; just give us a call…; After careful consideration following your recent interview, we would like to extend an offer to….* Ellen paced again, then tossed the letters onto the kitchen table and left.

MASS at the abbey was different from anything Kate had experienced in church. The chapel was a small rustic space of heavy wood, pale stained glass—the most beautiful she'd ever seen—and dozens of candles that served as the only light. There were ten pews, the first couple occupied by the abbey's eight priests who chanted the entire Mass in Latin, before which Father Elway had circled what Kate was told to be an eighteenth-century wooden altar, swinging the ornate silver thurible that emitted the fragrant, smoky incense. Kate sat toward the rear with Matt and three other parishioners, enjoying the deep peace of the sacred. By what grace had she gotten to this precious moment? She looked at Matt, his eyes closed in prayer, hands folded in front of him. She struggled against distraction but couldn't get him out of her thoughts long enough to give God proper thanks and attention. She had been much too close to him the night before, too close in so many ways and her senses could not move beyond the intimacy of it.

As was the abbey's custom after Sunday Mass, Mrs. Wick had set out refreshments in the library for the priests and parishioners—coffee, tea and a small spread of pastries and cake, some of which looked familiar. It was Kate's first chance to meet Father Elway, a meeting that proved pleasant and curious.

"Well, I am indeed happy to meet you at last, Miss Gannon. I pray you are finding that our little hamlet has the respite you seek. Issues and trials need not last forever, if we allow true peace to take hold in us." He placed his hands on her shoulders and leaned in, his eyes warm, deep and knowing. "Wondrous things are known to happen in Spiritu. So, as you can imagine, I'm very happy to have you stay another week or two. Stay as long as you like."

"Thank you, Father." Did they just assume that everyone coming to Spiritu had issues and trials? She hadn't thought of her own situation as such. Did the sweet old couple she'd met on the path that week have issues and trials? The grandmother of those two teenage girls? As Kate saw it, the fact that she seemed suddenly in the throes of some kind of revival of purpose had more to do with avocation than dysfunction.

"And one more thing," Father Elway said in a gleeful

whisper. "I see you've discovered Englert's. The sweets you brought us are wonderful."

The library was another richly old, traditional room—walls lined to the ceiling with book shelves, an abundance of mahogany along with a thick burgundy patterned rug that filled the center of the dark wood plank floor. Kate enjoyed the small talk with the priests and others from the local community who'd been at Mass, and it appeared that Mrs. Wick had come around. "They're taking my pantry," she whispered to Kate, as if by way of confession. "The two of them." She nodded in the direction of Father Elway and Matt. "The very thought of it turns me into a…well…you saw."

"It's okay, Mrs. Wick. I understand." She put her hand on the woman's shoulder. "I have a feeling from what little I've seen of Matt, that they'll give you something that may turn out to be even nicer."

"They'd better," Mrs. Wick said with playful gruffness.

In the midst of this pleasant mingling of people who were so quickly and easily no longer strangers, Kate once again had a sense of something that had been missing from her life—her job had lulled her into forsaking social and community opportunities, now and then even the spiritual. She'd like to blame Edward Darien for that, but the choice ultimately had been hers. School and work and, as she was beginning to discern, maybe not even the work she was meant to do. But just what exactly was she meant to do and how would she find out? During Mass, she had asked that question in the silence of her heart.

"Ready to go?" Matt asked, smiling. "The fish will be biting."

"Why don't you go on ahead, Matt. I think I'd like to walk back. It's such a beautiful morning."

He raised an eyebrow. "Don't tell me you're still concerned about taking me out of my way."

"You've managed to get me past that. Thanks." She looked about the room. "And thanks for this too. It's been wonderful."

As Kate prepared to leave, Father Elway approached. "Have you seen the garden?"

"Yes, Father. It's so beautiful and tranquil. And the cardinals seem…very much at home out there." She laughed. "I had an interesting meeting with one that has a clipped wing."

"Ah, Yes, Solomon."

"Solomon?"

"Oh, yes. That little bird knows things, which gives him… shall we say…no small measure of power." Father Elway laughed, then took Kate's hand and patted it. "I do hope you'll become a regular visitor to the garden. We can bring so much to it and take so very much away with us."

Kate left the abbey with a jumble of thoughts and emotions—uplifted, confused, mystified. A bird who knows things? Really? Father Elway so beautifully…odd. Mrs. Wick, dutiful and sweet. Matt, taking tighter hold of her heart. She had prayed for guidance and for clarity. Maybe for once in her life she would follow God's lead instead of her own. But where on earth was He leading her?

She was glad she'd worn her flat shoes because a short time later, headed back home with the sun warm on her back, she decided to meander the lanes again, noticing how many things constantly change in nature—types of trees she hadn't seen before, new flowers in bloom, colors shifting in the light of the passing hours. She enjoyed the stroll, content with the feeling of remaining unbound by time, hoping to see the cottage with the fantastic garden. But no matter which lane she chose, she couldn't locate it.

In one direction, then the other, she stopped and looked about, trying to orient herself. Something flashed red. A bird swooped, nearly brushing her shoulder. She jumped out of the way but managed to catch sight of something familiar. "Oh, my gosh, the clipped wing. It's that cardinal again." She began to hurry along in the opposite direction, her heart racing. *You crazy bird, stop making people feel like they're under attack.* The cardinal came back around, nearly stopping in mid-air in front of her, its wings aflutter. What was going on here? She was frightened. And no one around that she could call to? She looked about but saw only trees. She didn't even know exactly where she was. *What lane is this? How am I going to get back to my bungalow?* As the cardinal hovered, Kate put her arm up for protection and started walking away. Sooner or later, she would have to see a house. But the cardinal came around in front of her again, flew off to the left and came back. She stopped. The cardinal flew off again to the left, then came back, repeating this four or five times. A crazy thought crossed her mind—did he want her to follow him? Was she insane for thinking such a thing?

The next time he flew off to the left, she followed. He came back around, less frenzied now, then took off again in the same direction, and again she followed. She felt mesmerized. After a few minutes, the cardinal flew straight up and away. She shielded her eyes from the sun, looking up after him, and waited. He was gone. *What on earth was that all about?* A moment later, she realized she was standing in front of the flower cottage.

Chapter Fourteen

Kate could only stare. Was she imagining that the cardinal had led her here? Solomon, the bird? Was she losing her mind? Maybe this is what Ellen was so afraid of—that being in such a remote place, completely out of the ordinary from her normal life, would plunge her into some kind of alternate reality? Aberrations? Isn't that what this was—an aberration? She couldn't find the flower cottage on her own, so a cardinal came along and brought her there? She looked up, "Oh, God, am I going crazy? What kind of guidance is this?" But she knew better—one thing her faith had taught her all her life was that God does things in God's own way and in God's own time. So, if God were guiding her, what was he guiding her to? And for what reason? Just to take a photograph of a lovely little house? Well, beauty being what it is, maybe that would be enough.

The heat of the sun was getting to her. As striking as the flower cottage was, she felt the need to get back to her bungalow, wherever the heck that was. It would have been wise for her to have gone there directly after Mass to get out of the light wool jacket she'd worn to church, and put on some cooler clothing. She had taken off her jacket and folded it over her arm, but it wasn't enough. The sun had gradually become too intense and she had to take it seriously. She might be in the throes of a heat stroke.

She noticed a small post and leaned against it, and after a minute or two, turned back to the path to try and head home. Something moved at one side of the cottage. She strained to see what it was, her line of sight obscured by a cascade of arched pink tendrils. A woman. She could see her moving toward the front flower bed, a yellow watering can in her hand. Kate wanted to approach to ask about the garden. Who knew if she would get another chance? But she felt she'd better get home. At least, she would ask for directions to Hummingbird Lane. Still, she hesitated—this was so clearly a very private place; she felt sure she would be encroaching. When the woman reached the front door she turned, having noticed Kate.

"I'm sorry," Kate said, calling out to her, and stepped forward. "I'm just so overwhelmed by the beauty of your garden." She waved her hand in front of her face. "And by the heat. I'm not sure how to get back to my bungalow."

The woman smiled. "You'd better come up. It's cooler and I have lemonade."

"Are you sure?"

"Come," the woman said, with a friendly wave of the hand.

She appeared to be about fifty, with fair skin and soft blonde hair tied back with a blue checkered band. "It makes me happy when people love my garden as much as I do." She tucked her gloves into the pocket of her seersucker coveralls.

Kate approached. "I can't imagine what it takes to create something so spectacular."

"A labor of love," the woman said in a loud whisper, as if relaying a confidence. "Anything spectacular requires it. Don't you think?"

"Yes. Yes, I do."

The woman placed the watering can on the floor of the porch, and walked to the railing as Kate approached. "I'm Abigail Sweet."

"Hi, I'm Kate Gannon. Thank you for letting me see your garden up close. I happened upon it for the first time this week. I've only been here a few days. I'm just on my way home from Mass at the abbey. I have to confess I took a few photos of your cottage the other day. Maybe you wouldn't have wanted me to."

"Oh, please do," said the woman, offhandedly. "You're welcome to take all the pictures you want. I hope they come out. Matter of fact, next time you have your camera with you, I'll take you around back, where the gazebo and the rose trellises are. You'll definitely want to snap a few back there. But for right now, you need to have something cool to drink. Come have a seat. I'll get the lemonade."

Kate felt happy about the woman's kind invitation but wanted to be sure not to overstep. "I really can't impose. Lately, I keep pulling people away from what they're doing."

"I love being pulled away," the woman said, and went inside.

Kate took a deep breath, just now fully realizing how much she had needed to stop and rest. She had a way of getting so absorbed in nature that sometimes she lost track of everything else.

Abigail Sweet returned, carrying a bright green, lacquered tray with a round glass pitcher of lemonade and two frosted glass tumblers. "It's easy to overdo things, isn't it?"

"Yes, it is. I guess when it comes to nature, I don't even realize I'm overdoing."

"In time, you'll get a hold on things," the woman said, handing a glass to Kate.

The woman had a fragile beauty, soft and light. Kate could instantly sense a vibrant spirit. A kindness. "Maybe that's partly what made me decide to stay longer. At first, I thought just a week. But I'm finding it such a wonderful place to get back to…things."

Abigail set the tray on the side table and sat with her glass of lemonade. "Like what? What kind of things are you getting back to?"

"Writing, mostly. Taking photos." She laughed. "Exploring."

"Ah, wonderful. A writer. What do you like to write? I can't wait to hear more."

"I'm embarrassed to say I've never been published under my own name. At Milston, the school where I taught

Literature, I wrote articles and essays for our director. He actually won a few awards."

"You mean *you* did. You won the awards," Abigail said, smiling.

Kate felt herself blush. "Other than that, my writing has always been mostly about nature. A poem here and there. The milky scent of boxwoods, stuff like that. A short piece about a tree—the way it settles its shade over a yard, as if in some way to take command of the sunlight or to look out for those in need of respite."

"Very interesting." Abigail eyed Kate with an easy gaze, nodding. "Yes, I could tell you're a very interesting person."

The porch...the house...Abigail herself...all such a surprising respite, as welcoming as Kate would have expected, with a profusion of flowers spilling from the window boxes and the pots set near the railing. The breathtaking fragrance. Abigail's interest and kindness. Kate felt better already.

"Honestly, Kate. I'm baffled by what you're doing."

"I know it must seem strange, Ellen." Kate regretted answering the phone.

"How else could it seem? I've called you fifty times. I've opened letters that you apparently have absolutely no interest in, even though they figure heavily into a future where you don't become a bowery bum."

"I'm sorry for all the trouble. I've been very inconsiderate. I'd tell you what's going on but, odd as it sounds, I hardly know myself."

"That's exactly what I'm afraid of, Kate. Seriously." There was an audible gasp. "I think I should come out and see you. At least, let me have the reassurance that you're not in some kind of crack-up mode."

Kate laughed. "Ellen, I am not cracking up." She had suspected it might come to that, and even though Ellen sounded more exasperated than Kate was in the market for, she knew it was probably better to agree to have her come. Besides, she knew Ellen meant well and was acting out of friendship. Maybe it wouldn't be a bad thing to have her come and kind of touch base with the reality of life at home. On the other hand, letting Ellen in on some of the things that had happened would be like sending a bulldozer into a field of daisies. No, at this point, Kate felt things were best kept to herself.

"How about Tuesday?" Kate didn't want to miss out on getting back to the flower cottage as soon as she could. She and Abigail had enjoyed a nice little conversation on the porch. She was a pleasant person and Kate felt an immediate bond and great interest in getting to know her better. She wanted to return the next day.

"How about tomorrow?" Ellen countered, a definite edge in her voice.

"I'm sorry that won't work for me, Ellen. I've got a couple

of things going on that need my attention."

"There's nothing and nobody out there. What can be going on? And if you don't mind my asking, don't you think getting a job needs your attention?"

"I think Tuesday is going to work better. If you can make it, I'll look forward to seeing you."

There was a momentary pause. "Okay, my friend. Tuesday it is. But I have to say…I'm done caring more than you do."

"You're right, Ellen. And, honestly, that's exactly how you should feel. I've been having fun exploring and you've been pulling your hair out. I promise I'll make it up to you."

The next morning, Kate was ready by eight to head back over to Abigail Sweet's with her camera, but waited for a more respectable hour. Instead, she enjoyed her toast and coffee on the porch, while scribbling thoughts for a poem that had been tickling around in her head—she had seen a hawk on her railing the day before. She had never seen a hawk up close and couldn't stop thinking about it. At ten, she knocked on the cornflower blue door.

Abigail Sweet answered, fresh and friendly as the day before, and welcomed Kate in. The summer heat had settled in and once again the flower cottage was a cool respite. On entering, she noticed at once the place was nearly as dazzling inside as out, filled with quirky, artistic charm and whimsy. Birds, flowers and quaint statuary of every material—wood, pottery, porcelain, iron filigree—were set about, and on one cerulean blue wall a cuckoo clock decorously painted a yellow, green and purple plaid. There were chairs dressed in striped and floral slipcovers and beside them, painted side tables, one deep blue, one violet with painted stems appearing to entwine the legs. A ceramic cat holding a long-stem rose in its whiskered mouth sat in the corner by the fireplace along with an elaborate balustrade post that now served as a candlestand. Kate was as captivated as when she'd first caught sight of the cottage itself. "Thanks for asking me to come by. Your home is as beautiful as your garden. If you don't mind my asking, are you a designer of some kind…an artist?"

"Actually, yes," she said, heading for the kitchen. "An artist. Would you like something cold to drink?"

"Thank you. Maybe some of that wonderful lemonade, if you have it." Kate took a seat in the armchair by the window. "What do you paint?"

"Watercolors, mostly. Nature. I've spent many a summer trying to capture the full beauty of the garden. The birds. Flora and fauna, as they say." She looked toward the window with a wistful glance. "The light here is always just right."

Kate had never heard the name Abigail Sweet. She wasn't familiar with many contemporary artists, mostly the more famous ones like Georgia O'Keefe and Pollock. "Do you have any here? I would love to see them."

"Yes…in my portfolio…along with a number of unfinished works that I've been spending this summer completing." She brought in the tray with two glasses. Kate took one. "I'll be happy to show them to you another time.

This has always been a summer place for me, a studio really. I've gotten a lot done here over the years. My husband and I bought the place about twelve years ago, a nice retreat away from our busy life in Croton-on-Hudson."

This surprised Kate. For some reason, it hadn't occurred to her that there was a husband in the picture. "Is your husband here with you?"

"Not…anymore." Her smile faded. "A car accident, just about a year ago." She pointed to a small framed photo on the side table. "Ben was the love of my life and my most ardent supporter. A friend for all time. I miss him more than I can say."

"Oh, I am so sorry, Abigail."

"Letting go of someone you truly love can be an almost impossible thing." Abigail's gaze remained on the photo. "These past many months have been a time of great adjustment."

Kate nodded her understanding. Even though she had known that her grandfather's passing was imminent and that it would end his suffering, it had been hard to adjust once he was gone. She couldn't imagine losing someone you dearly love so suddenly and so horrifically as Abigail had.

Abigail rose from her chair and smoothed down the front of her blue cotton dress. "I promised to show you the gazebo and the rose trellises." She led the way through the kitchen to the back door.

Chapter Fifteen

MATT DUG THE hammer's edge into the baseboard and yanked it hard to pry it loose. "It's a cinch that new buildings don't have this kind of construction." He gave the baseboard another whack and ripped harder. "This place is built like a fortress." He tore at the baseboard again.

Father Elway chuckled, then gave Matt a sober look. "Is something bothering you, Matt? A baseboard can take only so much. What's really on your mind?"

Matt hesitated. "Nothing, Leo." Then he stood up, straightening himself. "She…she smelled of beer." He ran his fingers through his hair. "Beer. At three in the afternoon. When I picked her up from the Farmer's Market. And she tries covering up her problem with this…this…I don't know…cheerful innocence."

"Well…maybe…"

"There's more. During our little gathering after Mass yesterday, she apologized to Mrs. Wick for breaking one of the lamps in the bungalow, and promised to pay for it. Father Garrett was right, Leo. And if that's not enough, she dropped her purse the other day and when I helped pick up her things, there was a book of matches from Dusky's Tavern."

"Worse than you think, my friend." Father Elway took a few steps, rubbing his chin, then looked Matt in the eye. "You've come to care for her."

Matt looked away and said nothing.

"We're supposed to care, Matthew. But you know as well as I do that if they're not willing or ready to admit that they have a problem and get the help they need, there's little anyone can do. Just proceed with caution, my friend." He put his hand on Matt's shoulder. "And pray."

Matt turned and looked at him. "I've already sailed right past the warning signs. I was trying to help her, and now I'm not sure I can help myself." He slammed the hammer against the baseboard. "I can't believe how quickly she grabbed hold of me. We've only known each other a couple of days."

Father Elway folded his hands behind his back. "To be honest, Matthew, I can definitely see how that could have happened. She's quite lovely in so many ways."

"It gets even worse. I lied to her, Leo. I wanted her to be able to get to Mass, so I picked her up. But I told her that you and I were going fishing…just so I'd be able to stay away from her."

"Ah, Matthew," Father Elway uttered, pacing.

"I even lied about the station wagon. I told her that it needed more work than Father Garrett had figured, and that's why I had to pick her up at the Farmer's Market. That's the crazy part—first I lied so I would see her again. Then I lied so I wouldn't."

Father Elway stopped. "Trying to do a good deed, Matthew, seems to have gotten you into a bit of a pickle. We must be careful not to use a well-intentioned idea to rationalize sin, however noble it may seem. What now, my friend?"

"I want to help her, Father. I know she needs it, but I believe she's as attracted to me as I am to her, which makes us both vulnerable. Under the circumstances, that can't be a good thing, can it?"

"Not so much, Matthew. Not so much."

"WOW. Abigail. This is spectacular," Kate turned slowly to view every part of the backyard, dazzled by the sight and fragrance of eight white trellises massively overgrown with cascading roses of every variety and color. "You have your very own botanical garden. You did all this yourself?"

"It was Ben, mostly. He got it started…the design and all. I maintain it as best I can."

After a walk-through, they sat on the back porch having their lemonade. "I can't get over it, Abigail. Thank you again for letting me see it. It's been so nice meeting you. Truly. Maybe one of these days you'd like to go into Hicksville with me. The abbey has been kind enough to allow me to use their station wagon. Maybe you'll come with me to the abbey garden. It's a beautiful place. Have you been there?"

"Yes. Yes, I have."

"So, you know Father Elway and Father Garrett?"

"I do, although I haven't seen them at all this summer." She hesitated. "And thank you for the lovely offer, but I guess I'm now just too much of a recluse." She put her glass down and leaned toward Kate. "Isn't it strange that you should come around when you have…between jobs, as you told me yesterday? You, a writer, I, an artist"

Kate hadn't thought of it that way, but *strange* definitely had been the order of the day since arriving in Spiritu.

"I'm wondering," Abigail said, pensive. "Would you be interested in working on a project with me? After speaking with you yesterday, and especially now, today, I feel certain that I finally have found the right person."

Kate felt a surge of exhilaration. "What kind of project?"

"I did a series of watercolors a few years ago. I painted them from my husband's photos, subjects from the natural world—this garden, for example. The woods. Birds. A publisher my husband worked with over the years wanted to make a book of my art. About seventy pieces or so. Not a thick book. The ones I have here. Some aren't finished yet, but it won't take me long."

"Sounds wonderful, but what could I possibly contribute to that kind of project? Believe me, Abigail, I'm no artist."

"Oh, you will contribute a great deal, Kate." Abigail appeared excited by the conversation. She stood and went to the porch rail, then turned. "You may not paint, but you are an artist in your own right." She sat back down. "Writing is your art." She leaned in. "The way I see it—my work could be grouped by season or subject, the florals, including the trellises, then the birds, the woods and stream, and so on."

"But…"

"But where do you come in? Well, about every seven pages or so, there would be a poem, a verse, an essay. Reflection." She gestured to Kate. "Things that you would create." She held Kate in her gaze, waiting, her pale eyes eager.

"I…I have to admit, Abigail, I am extremely flattered… honored. But I'm only going to be here another couple of weeks or so. How could I possibly…"

"That's all the time we'll need. Think about it—couldn't you write what needs to be written in two weeks or three? About eight pieces? Eight, possibly nine?

Kate rubbed her forehead. "I don't know. Maybe I could. I guess I might be able to." The whole idea seemed preposterous. "But you don't know anything about what I'm capable of. I can't imagine that I'm the right person."

"You'll have to trust me. I believe if Ben were sitting right here, right now, he'd be one hundred percent in agreement. And more—you would definitely be a talent he would take under his wing."

"Sounds like your husband was very supportive."

"Most talented in his own right, and my biggest fan. Always." She rested her chin on her hand. "Even when my confidence sagged from time to time, Ben always managed to spark my passion and help me center myself. That might have been his greatest talent—helping artists, recognizing their gifts, supporting their achievements. Unknowns, always." She turned and looked at Kate straight on, and with a hint of pleading in her voice, "You will help me do this, won't you, Kate? For Ben?"

Kate marveled at this woman—so full of enthusiasm and charm, even in the face of great loss and grief. How sad to be widowed at such an early age, a loving husband gone too soon, and both of them with wonderful ideas that might never come to fruition. A reclusive woman alone in a garden that, for all Kate knew, might be her only world. And out of the blue, here was Kate, right in the middle of it. How odd life was. "I really don't know what to say."

"Well, I can make it easy for you—say yes." Abigail's eyes, bright with possibility, were fixed on Kate.

"I think the project is a wonderful idea. But I can't imagine that I'd be your best choice to do the text."

"That's because we're not talking about *text*. We're talking about writing, poetry. Expressions of the beauty you carry in your mind and heart. Your spirit. I have a very good feeling about you, Kate Gannon. Ben always said I have good instincts."

"You haven't read anything I've written. And it's been a while since I've done any creative writing. Just literary articles and essays. Academic journal type stuff. I've only just started scribbling around since coming to Spiritu."

Abigail gave her a gleeful side glance. "I believe there is going to be magic in your scribbling. I know you're the person." She walked over to the porch door. "Come inside. I want to show you the paintings. Then you'll see exactly what I'm talking about."

Kate followed, closing the door behind her while something occurred to her that was very unsettling. What if this woman were a complete kook? Living some fantasy about being an artist? What if Kate saw that her paintings were awful, and realized that her husband had merely humored her over the years? What would she do? It didn't take more than a split second for Kate to figure that out—she would be kind. This woman had been through a lot. Maybe in this private little corner of the universe, Abigail Sweet was entitled to live whatever fairy tale she chose. "It's so refreshing in here. The mornings heat up pretty fast, don't they?"

Abigail went to the closet in the hall. "These old houses are wonderful that way—so much better insulated." She let out a grunt. "If only these doors didn't stick so much."

"Can I help?" Kate gave the door a swift thump with her hand and pulled the round glass knob.

"Ah, that's it. Thanks." We were going to have the windows and doors replaced, especially after the last time Ben was here and had to take off the hinges to get into the bedroom closet." She laughed, as she removed one of two large black portfolios. Kate took the other, along with a small flat box. "Come into the dining room. We'll have more space."

It was another fabulous room. Smaller than the living room, and about as enchanting—wall shelves filled with decorative dishes, cups and platters in a mix of patterns and styles, from chic porcelain to hand-painted pottery. Nothing was formal. The wooden table appeared to be hand hewn as did the chair backs. Abigail unzipped the cases. "If you'll just move that," she said, pointing to the large pot of fresh geraniums that sat in the middle of the table, "I'll spread these out."

Abigail removed the paintings, along with the small stack of art from the box, one by one, all of them done on art paper, some as large as a wall poster, a number of them unfinished. She spread them out on the dining room table, the light from the windows playing across the images with a luminescent glow. They had an ethereal beauty, like the artist herself, soft edges and subdued radiance— hydrangeas in pink-cloud clusters as if they'd fallen from the heavens, yellow-breasted warblers, an Indigo bunting, its rare vibrant blue captured perfectly by the artist's deft touch, a woodland canopy, a riverlet glistening silver in the lateday sun.

Kate was speechless. How could she not know of such an artist as Abigail Sweet? Surely her talent had to be more widely heralded than one New York gallery. "Oh, Abigail, I've never seen anything like them."

"Now you can see why you're so perfect for this project."

Kate looked at the woman. "You can't be serious. My limited skill is no match for these…masterpieces."

"I see no limitations here. I see only one masterpiece finding its match."

Kate wondered how that could possibly be true. And, however fleetingly, Kate really did have to wonder if Abigail Sweet was all there. What did she actually know about this woman? Just because she was kind and artistic and extremely interesting, didn't mean she might not be a mental case. She'd only met her a day or so earlier. Besides, artists were famous for being crazy. Like writers. Yes, maybe that was the problem here. Maybe Kate wasn't yet crazy enough, although a few days longer with more of these odd happenings in Spiritu and she was certain to get there. She caught the look in Abigail's eyes—sincere, perhaps longing. This woman, possibly alone in the world—she had told Kate there were no children—so obviously trying to honor the wishes of her late husband.

Abigail reached out to touch Kate's arm, but held back. "I can see you are at a loss," she said with great tenderness. "Promise me that you will at least give this some thought. The only thing I ask is that you keep it between us. Please don't mention this to anyone. I have learned that true inspiration is very much a spiritual experience, often a fragile one, best served in the privacy of one's heart and imagination." She turned. "I have one more painting to show you." She carefully slid the piece from the portfolio.

Kate gasped as she looked upon the painting of a cardinal with one slightly clipped wing looking back the way he had looked at her to get her to follow.

"Please just think about what I've said, Kate. Surely you can see that you are indeed the right person."

Mystified, Kate took a deep breath. "I…I'll need a little time, Abigail."

Chapter Sixteen

On Tuesday afternoon, Kate sat on a bench at the Hicksville station waiting for Ellen's train to arrive. Although she was disappointed not having heard from Matt, she was still in a state of…what…bedazzlement…with the whole Abigail situation. This was not at all a state of mind that Ellen would be happy to see her in or to make sense of, but Kate was beyond caring. She was thrilled and confused, uplifted and yet anxious. And inspired, even as she saw things less clearly than she had a few days ago when she'd felt hopeful about getting clarity on a direction for her life. Most puzzling of all, she could not get Abigail's painting of the cardinal out of her mind—a cardinal with a clipped wing, looking toward the observer, just as Kate had seen a few days earlier when he had fluttered above, leading her.

She heard the train whistle. A short time later, Ellen stepped off carrying a weekender. "You are one terrible person," Ellen said, hugging her.

"Glad you could come." Neither the smile nor the sentiment was entirely sincere. Chalk it up to poor timing, Kate thought. Ellen was holding down the fort back in Brooklyn, collecting her mail, checking to make sure she was safe, nervous that Kate was losing out on opportunities that could help secure her future. Kate knew she had to put her own interests aside and find the spirit to be kind and welcoming to her friend. "Come and sit. Our taxi will be here in a few minutes." She had decided not to borrow the abbey's station wagon, not only because she didn't want to chance running into Matt and risk having him think she was pursuing him, but because she didn't want Ellen anywhere near the abbey, snooping and making judgments—it was one thing to be friendly to Ellen, quite another to let her know too much. The last thing she wanted was a lecture on how misguided she was.

On the ride to the bungalow, Kate made small talk about one thing and another, mostly turning the conversation back to what Ellen had been doing with herself and the goings-on in the neighborhood."

"People have been asking about you, especially over at Lenny's. Gloria is still trying to find you a job. Mrs. Palladino wants to know if you're sick. I was tempted to say yes, sick in the head, but I just told them you took a little vacation. And I'm being honest when I tell you that every time I said that, the person gave me a look as if to say, 'Who goes on vacation when they've been fired?'"

"Thank you, Ellen." She reached over and touched her friend's arm. "I appreciate you." However touched Kate was by her friend's gruff compassion, she was definitely not letting on about anything, least of all Abigail Sweet and Matt

Reagan. What would Kate even say about them? And she had promised Abigail not to discuss the project with anyone. In any case, she could only imagine that Ellen would meet all of it with scorn. The small blessing in all of this was that Edna Mallory had managed to get Kate's phone number and called her about meeting for lunch. Instead, Kate invited her to dinner—she had a feeling Ellen and Edna would get along fine and take the pressure off Kate to be more interested than she cared to be. "I'll bring the wine," Edna had said, delighted.

"A woman I met in town is coming for dinner. I'm making Cornish hens."

"Well that's good to hear. I was worried you were wasting away like a recluse." She put her arm around Kate's shoulder. "I've missed you."

"I've missed you too. And now you can see that there's no reason at all to worry." She gave Ellen a pleasing side glance. "Not every recluse wastes away."

"If you say so."

THE Cornish hens cooked up beautifully—the first time Kate had used the oven. With subtlety, she gave over the after-dinner conversation to Ellen and Edna, each of whom was taken with the other, trading bits of gossip about people the other didn't even know and agreeing to keep in touch after summer. Edna's husband was a mortgage banker. She appeared to relish the coincidence of Ellen having her own real estate business. "What are the chances," they both nearly chimed in at the same time. Both also commented favorably on the bungalow, Ellen backing off just a little in her criticism of the whole Spiritu idea now that she had gotten to meet an actual live person, enjoy a nice dinner and savor her third glass of wine.

"I'm looking forward to going to Hicksville. It's been on my radar for a long time because of my business," she said, "but I never really had a good enough reason to make the trip out."

Edna lifted her glass. "Maybe there will be a rental in your future too. Only…maybe closer to…you know, a bit more excitement." They both laughed.

With a mindless smile, Kate busied herself playing the good hostess, refreshing their wine glasses, while having none herself. She served dessert in the living room, unable to clear her mind of Abigail's project. Could Kate possibly be as capable as Abigail believed? Each time she considered it, she couldn't tell which was stronger, the tingle of exhilaration or the shiver of apprehension. The last thing she had wanted in the midst of all this was a visit from Ellen, or anyone, right now. Kate was relieved when they called it a night.

She handed Edna the sweater the woman had brought and thanked her for coming. "Drive carefully. It's pretty dark on these little lanes." What she really meant was, "You've had a little too much to drink." So had Ellen for that matter.

The last of the three bottles of wine Edna had brought was nearly empty. "Maybe have a nice cup of black coffee before leaving?"

"Oh, I'm going to be just fine," Edna said. "Don't you worry about me. I have a great sense of direction. Plus, I'm used to dark roads." Kate could tell that she was also used to wine.

Wednesday morning, they slept in, Ellen occupying the bedroom while Kate spent a familiar night on the couch in the living room, minus the paralyzing fear. The truth was she couldn't wait for Ellen to leave. She needed to think things through. Too much felt unsettled—Abigail's incredible offer, the amazing coincidence about the cardinal painting, Matt Reagan. She still hadn't been by the abbey to have tea with Father Elway, as she had promised. Besides, if she agreed to work on the project with Abigail, she would have a lot of work to do in the next two weeks. She had tossed about half the night, unable to sleep, trying to make sense of this whirl of the unexpected, and remembering what Father Elway had said, "Wondrous things are known to happen in Spiritu." But as it turned out, she was left to consider exactly what his definition of "wondrous" was. Was it wondrous that a man she was attracted to and who seemed to be attracted to her had not called or come around, although how would she know—she was out most of the time?

"Everything okay?" Ellen had asked over lunch at The Sweet Shoppe in Hicksville. They had walked up to Old

Country Road and taken the bus. "I feel like you're someplace else."

Kate was disappointed that Sal was not the driver. Ellen would have liked him. "Just a little tired, I guess."

"I have to admit this whole place has turned out to be much nicer than I expected, although there does seem to be a lot of walking to get anywhere. Then again, who knew I'd make a good contact like Edna Mallory? Pretty swell. In a way, I can understand why you'll miss it a little. A little," she repeated.

More than a little, Kate thought. Missing it meant leaving it. She took a sip of her chocolate soda. George refilled Ellen's coffee cup, glancing curiously at Kate. She could see that even he sensed something was different about her than the first time she had come in. "This is George. My friend, Ellen."

George nodded. "Pie?"

"So, you've got four top colleges interested in you," Ellen said as they left the Sweet Shoppe, "and a cryptic note from Edward Darian. Can't wait to find out what that's all about." They were headed over to Hughie's Pharmacy where Kate could drop off her first few rolls of film.

"I'll give all of them a call tomorrow after you leave. As for Edward, I have no idea what 'things are going on here' means."

"Well, if you hadn't fallen off the planet, you'd know by now. How many times did he say he'd called you? If he's gotten you your job back, he may not be able to wait forever.

Get a move on, Kiddo."

Kate realized that Ellen had always been this way, bossy and brash. True, her care and kindness had helped her get through those rough days following her firing as well as her grandfather's passing. She would always be grateful to her. But since being in Spiritu, she found herself less patient with her friend, less interested in being around her. Was that a wondrous thing? "You want to believe he's going to offer me my job back, Ellen, but it could be nothing more than Edward needing the ear of a trusted colleague. I hope he realizes that is definitely no longer me."

"Please don't do or say anything in haste, Kate. Be prudent. Your future depends on it, remember."

Kate stopped. "Do you really believe that, Ellen? Do you really believe that something as big and potentially breathtaking as a future, depends on someone like Edward Darian? On one school? On Milston? No other possibilities?"

"What's gotten into you?

Kate didn't answer.

Ellen gestured to the surroundings. "Well, you'll never convince me that the potential for a breathtaking future, as you put it, is here. Not in a place where you've squirreled yourself away like a bear in hibernation. Okay, that's either a mixed metaphor or an oxymoron—I get it. But seriously, what kind of a choice is this? Granted, the place is lovely and rural. Birds sing and flowers bloom. And the bells of the quaint little abbey hidden somewhere in the woods chime.

But what's here for you that has anything to do with real life? Anything to do with what you're all about?"

Kate glanced off, noticing a few passersby chatting. A bus went past and she wondered if it was Sal's. She hoped his wife had liked the turnovers. She looked Ellen straight on. "What am I all about, Ellen?"

"You don't need me to tell you, my friend. You're about excellent teaching and routine. Tradition. Passing what you know on to others. Making things better for others. You remember the movie, *Goodbye, Mr. Chips*."

Kate nodded slowly. "Hmm," she said, as they entered the pharmacy, recalling the movie about a lonely and unappreciated professor who finally got some recognition in his old age right before he died.

"You can pick 'em up next Tuesday," the man said.

It was a beautiful day. They browsed the shops and bought a few pastries from Englert's before making their way to Nicholai Street and the art gallery. There was a different woman working there.

"I'm wondering," Kate said, "do you happen to have anything by an artist named Abigail Sweet?" Ellen had wandered away to browse the collection, but it didn't matter— she wouldn't have any idea why Kate was asking.

"Doesn't ring a bell," the woman said. "We get new arrivals about every two to three weeks. Something may come in. Check back with us."

Afterwards, they walked over to Marie Street to catch the

bus. Kate wished she could show Ellen the flower cottage, have her meet Abigail and Matt. And Father Elway. But she was determined to keep things as uncomplicated as possible—the more Ellen knew, the more she would interrogate Kate, and Kate wasn't up for any of it.

Late in the afternoon, it was sandwiches and Cokes on the front porch. "So, this is your new little domain," Ellen said. "Sweet."

"I actually love it, Ellen. I do my writing out here. I've started doing some poetry again."

"Good for you, my friend. Enjoy it while you can—there's likely to be little time for all that if you land Fordham."

Before bed, they enjoyed another little treat from Englert's. Ellen managed to finish the last of the wine from the night before. "Edna's a nice person, isn't she, Kate?"

"Seems okay." Kate had mixed feelings about Edna Mallory. A touch elegant but still a little rough around the edges. Still, she appeared authentic; nothing put on. She'd give her that. Kate had been sure that Ellen and Edna would enjoy each other's company.

"Thanks so much for coming out. Thanks for everything," Kate said, as Ellen boarded the train back to New York the next afternoon. "I'll call. I promise."

Chapter Seventeen

T HE NEXT DAY, she called Edward Darian.

"Oh, Kate. So glad to finally reach you. I have really needed to speak with you. It's so good to hear your voice. How are you?"

"Fine, thanks." She wasn't at all in the mood for small talk with him. "What is it you've been in such a hurry to speak with me about, Edward?"

"As I hinted in my note to you, things have really happened around here. Rorimer is out. The board fired him the very same day that I fired Lonny Kagan with the threat of criminal charges of embezzlement of college funds."

"Whoa." Kate sat back in her chair. "That's not something I expected to hear, although I can't say that any of it surprises me."

"Seemed that it was bound to happen. Lonny had been teasing around the edges of corruption for some time. You, more than anyone else, know how people covered for him. But embezzlement is a whole different game. This time, it's money and a lot of it—$50,000, to be exact. Even Rorimer can't pull him out of that."

"How on earth was Lonny able to have access to that

much of the school's funds?"

"Even as we speak, the board is trying to figure it all out. But perhaps more importantly, for the moment, they're also trying to come up with the best way for Rorimer to make good on the money without having to put him in jail along with Lonny, which, of course, would put Milston on the front page of every morning paper."

"Hmm. Thanks for letting me know, Edward. I appreciate the call. You sound jolly about the whole thing."

"You have no idea how glad I am to see them both gone. But there's more, Kate, and this is where you come in. Now that the board is free of Rorimer, they are also free, shall we say, to have you back. We all want you back. And…" He took a deep breath. "they're going to award you early tenure along with a twenty-percent increase in salary."

She fell silent, stunned.

"Aren't you excited?"

As much as she had vowed to maintain a distant civility on the phone with Darian, she couldn't help feel exhilaration at the most unexpected prospect of having her credentials restored, to say nothing of the early tenure and the increase in salary. "I guess I'm just a bit surprised, Edward. This is a very different conversation than the one we last had."

"Circumstances have changed, Kate. I couldn't wait to tell you. It's going to be wonderful having you back in the fold."

Even if Kate were to accept the school's offer, she had no intention of ever being back "in the fold," that little pen where sheep are kept. No, never that. Once around was once too many. Things have changed. Surely, Edward wasn't so clueless as to believe everything could be the way it used to be. Then again, hadn't she recognized how shallow and clueless he was the day he let her go, showing no sentiment whatever for their long history of working together, avoiding any risk at all by not defending her? Having delivered the news to her in such a perfunctory way, as though she should completely understand that "these things happen" was suitable reason from an institution to which she had been so devoted?

Her exhilaration was fleeting, tainted by the bad memory of that moment, of losing it all, of seeing Edward Darian so pleased by his own sense of goodwill in handing her an envelope containing a check and an "outstanding letter of recommendation." His cavalier advice: "Just pretend you're taking the summer off to look for a new position." She imagined for a moment what it might have been like to receive this kind of appreciation six months earlier… when she still believed Milston was her whole life. "Don't do anything hasty," Ellen had cautioned.

"Kate? Are you there?"

"Yes, Edward," she said, her tone sober. "I guess I'm still… pondering your offer."

"I understand. This may help. When I was unable to reach you, I received special permission from the board to extend your start date to a week from next Monday for the last of our faculty meetings before the fall semester. I'll mail you a packet containing the notes from the first two meetings."

A week from next Monday. How could that possibly work? She had two more interviews scheduled, but it should be no problem cancelling those, if she chose to. The big consideration, of course, was Abigail's project. Right after Ellen had left for the City, Kate accepted Abigail's offer and the two had sat down to plan the layout of the book. Kate had even started noodling ideas and completed a poem about the rose trellises, an accomplishment so gratifying that she had to read it over and over to believe the words were hers. She had also begun to find Abigail a great partner—easy to suggest ideas to, appreciative, supportive. How could Kate go back to her now and say she had changed her mind, that something else had come up? Abigail seemed at times to have a fragile constitution. Kate wouldn't want to do or say anything to derail this lovely woman's plans. Quite apart from what might be Abigail's tender feelings, was Kate's own situation. Was she ready to abort this intriguing and satisfying endeavor? Yet, how could she pass up Milston's offer of a full-time position with the kind of benefits Darian had presented to her, benefits that could guarantee a comfortable livelihood for some years to come and put her whole career back on track? But there was something a little bristling now about the word "career," and the whole idea of being "back on track." If these days in Spiritu had meant anything, they had shown her that there might possibly be something else.

"Let me get back to you in a day or so, Edward. There's

a lot to process and, frankly, a week from next Monday just won't work for me in any case."

"Are you telling me you may not accept Milston's offer? Isn't it everything you wanted?"

"Definitely an outstanding offer, Edward. One that I would have relished some months ago. But now…well, I just need to sort out a few things I've been involved with over the summer. You understand."

"I suppose I'll have to, but I must admit I'm taken aback by your hesitation. I figured we had worked everything out."

"We? There hasn't been a 'we' since you let me go, Edward. You recall, don't you, that in your goodbye speech, you suggested I treat my dismissal as a summer vacation while I looked for another job. Did you not seriously think I might find another job over the summer?"

"Oh, Kate, have you?"

"Frankly, in a sense, yes. So, please, David, give me some space as I sort things out. And, by the way, you have offered Mrs. Stanek her cafeteria job back, haven't you?"

Darian cleared his throat. "Well…if you think that she… that Mrs. Stanek would be open to that, I'll gladly mention it to the board."

"Yes, do mention it, Edward. You can tell me all about it when I get back to you."

"Kate, I have to say I'm surprised by your attitude. I was certain that…"

"You know, Edward, it's been several months since I

learned that it isn't such a good idea to be too certain about certainty. I'll be in touch. And please convey my sincerest thanks to the board."

FATHER Elway closed the door to his private office. "Have a seat, please, Matthew." Father Garrett was already seated.

"You're looking serious this morning, Leo," Matt said.

"I'm very sorry for the need to be serious, Matthew, but Father Garrett has some information that he believes supports his initial impression regarding Miss Gannon." Father Elway looked to Father Garrett. "John, please repeat what you told me earlier."

"Well, allow me to first say what a lovely and otherwise remarkable woman Miss Gannon is. But when I went by her bungalow a few days ago, I couldn't help notice a bag containing empty wine bottles. There were three of them and they had not been there a day or so earlier."

Matthew put his head back and looked at the ceiling. Father Elway remained silent.

"Sounds like she's drinking alone and, apparently, a lot." Matthew said. "It's even worse than I thought."

Father Elway rested his hands on the desk, lacing his fingers. "Let me caution both of you again about jumping to conclusions. I'm hopeful that if she comes back for tea one of these afternoons, then perhaps I can find a way to ease her into a conversation about…things."

"I understand," was all Matt said, before moving slowly out the door.

Chapter Eighteen

K ATE BUSIED HERSELF pouring over Abigail Sweet's art, happy in a way that she hadn't felt in years. On some mornings, she did her writing at her porch table before heading over to the flower cottage to work in Abigail's dining room, while the artist herself worked in the accommodating light of her garden in the rear of the cottage, never failing to heap praise on Kate for her writing. Other mornings, Kate visited the abbey garden, which she found a well of inspiration, capped off by a cup of tea with Father Elway.

"You are most welcome to delight in the many healing benefits of our beautiful garden," Father Elway had said. "There is great power in the mingling of the creative and the spiritual. With a proper heart and purpose, they very likely are the same thing, drawn from the same well, so to speak."

Kate enjoyed his company immensely. He was both interesting and interested as they talked about this and that. He had a way of combining an inquisitive disposition with one of encouragement and affirmation that she found helpful and touching, but still a little enigmatic. "Spiritu can be that place where you free yourself of unwanted earthly burdens, if you allow it."

One late morning on the way out to the prayer garden, she caught sight of Matt. He was working in what had been Mrs. Wick's pantry, but she continued on her way out the back without stopping to speak with him, uncertain as to whether he would welcome seeing her or view her showing up as a distraction, maybe even an imposition—she still wasn't sure that their relationship was on solid footing.

The foot of the cross had always been a place of spiritual nourishment for her. She stood in silence, breathing in the sweetness of the garden, mindful that her little clip-winged friend might suddenly appear. She asked for clarity and guidance, yet knew also that this was a moment for gratitude. However confusing the events, however much these odd happenings were beyond her ability to fully grasp, she knew above all that this place, these days, these people were a gift. It surprised her how strong she felt, how ready, come what may. "Thank you," she whispered after a while, and turned to leave.

Matt Reagan was waiting for her at the back door. "Well, at least our little cardinal friend has decided to leave you alone."

She smiled. "Yes." If Matt only knew about 'our little cardinal friend,' what on earth would he think?

"Haven't seen you lately," he said.

"I'm still here." Something about his voice was comforting, like a sip of warm tea.

"I came by your bungalow a few times, but you weren't

around."

Her heart skipped. No matter how involved she had been in Abigail's project, she had not stopped thinking about him. Each time she had come to the abbey, she hoped for a chance to see him. Here was a man she could tell everything to. She had believed that from the very first time they rode together in his truck, then later, during their dinner at Angiolini's. But she had made a promise to Abigail. "I'm out a lot. Long walks with my camera. A little writing project I'm working on. I'm sorry I've missed you."

"I was thinking maybe you'd like to go into Hicksville. Or back to the Farmer's Market. My truck's right outside. It's easier than the bus. How about it?"

Was he as interested as she was? She wouldn't want to end up making a fool of herself like some love-struck school girl. She was sure of only one thing—she wanted more of him. To see him, spend time with him. *Those hazel eyes.*

"I'd like that," she said. "but I can't go today. Maybe Saturday? In the afternoon? I have a few things I'm in the middle of. I'll need a couple of days." She had no intention of passing up the opportunity to be with him again. At the same time, she had made a commitment to finish the project.

"Something I might be able to help with?"

"I wish it were."

"Sounds interesting. Maybe one day you'll let me read some of your writing."

"I'd really like that, Matt."

He stopped and touched her arm. "It may not always be a good idea to spend too much time all alone around this place, Kate, or any place for that matter."

A curious thing to say, but thoughtful. "I'm doing fine, Matt. Honest."

He didn't answer, but opened the door and walked with her across the great room.

"If you're headed back to your bungalow or elsewhere, can I give you a lift?"

"Sure. That would be nice."

When they arrived at Kate's bungalow, she invited him in. "Cozy little places these rentals, aren't they?" he said, sitting in the armchair.

Kate brought lemonade and they sat for a few moments in a bit of an awkward silence. What was going on, anyway? What was this uneasiness that she sensed? "I do love it here. I'm writing. I'm happy." She wished she could tell him the rest. He was a man she would never want to keep anything from.

"You can't be writing all the time. All work and no play. You know how that goes."

"Of course not. But I have my camera. I've already dropped off a few rolls of film at Hughie's. I can't wait to get the pictures back"

He turned the glass of lemonade in his hands. "Kate." Without understanding why, her heart began to race. "I can't help getting the feeling that you're…you're not being open about something. That you might be holding back."

How could he possibly sense that? She didn't know what to say. Be as honest as you can, she thought. She took a sip of lemonade and set the glass beside her on the table. "I'm baffled as to what would make you think that, but there actually is something." She pushed a curl of hair back behind her ear. "I just can't talk about it right now."

He leaned forward. "Wouldn't it be good if you were able to?"

Is this what it meant to have a soul mate? "It would be great." It really would. She could open up about how excited she was to have such an unbelievable opportunity with this amazing artist and, now, friend. "But no reason to look so solemn—you'll be the first person I talk to about it. I just can't right this minute. Please understand."

"Sure." And after another quiet moment between them, "You must know by now that I care about you, Kate. I care a lot." He laughed. "From that first time when I helped you up after our little cardinal friend did his dive-bombing act. So, I'm hoping you at least see me as a friend. And maybe you can sense that I would like much more than that."

His words sang to her. Oh, if he only knew. She went over and knelt by his chair. "I can't tell you how happy I am that I came here to Spiritu. That I met you."

He set the glass down, and gently ran his finger along her cheek. Then he stood and drew her to her feet. "I'll pick you up at three on Saturday. Will that work?"

She nodded, her face still holding the flush of excitement.

Chapter Nineteen

IN THE WEEK and a half that followed, Kate and Abigail worked long, wonderful hours. "Kate, I cannot believe how much we've accomplished. Your pieces are beautiful. The imagery is so rich, the words you choose perfection. I couldn't possibly have wished for anything better. Where did you come by such eloquence? Must be the Irish in you." She laughed. "What were your parents like?"

"I never knew them. My mother died giving birth to my sister, who was stillborn." She shrugged. "I was two. I've only seen pictures; sometimes I pretend to remember her."

Abigail's demeanor shifted. "So sad and yet so lovely. What about your father?"

"I have only the slightest memory of him. He was a big man. A trolley driver on the Manhattan Avenue route in Greenpoint Brooklyn. My grandparents always said what a good and hard-working man he was. They told me that he tried very hard to keep me and raise me, but it was too much for him, working full-time and all. He died young from an infection that got out of control. I had gone to stay with my grandparents and, of course, after he died, I made my permanent home with them. They were wonderful. My grandmother passed away about twelve years ago. Hardly a day goes by that I don't miss them both. I've been so blessed."

"Well," Abigail said, with a sigh, "they left the world a lovely, talented woman who has turned out to be the perfect person for our book, just as I said." Her eyes brightened. "And it appears that we will definitely be done on time."

On time. Abigail had mentioned this before, a curious choice of words, Kate thought. Did the publisher give her a deadline? Kate had asked her about it more than once, and each time Abigail appeared to become conveniently distracted, cleaning brushes, mixing colors, moving in and out the back door. Kate wondered if Abigail had even heard Kate's question. But no matter. Kate had become accustomed to the woman's quirky ways—her whims and fancies, as she herself would say.

"I'm very excited, Abigail."

"You have every reason to be. I am too." She rubbed her hands with a towel. "How much do you have left to do, my friend?"

"About four pieces." She tapped her pencil on the table. "Let's see. I've already completed the essay about the woodland stream. The poem about the hydrangeas is done, but I still need the final quatrain for the one about the hawk that I showed you the other day. I think that one might be my favorite."

"Oh, yes, I love that one," Abigail said, gleeful. "But they're all wonderful."

As planned, Kate had been to the Farmer's Market with Matt. This time, they had gone through together—"the obstacle course," as Matt called it. They had laughed looking at some of the odd things the market had to offer—the do-it-yourself fly-swatter kit and the double bicycle tire, "so you never again have to worry when one tire goes flat." They'd stopped for a Coke and a slice of pizza and picked up an order of zeppole to take home.

"Can you go to a movie tonight?" Matt had asked.

"I'd better not, much as I'd love to. I'm in a bit of a hurry to finish up a few things." She touched his arm before getting out of the truck. "Ask me again, okay?"

He winked. "Again. And again. Count on it."

She had wondered if he grasped the fact that her time in Spiritu was coming to an end. Did he care enough to think about what would happen when she returned to Brooklyn? Would they see each other again? Was this just one of those summer romances? In fact, was it a romance? They hadn't even kissed. In any case, this was no summer romance for her—she was in love. And it scared her to imagine how it could possibly work out. Did she care more than he did? It had never come up.

KATE spent another morning working on the last of two pieces she needed to edit. When the afternoon sun on the porch became too oppressive to continue, she collected her things and went inside to finish at the kitchen table. Before long, she was ready to clean up and head over to Abigail's. She was nearly in the shower when the telephone rang. She grabbed for the bath towel and rushed into the living room to answer. "One of these days, I'm going to make sure every bathroom has a telephone.

"Kate. Thank God." It was Edward Darien.

"Edward. Hi. You sound frantic. Are you okay?"

"Kate, you have no idea how glad I am to reach you. Something awful has happened."

"Please, Edward. What is it? What's going on?"

"Jonathon Rorimer just paid me a visit."

"Oh, Edward. He didn't bring the money, did he?" She twisted the telephone cord into ringlets as they spoke.

"No, Kate. Even after I gave him more time, he didn't bring the money." Kate heard a deep sigh, more a gasp. "But that's not the worst of it," he said.

She wished she could feel more sympathetic about Edward Darien's trials and tribulations having to deal with Jonathon Rorimer and that felon of a nephew of his, but she was too far past caring about any more Milston drama. To be kind, she would hear him out. Beyond that, no more shoulder to cry on. Those days had come and gone. "Edward, please just give me a minute. Hold on." Knowing Edward's tendency to go on, she figured she'd better slip into a bathrobe instead of sitting around in a bath towel. "I'm back."

"You know how Rorimer can be, Kate. Demanding. Oppressive."

"Edward, tell me. What's he done now?" She was growing impatient. "I don't have a lot of time." She wanted to get back to Abigail's—their project was so close to completion, and she wanted to make sure that they met the deadline that Abigail had committed to.

"Rorimer said that if the board pursues an embezzlement charge against him, he will go to the newspapers and declare that it's all a lie, a cover-up."

"That's crazy."

"You have no idea, Kate." Darien was nearly breathless now. "He…he said that he would cite your termination as proof that it was actually you who had embezzled the money and that the board fired you to bury the scandal."

"What! Oh, my God. Edward." She began pacing, nearly pulling the phone to the floor. "He's not really serious about this, is he? Can he do this?"

"The auditors will be here next week, Kate. They'll find the money missing. And it's a lot of money. Even before going over everything with a fine-toothed comb, they'll spot a $50,000 short fall in the blink of an eye. Rorimer believes it will be harder to prove that he had anything to do with it than that you did…because of the unusual manner in which you were…you were released."

Kate dropped onto the sofa, the phone in her lap. "Is he right? Would they believe I could have done it?"

There was a long silence.

"Edward!"

"We…we think maybe they would."

She threw her hand to her mouth. "Lord have mercy, Edward. I could go to prison."

"Kate, we want to support you every way we can, but Rorimer's not planning to take the wrap. And he won't let Lonny take it either. You know all those times you covered for Lonny to help him keep his position. They were minor infractions, and we all know you covered for him out of the kindness of your heart, but there's documentation in the files, and if the authorities go after Lonny, he and Rorimer are prepared to say that you covered for Lonny in an attempt to coerce him into taking the money, but he refused. They'll swear that you did it and when the school found out, they released you.

Her mouth was dry as sawdust, her heart pounding in her ears. "And you, Edward—you will let this happen to me? Et tu, Brute? You and the board. The wonderful Milston board will put a knife in my back for the second time? How could you do this?"

"Kate, please, listen. We're working on this from every angle we can. Our legal team is involved. Please don't jump to conclusions"

"Don't jump to conclusions? I could go to jail. Prison. And what you're telling me is that I really have no defense? How's that for a conclusion?" She slammed the phone down and sat for a long while, trance-like, her life flashing before her eyes. She'd be ruined. Her mind was a scramble. Even if a good lawyer got her off, it was bound to make the papers, and after that, no school would consider hiring her. Or keeping her on staff. She'd be done. How do you get a job anywhere, in any profession, with a conviction or even an accusation that goes to trial for embezzlement? Good grief, what would Abigail think of her? And what about the project, the book? What publisher would invest in something a felon contributed to? And then there was Matt Reagan.

Distraught, Kate finally stepped into a hot shower and let it run for who knew how long. How much was Matt expected to believe about all this? About her? So far, he knew only what she had told him about how she lost her professorship at Milston. What made her think that he wouldn't find Rorimer's accusation plausible? The only person she could imagine talking to about this right now was Abigail Sweet.

EVEN before this horrifying turn of events, the idea of nearly being done with Abigail's project had, on its own, felt unsettling to Kate. She loved working with Abigail and just like with Matt, she wondered what would happen next. Would she and Abigail work on something else together? Would they still see each other? Abigail lived a quiet life, almost reclusive, it seemed to Kate. She had wondered if

Abigail would be open to Kate visiting her at Croton-on Hudson once there was no project to work on. She had never said anything about Kate visiting her there. But now, how did any of that even matter?

And what about the book? If Rorimer followed through on his threat, might it be scrapped? Even though Abigail had a relationship with the publisher, would they even consider going forward? Maybe they would assign Kate a pseudonym, so no one would connect her to the book. At this point, with the darkest of possibilities looming, it certainly didn't matter to Kate, but it would definitely matter to poor Abigail. How could this be happening? After all the work she had done to put Edward Darien and Milston behind her, here they were again, like a sickness that takes hold and just when you think you've beaten it, here it comes all over again, only this time, with deadly consequences.

Kate needed to find a way to protect herself, but she also felt she had a moral obligation to protect Abigail. She had developed great respect and fondness for this sweet, quirky woman, a humble woman, Kate thought, always managing to turn the focus from herself, genuinely interested in Kate's plan for continuing her "writing endeavors."

"Don't be surprised," Abigail had finally offered one day with a hint of mischief in her eye, "if this book leads to something more."

In the best of moments, Kate had pondered the possibility, but even for a good artist, it was no easy thing to sell a book of art to a publisher, no matter how much of a relationship he'd had with Ben Sweet. She had considered all of that, and weeks back had made the decision that the project was, in many ways, more important to her than the outcome—she had returned to writing. It had been a time of discovery and of grace. Mercy, also, for she had come to Spiritu half full.

But now, with one phone call, the earth underfoot had shifted and Kate was completely off balance. A shameless scoundrel named Jonathon Rorimer once again had gotten the upper hand. And once again, the news from Milston was devastating, only this time it made her termination look like child's play.

Abigail Sweet clasped her hands, prayer-like, great satisfaction in her voice. "So nearly done. I knew you would do it, Kate Gannon. And once they do the photo shoot of all the art work and text, complete the editing and proofing, and pass it along for layout and mock-up, the book should be ready to go into production pretty quickly. Surely by late fall. Of course, they will be in touch long before that. Have no doubt."

"Sounds wonderful, Abigail," Kate said, her voice flat. How could she broach the whole situation with Abigail?

"Yes, wonderful," Abigail said, nearly in a whisper. "But then tell me, my dear Kate, why do you look so forlorn?"

"I…I feel I have to tell you, Abigail…much as I hate to bring bad news here into your happy little home." She fidgeted with her hands. "I've had some very bad news this morning, and I'm…I'm scared."

"Oh, my goodness." For a moment, Abigail said nothing, then headed into the house. "Come with me," she said, and led the way into the living room. "Now, sit right there and tell me everything."

And with that, Kate started at the beginning, sharing the details of her termination that she had not shared before, and about Lonny Kagan and the board. She talked about how her termination had affected her and the long weeks she'd spent recovering, as she called it. She told about the odd circumstance of seeing the ad in the paper for a last minute Spiritu rental, and how transforming she had considered these summer weeks. Then, the phone call this morning from Edward Darien. For a moment, she put her hands over her face. "Abigail, I could go to prison. And even if I didn't, the mere accusation of so terrible a crime could get me blacklisted. Schools abhor scandal or impropriety of any kind. My career, my life would be ruined."

Abigail listened without expression. "Yes, dear Kate, that certainly does appear to be bad news. I saw it in your eyes the minute you walked in the door." Then she looked away, as if searching.

Kate was concerned. "I'm sorry, Abigail. I shouldn't have burdened you with this. I don't know what I was thinking." She stood, straightening herself. "Why don't we just get back to work. I'll finish up and we won't talk about it again."

Abigail stepped in close and looked directly into Kate's

eyes. "You're right, Kate Gannon, we won't talk about it again."

Kate's heart dropped. What had she done?

"We will not talk about it again because, I promise you, it is all inconsequential."

What was this woman thinking? Kate took a step back.

"Wondrous things happen in Spiritu," Abigail said in a whisper, then walked into the dining room where the last of her canvases were, and picked up a small tube of cerulean blue.

ONE thing Kate had come to feel strongly about, perhaps for no particular reason, was that she could trust Abigail Sweet. Without another word between them, Kate returned to the back porch with her pad and pencil to work on her poems. Inexplicably, she was swept by a sense of…what was it exactly…confidence, loss of fear? Strange as it seemed to her under the circumstances, she felt the return of creative energy and allowed herself to become fully engaged in her work. Somehow, with a glance and a whisper, Abigail had managed to quell her anxieties.

But at some point, later in the day, she had a clutch of urgency. "Oh, my gosh, the time." Neither she nor Abigail had noticed the hours passing into sunset. She rushed inside. "Abigail, I've got to hurry before it gets dark."

"Oh, Kate. I wish I had a car. Or a phone to call someone

for a ride."

"If I hurry, I think I'll be okay. See you tomorrow," she said, heading out the door. "And thank you, thank you, Abigail. I love you."

Chapter Twenty

BUT SHE WAS wrong. Not only had she miscalculated the onset of nightfall, but she quickly lost her bearings so much so that she couldn't even return to Abigail's for help. She was terrified. If she could only see a light in a window somewhere before the darkness set in, but her hope was in vain. Father Garrett's warning had come to pass. As she hurried across one of the lanes, looking in this direction and that, frantic, she noticed passing car lights in the distance and realized that had to be Old Country Road.

As the darkness intensified, and the night noises started, Kate felt as if she were running for her life. More than once, she thought something touched her shoulder…maybe a bat. Would her crazy little cardinal be out at night? Even he might be scared.

By the time she made it to Old Country Road, her heart was nearly pounding out of her chest. The ends of her hair were soaked with sweat. Jack Yerk's was closed, but she collapsed onto his bench to catch her breath and tried to figure out what to do next. She had no watch, and in her rush to leave Abigail's, she had left behind her purse which meant she had no money and no house key either.

She looked about. All was dark. No houses, no stores. She could flag down a car, but how safe would that be and where would she have someone take her? Who would even know how to reach number 7 Hummingbird Lane? She herself wouldn't know. Lord have mercy.

The night air was chilly. She had also left her jacket at Abigail's. She was in a cold sweat. After a few minutes trying to collect her thoughts, she started walking in search of any place where she saw a light, any place where she might ask for a ride or use the phone. Maybe she could call the abbey. She would be embarrassed beyond belief and how would she explain herself? What a mess.

About a hundred yards or so up the road she spotted a light in the window of a house at the end of a gravel driveway. She made her way toward the front door, moving slowly as much from caution as exhaustion. It looked to be a simple Cape Cod with a light in the kitchen. Kate could see a woman, perhaps at the sink. She breathed a sigh of relief and knocked on the door, which startled the woman, who then went to the window to see who was there. Kate waved to her and the woman edged the door open.

"I'm so, so sorry. Can you please help me? I'm staying in one of the abbey rentals and I've lost my way. I don't know how to get back to my bungalow."

"Are you alone?" the woman asked, glancing past Kate to try and see for herself.

"Yes, completely."

"Well, I can let you use the phone," the woman said in a flat tone. "But I can't do much else for you. My husband is a milk man and has to get up at 2:00. I can't wake him now."

Kate rubbed the side of her head. "Thank you." She spoke in a whisper. "The problem is I don't know who to call. Do you think it's possible to get a taxi?"

The woman glanced over at the oven clock. "That would be very unlikely. It's after nine."

Kate felt frantic. She began rubbing her neck, aware that she was pretty much out of choices. "The only place I can think of calling is the abbey, but…I would have to dial information. I'm so sorry. I promise I will repay you. Honestly. I will."

"No need." The woman gestured, unsmiling, to the phone which was set on a wall shelf by the refrigerator. "No young lady should be out this time of night wandering around by herself."

KATE sat in silence in the front passenger seat of the station wagon nearly the entire way back to her cottage, Father Garrett glancing over at her a few times, barely saying a word himself. She had awakened Mrs. Wick who then roused Father Garrett out of bed. For all she knew, the whole abbey had been awakened. What must Father Elway think? What would Matt think—he was bound to find out. And, if so, where might he think she had been and with whom?

"Please forgive me, Father Garrett. I'm so grateful, and really very sorry. Time just got away from me."

"Ten o'clock at night. No purse. No key. No jacket." His tone was somber. "You look like you'd been running for hours."

"I know how awful this looks. I lost track of time and it was too dark to find my way home and I was scared."

"Home from where, Miss Gannon?"

"From…a friend's house."

"What kind of a friend lets you leave in the dark? With nothing. Not even a phone call. Miss Gannon, I do not understand you and, clearly, I do not understand such a friend. I hope you're being truthful. I hope you were not escaping from some bad situation."

"Of course not. It wasn't like that at all. Honestly." Kate could not remember a time when she had felt such humiliation. She couldn't even offer a cogent explanation. Although she was tempted to tell the truth, she resisted because of her promise to Abigail.

They rode in silence the remainder of the way until Father Garrett used his master key to let Kate into her bungalow. "Miss Garrett. Kate." His tone had softened. "Are you sure there is nothing any of us can do for you?"

"I…I'm okay now, Father. Truly. Please apologize to Mrs. Wick for me. I feel so bad to have gotten her out of bed. And you, of course. Thank you again." She felt like an undisciplined schoolgirl facing a week of detention. As if this weren't humiliation enough, she had to wonder if she would now be viewed as some kind of incorrigible and would have to give up her rental. What if they decided never to rent to her again?

Father Garrett took her hand and smiled. "Come back and talk with Father Elway again, my dear. It will do you a world of good, I promise."

She closed the door behind him, too exhausted to consider any deeper meaning behind his comment, and went to take a shower before bed.

"GOOD grief," was all Matt Reagan could say, pacing the floor in Father Elway's office. "She could have gotten herself into real trouble out there that time of night, and in that condition."

"I have to admit, I was a little angry with her at first," Father Garrett said, "but then I could see how alone and anxious she was."

Matt ran his hand across the top of his head, then turned to Father Elway. "Now do you still think we're jumping to conclusions, Leo?"

Father Elway rubbed his chin. "I just have a hard time believing the worst of the Kate Gannon who comes to see me."

"Well, she did say she'd be in to see you this week, Leo,"

Father Garrett said. "Let's hope she keeps her promise."

Matt turned to Father Garrett. "There was no indication where she'd been?"

Father Garrett shook his head. "She wouldn't say?"

Matt dropped into a chair opposite Father Elway's desk. "I'd hate to think she had been to Hicksville. To Dusky's." He looked up at Father Garrett. "Did you smell any alcohol on her."

"No." He shook his head. "No, I can't say that I did."

"She said she'd been to a friend's and lost track of time?" Father Elway asked. "And she stopped at the first house she could to make the call? Correct?"

"That's right. The house was an ordinary little Cape Cod. The woman who opened the door seemed stern. She had an apron on, pots on the stove. Didn't look to be happy about any of this. On the way out, Kate thanked her and said she'd repay her for the phone call. Didn't seem at all like she knew the people. The woman asked us please to be quiet because her husband was sleeping. Said he was a milkman."

Father Elway came around from behind his desk and put his hand on Matt's shoulder. "Might be a good idea to take her at her word. Things happen. I'll see if she brings it up when she comes."

Chapter Twenty-One

KATE TAPED THE last of the parcels and set it on top of the other two in Abigail's living room. "I can't believe we're all done. I'm feeling a little sad." More than a little. Abigail had managed to sidestep Kate's curiosity about what would come after summer, but she had also been adamant about their remaining friends, continuing to reassure Kate that all would be well and not to worry about…things.

"I guess I'm just like you, dear Kate. I, too, have always felt a little sad at the end of a project or a painting. We put so much of ourselves into what we love that sometimes there's so little of us left. Look what happened when we were both so involved the other night that you dashed out, leaving everything behind. I still feel very bad about that, Kate"

"Please don't give it any more thought. It was my fault for not keeping track of time." She could see the garden through the window. How she would miss it. "This has been the most meaningful, beautiful thing I've ever done, Abigail. When do you suppose we'll hear about the book? Maybe it'll take longer than you think." She turned, laughing. "I'm full of questions this morning."

Abigail set her coffee cup on the small table near her

chair. "I have no doubt, Kate—the publisher will respond very quickly. Kyle Tillis is a longtime friend. Ben spoke about this project more than once. Although I do believe Kyle will be shocked when it arrives."

Kate went over and sat on a footstool near Abigail. "But I'm such a nobody. Won't they wonder? Shouldn't you talk to them about me before we send it in?"

"Surprises can be fun. I hope you think so too. This will be a pretty big one, but I promise it will all work out. You are exactly the kind of undiscovered talent my husband always went out of his way for."

Abigail took the coffee cups into the kitchen, where Kate noticed that the morning sun coming through the back door surrounded her with a kind of aura. She would miss this dear, wonderful and intriguing woman, miss her artistry, miss the daily routine they'd established.

More than once over these many days, well before Kate had shared her news about Rorimer, Kate had noticed that Abigail would glance off, wistful, somewhere else. Was it about Ben? All of this had been for him—Abigail had made that clear. She missed him very much and Kate knew this book was Abigail's way of honoring his memory, of staying connected through some tangible effort.

Kate waited until Abigail returned to the living room. "Abigail, is anything wrong. I hope I didn't make you unhappy with my…news."

"No. No, dear Kate. Please don't think that," Abigail said.

"I guess I'm just a bit…sad…that all our wonderful work is coming to an end."

"It's only the beginning, Abigail. Isn't that so? Isn't it?"

Abigail didn't answer.

"Come with me, please, Abigail." Kate opened the back screen door and stepped out onto the porch, Abigail following. "Look at all this. You've tended these gardens, front and back. You've managed as no one else could to capture their beauty on canvas. To memorialize rivers and trees and birds…and…the very soul of nature. This book will preserve that. It will always be yours and Ben's. Yours and Ben's, Abigail. And there's no reason to stop. You have so much beauty and talent in you."

Abigail looked into Kate's eyes with a gaze that was deep with…what…Kate couldn't tell. "And by the way, you make the best, most refreshing lemonade." They laughed. Everything about spending time with Abigail Sweet felt refreshing. She was as ethereal as her artistry, as calming and yet as vibrant as her surroundings. What a joy, a miracle really, to have met her the way she had, taken as she had been when this amazing cottage first caught her eye. Kate may not know what the future would hold, but she knew she had a special friend for life…wherever their lives would take them. What a marvelous gift.

"Thank you, dear Kate." They sat for a while in silence, enjoying the occasional lush swirl of breeze and the delight of bird chatter. Abigail took a deep breath. "I have loved this project more than I could ever have dreamed. More than Ben could have imagined. You are an extraordinary writer. I knew that you would be. I know what a disappointment it was to Ben that this book wasn't finished. I think this will make up for it."

"I will never be able to thank you enough, Abigail, for the opportunity, and for having faith in me."

"My great honor, dear Kate." She got up. "So…you do what you need to, and I'll finish signing all of the art then put the canvases in order with the appropriate pieces of writing—*your* wonderful writing. I'll put everything in the portfolios. The gallery will have everything they need."

"Perfect," Kate said. "I'm excited."

About an hour later, Abigail asked Kate if she would call the courier. "You're the one with the phone," she said, gleeful, as if pleased with herself for not having to bother with annoying necessities. "Their card is on the little table there. They're very good. Ben used them for years. And I think it would be best to have them pick the packages up at your bungalow, if you don't mind—can't imagine they'd find this one very easily."

"I have a feeling you're right about that." They both laughed.

"As for any end-of-summer down-heartedness, let's promise to never lose track of each other. Never. I would always hope you will come to visit me, wherever I am."

Kate turned to look directly at Abigail and leaned in.

"Abigail, when did you truly know what you wanted to do with your life? Your art?"

"I'm not sure. It came to me more like a gradual awakening once I realized I was avoiding it, much as I believe you did with your writing, if you don't mind my saying. I loved teaching but much preferred painting and creating."

"I can't imagine you doing anything else. Although I also can't imagine a better teacher. Your students must have loved you."

"Thank you, Kate." Abigail laughed. "Actually, I should have gotten a clue long before I finally decided because at the end of the day, after we'd gone to bed, I would get up and do a watercolor or work on an oil." She sighed. "And one day, something just clicked. Well, the truth is I had prayed constantly for direction. And I have to say my prayers were answered."

"And Ben supported your new direction?"

"One hundred percent. Such an amazing man. He helped me get that first gallery showing and next thing I knew, people were asking for my work. Can you imagine? I hope so, Kate. I hope you can imagine because that's the kind of success that I believe awaits you."

Kate wanted to believe in that possibility, but summer was quickly coming to an end, forcing her to consider the practical side of things. She had no job and no income. Before she knew it, winter would set in and it might be long, cold and hard if she refused to face reality. She hated to find herself thinking like Ellen, but how could it not make sense to make sure you were able to make a living. It would take time and a bit of magic for their collaboration to be a success, and then perhaps only for Abigail. It was a longshot for Kate.

Kate set the packages on the small trolley that Abigail kept in the hall closet. "I think I'd better get these packages over to my bungalow and get hold of the courier."

"Oh…and take these," Abigail said, handing her a pair of short white cotton gloves. "I'd like you to have them."

Was there no end to the kindness of this woman? "I don't know that I should, Abigail. You'll need them, won't you?"

"I have others." She chuckled. "I never leave home without them."

"This is a wonderful gift, Abigail. I left mine on the subway and didn't have a chance to buy a new pair. Thank you."

Abigail clasped her hands in front of her and with that smile that had always indicated warm acceptance and endearment, she whispered. "Blessings to you, my dear and beautiful friend."

THE publishing house of Tillis, Wilkes and Gorman occupied the entire twenty-seventh floor of the historic Chandriss building in midtown Manhattan. Because he had to use a small trolley to transport the three large black portfolios and a much smaller manuscript box, the courier was required to utilize the service elevator. After clacking along the seemingly endless terrazzo corridor, he used a side entry instead of the art deco double doors bearing the name of the company that had occupied the lavish space for more than thirty years.

"Hear the game last night?" he asked the woman at the receiving desk.

"I told you, Tommy, I'm not going to waste one minute of my time on those bums."

He laughed as he placed the items in the space the woman had designated, and began filling out the paperwork.

The woman looked at the name of the sender. "Katherine Gannon. Hmm. That's a new one." She looked over her shoulder at the items. "Quite a batch." Then glanced again at the paperwork. "Hummingbird Lane, Spiritu, New York. Wow. Where the heck is that?"

"Way out on the Island. A Brooklyn girl though. I was surprised. And it's all for Tillis only. Hmm."

"Mr. Tillis, if you please."

"Yeah, yeah. Whatever you say. See you tomorrow. And remember, Jean—the bums in Cincinnati today."

"Never."

Chapter Twenty-Two

"Okay," Ellen said, putting one of the warm dinner rolls onto her plate, "you are going to have to run this by me again because none of what you're saying makes any sense." They were having a late lunch at DiMarco's, their favorite local restaurant, after Kate returned from her second interview at Fordham up at Rose Hill in the Bronx. By the gift of grace, she had done what Abigail had directed her to do—put Milston and Rorimer out of her mind. Whenever those frightening thoughts surfaced, she pushed them back down, and had actually started to feel hopeful, without understanding why. She now also felt relieved since she no longer had to keep Abigail's project a secret. She could tell Matt about it when she returned to Spiritu the next day. As usual, Ellen was difficult and Kate hadn't even told her a word about Rorimer—Abigail had told her not to speak of it again, and perhaps out of some odd sense of respect, she did not intend to. Nor would she tell Matt.

"Really, Ellen? None of it makes sense?" Even though they had already placed their order, Kate kept looking over the menu, as if using it as a boundary of sorts between the two of them. "Exactly which part don't you get?"

"The whole thing. Just like that, some woman you never saw or heard of before in your life…an artist…offers you this job…or project…whatever you call it…without pay…to help her create a book of art?" Ellen raised an eyebrow. "What do you know about art…or writing about art? Or artists? The Guggenheim makes you dizzy. You see why this sounds just a little bizarre to me?"

"She told me she's had showings in galleries. And, by the way, my friend, I've been to the Metropolitan Museum of Art a zillion times and never get tired of it."

"On top of which," Ellen went on, ignoring Kate's comment, "you send this book to a famous Fifth Avenue publisher by courier? All of it taking place in this little village in the middle of nowhere?"

"The people in Hicksville believe it's somewhere, Ellen. Sal, the bus driver believes it's somewhere. The priests at the abbey believe it too. So does your busy-body gossip-queen friend, Edna Mallory." Kate looked up to thank the young man who brought their salads. "What's the problem?"

Of course, Kate didn't dare mention her little clipped-wing friend who led her to Abigail's. Didn't dare mention running around terrified in the dark of night until Father Garrett rescued her. Ellen would be booking her a room in Belleview Hospital's cuckoo ward before Kate had finished digesting her first crouton.

"How come you never said a word about any of this the whole time? Not even when I came out to visit. That's why you were so…so distant."

"I promised Abigail I wouldn't mention it."

The server returned to refill Ellen's wine glass. "Abigail. That's great." Ellen looked around the dining room as if to summon the right words. "I have to say, that stings. I've been your friend for how many years? And suddenly, your loyalty is to this woman you know for a week? This stranger? When I'm the one who's been so concerned about you? And with good reason, by the way, when you tell me this fairy tale." She reached across the table and touched Kate's arm. "What's happened to you?"

"Good things, Ellen. Mostly. Good things have happened to me." She put the menu down. "And I knew that if I had told you about Abigail when you visited me, you would have wanted to meet her, investigate, see where she lives, question her, look her up. And you would have nagged at me the way you're doing right now."

"Nagging. Hmm." Ellen took a sip of wine. "Have you looked her up? Who exactly is this great artist named Abigail Sweet? You can bet I'm going to look her up because there are all kinds of schemes in this world and even though I don't know what this one is about, I do know that art books don't sell. It's like poetry. And she's got this deadline? In this tiny hamlet she just happens upon the one person who is the perfect partner. Get real, Kate." They both looked about, concerned that she had raised her voice. A woman at the next table smiled at them. They fidgeted with their napkins, then for a few minutes continued their meal in silence.

"I thought your expertise was real estate," Kate whispered. "And yet, you know everything that concerns me. Maybe I should be asking what's happened to *you*? Tell me this still isn't about the Berkshires." After a long moment staring at each other, they laughed.

"No. No, it's not. I swear—it's not about the Berkshires. I don't want to see you get hurt or get into trouble, that's all. You've become a dreamer, Kate, and this whole scenario you've described is usually the destiny of dreamers."

"What harm, exactly, do you think has come to me, what offense? Did she ask me for money? Or for anything?"

"You were vulnerable. Some people…the wrong people… see that kind of person as an easy target. And even if you're right, Kate. Even if this Abigail person is on the up and up, I don't care how gifted she may be, it's likely no one has ever heard her name, even if she did have a gallery showing at one time. It happens—because the truth is it's hard enough for true artists to sell anything. That's why they're all selling their paintings along the sidewalk down in the Village. Trust me, they'd never sell an art book." She took a bite of salad. "And… maybe even worse…what if she is a famous artist somewhere and they buy this great book. Did you sign a contract? What makes you think this woman will square with you and give you anything at all if the book actually sells?"

It was likely that the thing that bothered Kate the most about Ellen was not that she was often cynical and annoying, but usually made sense. Ellen Castle was not a dreamer. It was possible that her last dream died with the end of her troubled marriage. She lived her life dependent on logic. Maybe that's why she was so successful in real estate—her ability to translate a young couple's dream of a beautiful family home into a floor plan, square footage and a preference for north/south exposure.

"Ellen, I know that there's an element of truth in everything you're saying. Abigail Sweet saw that I was searching, examining my life, questioning my direction. But unlike you, she offered me something besides criticism, which is really interesting because during those first dark weeks after I lost my professorship, weren't you the one telling me this was a moment to consider different things. That this was 'providential'? Remember?" Kate lifted a forkful of salad. "Believe it or not, my friend, I followed your advice."

The server brought their entrees and Ellen dug into her chicken tortellini. "All I'm going to say…"

"Really? You've already given me the Old and the New Testament according to Ellen."

"All I'm going to say is that you've let a lot of precious time go by and if you have to return to Milston because it ends up being your only option, then it serves you right."

Chapter Twenty-Three

Kate pushed open the door at Hummingbird Lane as the cab pulled away. A small folded paper fell to the floor. She picked it up and entered with a deep sigh of joy and relief. *Oh, my goodness, this feels so much like home*, she thought— How she would miss it. She set her bags down to read the note, hoping it was from Matt.

"Please call as soon as you can. Father Garrett."

Well, she was right—they were going to tell her she couldn't stay the extra week. Thank God she'd been able to finish Abigail's project. But what about Matt? If they decided she had to leave, when would she see him again? She decided to take her time responding. The practical and sometimes scared part of her brain kept reminding her that as much as she had shoved the Rorimer issue aside, the tax auditors would be looking over the books in just a few days. She had still heard nothing from Edward about a solution and there were moments when the knot in her stomach felt as if she'd swallowed a medicine ball. "Have faith," Abigail had said.

She heard a noise and turned to see the familiar dark blue truck coming down the lane. Her heart raced. She set the note aside and took a quick look in the mirror to straighten herself.

The truck pulled alongside the curb and Matt stepped out. "Well, here you are, Miss Kate Gannon."

She laughed. "You've got perfect timing." Perfect everything, she thought.

"I'd like to take credit, but I'm getting ready to do a small remodel in the neighborhood. Would you still call it perfect timing if you knew I drove by here every spare hour I could?"

They sat on the porch. "I can't even offer you anything cold to drink."

"That's okay because I have a better idea. Dinner and dancing. I'll pick you up at seven, and you can tell me all about Brooklyn." He looked at his watch. "It's a little after four. You'll have a couple of hours to settle in. How about it? We'll go to the Valley Stream Park Inn. Food's great. So's the music. You'll like it. It's…beautiful."

Did she only imagine that he looked at her more deeply when he spoke the word "beautiful?"

"How can I say anything but yes. Yes." She was tempted to tell him how much she'd missed him but she didn't want to appear too eager.

"I've missed you, Kate." When he stood to leave, he took her hand. "Summer's coming to an end. You'll be leaving. We have to talk."

As she watched him walk to his truck, she could hardly contain her excitement. How was this possible? Ah, yes, Father Elway, wondrous things certainly are known to happen in Spiritu. She went into the house and put her things away, then showered. She had hoped to get around to Abigail's, but there wasn't time. Oh, why didn't the dear woman have a phone?

CARL Hoppl's Valley Stream Park Inn was everything Matt had said it would be. Large and festive, elegant, white tablecloths and a full orchestra. Just the boost that her spirit needed. Kate thought the robust noise of the room was the kind you would hear from a big, happy family on Christmas morning. Luckily, she had a habit of always taking along a piece of dressy evening wear. "You never know," her grandmother once had told her. From the look on Matt's face, she had picked wisely. When she opened the door of her bungalow, he looked her up and down, smiling. "I've never seen you with your hair up like that. It's pretty. You're pretty."

In between courses of escargot and prime rib, he held her close on the dance floor. He had ordered champagne and then for dessert cherries jubilee prepared by the waiter table-side. For Kate it was a night of nights. Not since her prom, had she been treated to such extravagance—a dazzling sensation. The best, of course, was being this physically close to Matt. The feel of him. The smell of him. His strength. His face against hers as they danced. Her hand in his. She wished she knew how to flirt. She had never been any good at it, and had envied the girls who were—the ones who always had a date to the school dance and homecoming. They knew how to dip a shoulder and curl a long strand of hair around their finger. So now, instead, she was comfortably resigned to just being herself and letting the evening unfold. "This is wonderful, Matt. I'm having such a good time. Thank you."

Back at the table, he was curious about why she hadn't touched her champagne. "I'm sorry. Would you mind if I ordered a club soda?"

"I apologize, Kate. I should have asked." After a while, they settled into a conversation, one that Kate had high hopes for. "Any news about a school?" he asked.

"Just Milston, so far. And Fordham is looking pretty good. I should know in a day or so, although I'm not so certain any longer about a clear direction." The truth was that when she was with him, her hopes were different. "This whole Spiritu experience has thrown a little bit of a monkey wrench into things."

"How so?"

"I've somehow managed to come face-to-face with myself, odd as that may sound."

"Not odd at all. Matter of fact, I like what I hear."

His response surprised her, disappointed her, actually. What was it about her coming face-to-face with herself that he thought was good? Had he wanted her to be different in some way? "What is it that you like about that?"

"I'm…I guess I'm always pleased when I see that people

are willing to make a change."

In her crazy, romantic way, she would have hoped he liked her just the way she was. Wasn't that how the song went—"Don't change a hair for me, not if you care for me…" Maybe she was not the Valentine he had hoped she was, after all.

The music swelled, making it difficult to talk the way they did that night at Angiolini's. "Would you mind if we dance some more?" she said, still wondering what it was he felt they had to talk about. Her heart skipped when she thought of the possibilities. She hoped he was interested in pursuing their relationship once she returned to Brooklyn. "I'll be leaving next week. I'll miss it here."

He pulled her closer. "I was hoping you could stay longer." The rhythm of their movement in each other's arms created an aura of dreaminess, but once again she sensed that something was off. "I guess this place wasn't the best choice for a serious conversation," he said.

She looked up at him. "How serious?"

"Serious enough." They stopped moving. On the dance floor, but not dancing; caught in each other's gaze. "I don't want you to go." He took her by the hand, and after signaling to the waiter to save their table, led her out onto the veranda. The night was balmy; the mild breeze coming in gentle waves, like a swoon and, somewhere, the scent of honeysuckle.

"Matt, what is it?"

He looked about and finally led her to a low brick ledge beneath a slight overhang of wisteria, where they sat. "You said you needed a little more time before you told tell me about…things. Can't you tell me now?"

How curious his behavior could be? He was always sweet, just more solemn at the moment than she'd known him to be. "Yes, I'm happy to." She told him about meeting Abigail Sweet and her amazing invitation to work on this project with her. She talked about those many wonderful, gratifying days with work that satisfied her renewed passion. About the artist herself—amazing, generous, gifted.

"That's where you've been these days, in and out? Nothing more?"

She laughed. "There wasn't much time left for more."

"Odd, though, isn't it, to just randomly run into such a person. Out of the blue, I mean. A little…unbelievable… maybe. Where is her house, exactly? I think I know most of the houses in the area."

She took a moment to think about it. "I…I don't even know the address." It had not even occurred to her until that moment. She laughed. "I could take you there quicker than I could explain where it is. Crazy as it sounds."

"Crazy is probably a good word."

First, Ellen, now Matt. What was it about providence or serendipity that puzzled people so? Why was it hard for people to grasp anything that involved what some might call a miracle? They never have any difficulty accepting the unexpected tragedy—sudden job loss, train wrecks, a broken engagement, a bad storm that rips the roof off of only one house in a neighborhood. True, they might wonder about it. But they don't get confused by it, probe, grow suspicious. Why was bad news so much easier to make sense of than surprisingly good news?

"Matt, is something on your mind? Is anything wrong? You said you wanted to talk but, so far, something about the conversation…or maybe something about me…seems unsettling to you." They were as close as a whisper, the music soft and slow in the background, the night air circling them like an embrace.

He hadn't taken his eyes off her. "Kate."

Their kiss took her out of her senses. Wrapped in his arms, his lips against hers—strong, soft, sweet. The power and magic of an eternal moment. "I love you, Kate."

"Matt." She was breathless. "Matt."

"We'll work it out, Kate. We'll work everything out, I promise."

Later, outside her bungalow, in the accommodating darkness of his truck, they kissed again. And again, at her door. She dared not ask him in. He squeezed her hand, nodding his goodnight, but before he headed down the path, she moved close and put her hand to his cheek, then her lips. "I love you, Matt." And when he turned to meet her lips, she knew that the heat of Matt Reagan's kiss would burn in her dreams all the rest of her days.

Chapter Twenty-Four

Thank God Abigail's project already had been completed. Kate knew she would have no mind for it now, no focus of thought or energy, no ability or desire to come to her senses in time to accomplish anything, let alone by some deadline. She was lost in a rainbow. What sense did that make? None at all. Who cared?

She undressed on the way to the bathroom, slipping off her shoes as she went, letting her dress fall to the floor before picking it up and tossing it onto the sofa. She held a steaming washcloth to her face and brushed her teeth, then changed for bed without realizing she was still wearing her pearls. Matt Reagan loved her and they would work it all out.

She had hardly been asleep ten minutes, when the phone rang like a fire bell. Kate sat straight up in bed and tried to orient herself. The clock said 11:40. It had to be him. Who else would call at this hour? She rushed into the living room to answer. "Matt?" she whispered.

"Matt?" However much of the magic had lingered, it was vaporized by Ellen's strident tone. "Who's Matt?"

"Oh. Ellen." Kate's voice was tranquil, faint. "Hi. It's…it's so late. Can we talk tomorrow? I'll call. I promise."

"Okay, but are you all right? Who is Matt?"

"Honestly, I'm fine. I'll tell you all about it in the morning."

"Well, then, sleep on this, my friend. I've checked three Manhattan galleries and everywhere else in between. They have no record at all of an Abigail Sweet.

THE next morning, Matt Reagan, slow and purposeful, walked across the main room of the abbey toward the library, where Father Elway sat in his winged-back chair reading.

"I see that our project is nearly done, Matthew. You were right—the perfect solution to enlarging the main reception area. I'm so glad you saw it when it had never occurred to me."

"Just one more coat on that far wall in Mrs. Wick's pantry and the painters will be done." Matt took a seat opposite the priest. "A little slow this morning."

Father Elway gave him a long discerning look. "Mmm. Are you slow this morning because you're carrying something heavy? Is that it, Matthew?"

Matt hesitated, then leaned forward, resting his elbows on his knees. "I lost my courage last night, Leo."

Father Elway set the book on the lamp table beside him. "Am I wrong to guess that our lovely Miss Gannon has tied you up in knots?"

"To put it mildly." He stood and circled the chair, then sat again. "I can't make sense of any of this. She's beautiful and evidently talented and so easy to talk to. But then, she tells me this story about where she's been spending most of her time. A woman…an artist…in one of the rentals, not ours, offered her an opportunity to work on an art book for a big New York publisher. A woman she'd never met before. Sounds fantastic. But she makes such sense when she tells me things. I can't figure any of it out, except that when an alcoholic is hiding in plain sight, they can appear so normal, successful. Then the delusions start. I remember that part from the man I told you about…the one that I worked with years ago. We all thought he was so accomplished, just an everyday kind of a guy, before his life blew up before our eyes. No kidding, Leo, I had planned to have this long conversation with her to get her to open up and…well…I allowed myself to be side-tracked."

"No point beating yourself up over it, Matthew. She'll be leaving us soon."

"Yes, and we'll send her off with a blessing and a friendly farewell. That would finish things off, all right, if it weren't for the fact that I'm in love with her."

Father Elway rose and walked over to the bookshelves. For a moment, he appeared to mindlessly finger a few of the titles. Then he went and stood behind his chair, looking at Matt. "I'm wondering." He rubbed his chin. "Are you sure, Matthew, that it hasn't all been a grand mistake. What if we've been wrong? What if Kate Gannon is everything she appears to be?"

Matt looked up with a smirk. "I know you'd like to see it that way, Leo. You've been a mentor, an uncle these past years. My spiritual director. You know how much I respect your counsel. But there's too much evidence. You know me—I'm a nuts and bolts kind of guy, two-plus-two-equals-four all the way."

"And so?"

"And so, I just can't dismiss the fact that she was stumbling about in her bungalow, breaking things. Okay, maybe not that alone, but the smell of beer on her clothing that afternoon, the matches from Dusky's Tavern, the wine bottles…three of them in little more than a day." He got up out of his chair and put his hands in his pockets. "And what about Father Garrett having to go pick her up at some house out on the road that night? How do I chalk all that up to anything but the fact that she has a problem? I can't even be sure that the story she told me about getting fired from her teaching job is true. A year before reaching tenure? What university would do that to a good professor unless there was something wrong? And the part that's making me crazy about loving her is how can I commit to spending the rest of my life with someone who lies so beautifully, so convincingly? With such innocence. I would never be able to trust her. Our life together would be a nightmare."

"And yet, you said nothing."

Matt looked away. "I said nothing. I said nothing because

I knew that if I went down that path with her, I could lose her. She would bolt. I know it, Leo. That's what they do. Isn't that usually true?"

"I'd have to agree—many times, in situations such as the one you have in mind, denial, yes…then sometimes flight. But I must say I have my doubts about what you and Father Garrett are telling me."

"I have no doubts at all, Father. I know she'd go back to the city in a heartbeat and it's likely that whatever good there is between us, I would lose forever. She'd never want to speak to me again. And God knows where she might eventually end up."

"And just what is it all costing you to be so fearful, Matthew? What nightmare are you living right now by not using the courage God gave you for so many things in your life? Is this any better?"

Matt didn't answer.

Father Elway walked over and put his hand on Matt's shoulder. "Keep in mind, Matthew, that this all started because you cared about another person's well-being. You were compassionate. You had good intentions. I know what they always say about good intentions. But we never consider the other side of it. Nobody talks about how the road to *Heaven* is paved with *good* intentions, the vast majority of which turn into good deeds, wonderful deeds played out with kindness and love, that make a difference for someone somewhere and perhaps forever change a life." He patted

Matt's shoulder. "Why not spend a little time in the garden, my friend? Might be a good place right now to find a bit of clarity, calm and grace."

Matt sat silent for a moment. Then he touched Father Elway's hand. "There are times, Leo, when it doesn't seem that anything can help."

"And yet?"

Matt looked up at the priest, then turned to leave. "I'll be in the garden if you need me, Father."

Chapter Twenty-Five

ABIGAIL SWEET SMILED at the photo of her husband and set before it the pink rose she had snipped from the trellis in the backyard. "You were right about the fragrance—the sweetest in the garden." She touched the frame. "I miss you, my love." The morning sun lit the room, metal objects gleaming with sparks of light, the vibrant palette fiery with illumination. She folded her arms and took in the surroundings with a deep sigh. What a lovely summer. What a lovely new friend... "I wish…ah, well."

She sat in the chair, keeping her gaze upon the photo. "She's wonderful, Ben. Just the kind of talent you would have taken under your wing if you had seen her first. So gifted. The book is even more beautiful than you and I had imagined, thanks to her writing." She laughed. "I can't say who will be in for the bigger surprise, Kyle Tillis or Kate Gannon. Ha."

She opened the front screen door and stepped out onto the porch. "A whole year gone by without you." She felt her spirit heave with melancholy. "But the garden has been fabulous. It's what brought her here, you know, even if my little bird friend had to help her find her way back." She laughed. "I must admit that in a way I'm a bit nervous about the whole book thing—an unknown writer. Then, throw me into the mix—Abigail Sweet. A bit of mayhem, I suspect. Oh, my."

She lifted her face to the sun. "Oh, how I wish you could make everything right the way you used to. What a life you gave me—supporting my efforts, helping me stay on track, keeping my whims and fancies at bay. You always knew how distracted I could get. But I did have some grand moments, didn't I? Thanks to you. Is it possible to still make you proud?" She picked up the yellow watering can and allowed a gentle spray to shower the window boxes. "Look at these snapdragons and petunias. The begonias and caladium. My goodness, how fresh, how full of life." She paused, pensive. "Forget-me-nots." She set the watering can down and walked to the far end of the porch, looking toward the woods. "Those desperate last words haunt me still—breathe with me, breathe." She looked up and down the lane. All was quiet, as if the whole world in that one moment had closed its eyes. "Summer's winding down, Ben. People will be moving on." She took a deep breath, drawing in the earthy scent of woodland must she loved so well. "What next, my love? What next?"

Chapter Twenty-Six

KATE AWOKE WITH the slow, dreamy recollection of Matt Reagan's kiss. *He loves me.* The thought tumbled over and over again through all that had happened the night before. She sat up in bed just as the phone rang, then clumsily scrambled to toss back the covers and get to the living room without knocking over the furniture.

"Hey, good morning, sleepy head." Matt Reagan's voice was deep and soothing.

"Good morning," she half-whispered, swept by a sense of something warm yet very unfamiliar to her life before Matt Reagan—intimacy.

"I want to get my bid in early—have lunch with me," he said.

"Sounds wonderful."

They made plans for him to pick her up around 11:30 to head into Hicksville. In the meantime, she was determined to see Abigail Sweet, but as she headed to the shower, the phone rang again. This time it was Fordham. The professorship was hers.

"Ellen, I can't tell you what a fantastic day this is. It's like a dream come true. And it's not even ten o'clock yet."

Lurking somewhere in the back of her mind was the fact that the auditors would soon be at Milston. She couldn't imagine why, but she had allowed herself to fully believe what Abigail had told her—she was not to worry; all would be well.

"Okay, slow down, Kiddo. Just what have you been up to now? I'm afraid to ask."

"I got the job at Fordham. The money isn't as good as Milston, but then Fordham is paying me fair market value and not an inflated guilt offering. Oh, yes, and I'm in love with the man of my dreams."

"Wait. What?"

Kate took a hurried few minutes to explain as much as she could without risking a quick visit to Abigail's and getting back in time for Matt.

"I'll say this about you, Kate Gannon—when you leave town, you really leave. I never saw any of this in you all the years I've known you."

"What do you mean?" Kate asked.

"These people you say you meet, these unbelievable things that happen—famous artists, the love of your life, the job of your choice. You realize this is beginning to read like a novel, right? We're in fairy tale territory here. And, by the way, you remember I told you that there is no evidence of an Abigail Sweet."

"Right. Yes. Exactly," Kate laughed her words into the phone. "But I've got to run, Ellen. I'm…"

"No, wait. You just can't hang up like that. We need to talk."

"Yes, I know. Later. I promise. Hugs to you, my friend."

ELLEN hung up the phone and sat for a moment staring into space, troubled. "It's too much," she thought. "Too much." No one wished more good things for Kate Gannon than she did, but something had happened to her out there, and it all sounded too good to be true. Every time she spoke with Kate, something extraordinary had happened…just like that. In just a short month's time, it had turned out to be one remarkable event after another. Now, after breaking up with the only man she had dated in years, she had suddenly found the love of her life, and Ellen found it all unsettling.

But what could she do about it? There was no talking to Kate. Odd as it was, Kate had even kept things from her when she went out to visit her. Was it possible that she did that because there really had been nothing to report? Ellen poured herself a cup of coffee and leaned back against the kitchen counter, pondering the situation, as her boxer, Tony, sniffed around. She looked down at him and patted his head. If there were only some way of checking things out to see if any of this were true. But who could she ask? How could she verify anything? Ellen didn't know any of these people or anyone else out there except Edna Mallory, and it was clear to Ellen that Kate wouldn't have shared anything personal with Edna. Who then?

Chapter Twenty-Seven

AT ABOUT 10:30, as Matt Reagan loaded the last of his tools into the back of his pick-up, Father Elway called to him from a side window. "A minute, please, before you go, Matthew."

"You've got that serious confessional look on your face, Leo," he said, and took a seat in Father Elway's study.

"It's Kate I want to talk to you about, Matthew."

Matthew got to his feet. "Is everything all right? Has something happened? You're scaring me, Father."

"I don't mean to." Father Elway ran his hand across the top of his head. "I don't mean to. It's just that I…I just received a call from a woman named Ellen Castle, Kate's closest friend. She lives next door to Kate in Brooklyn. She actually visited Kate here, but for whatever reason, Kate never told her anything about what she was doing, nor did she bring her friend here to the abbey. Nothing."

Matthew sat back down.

"We didn't share with each other any specifics about Kate. I would never do that and, evidently, neither would Miss Castle. But she did mention that she has concerns."

"About Kate's drinking?"

"That was not mentioned directly. But Miss Castle is extremely worried about what she says are Kate's increasingly strange behaviors. Fantasies. Delusions perhaps. Do you know anything about this friend of Kate's, Matthew?"

"My God, Leo." Matt got up and paced the floor, then stopped. "Did she give any examples?"

"Nothing. And I did not mention any of what you or Father Garrett had reported."

Matt turned. "This is all out of my league, Father. What are we going to do? How did you leave it with Miss Castle?"

Father Elway shrugged. "I didn't commit to anything. I don't know anything about this woman or exactly how she fits into Kate's life. Do you?"

Matt narrowed his eyes. "Kate mentioned her to me. She described her as caring but bossy. She was probably offering to help Kate and Kate wouldn't have any of it."

They were both silent for a few moments before Father Elway spoke. "Matthew, I'm curious. You mentioned the other day that Kate told you she was involved in some special project with a local artist. Do you happen to recall the artist's name? If she is really someone legitimate, maybe that would help us find something out…discreetly, of course."

"Not off hand. No." Matt dropped into a chair. "She had a different kind of last name. Began with an S, I recall. Ss… sp…sm…Sweet. That's it. Sweet."

Father Elway stood and walked over to Matt. "Abigail, Matthew? Was that it—Abigail Sweet?"

"That's it, Leo. Abigail Sweet."

Father Elway reached out and gently took hold of Matt's arm. "I can't tell you how sorry I am to hear that."

MATT Reagan got behind the wheel of his truck and just sat there, a hollow feeling in the pit of his stomach. This whole business with Kate had been bubbling up nearly from the very first day she'd arrived in Spiritu. He had been given fair warning, but he'd been foolish enough to believe he could help. Not foolish, arrogant, so sure of himself. The great Matt Reagan befriending a troubled woman in order to save her. And what happened? Nothing. What a joke. What a miserable joke because now he was deeply in love with her. Or with some version of her. Now, he had the toughest choice of all—get tough and make her listen, make her get help. Tell her they all knew everything. Or…just break it off and let her be. How could that even be a possibility? He pounded his fist against the steering wheel.

A few minutes later, he headed down the drive to pick her up. At the same time, a black Cadillac sedan made its way around the circle to the front door of the abbey. He'd never seen the car before or any car like it at the abbey. What now?

When he reached Kate's bungalow, he waited, uncertain. Be kind, he thought. No matter what, she's someone with a problem. *There but for the grace of God…*

She opened the screen door and waived to him, smiling. That beautiful face. How was he going handle this? Should he bring it up over lunch? How would she react, especially in a place where there were other people? Maybe he should sit her down and talk with her about it right here at the house, right now, just the two of them, no one else around.

"Come in," she called to him and when he entered, she put her arms around his neck and kissed his cheek. "I'm so happy to see you. And I have news."

"Oh?"

"I got the professorship at Fordham. Found out bright and early this morning."

"That's great. Congratulations." He wasn't even able to fake it.

She took his hand. "Are you okay?"

He hesitated, holding her in his gaze. "Not really, Kate. I'm not really okay."

"Oh, please, Matt, come and sit. What is it?" She led him to the sofa and sat beside him. "Are you sick? Let me get you something. I have stomach tablets. Aspirin?"

He put his hand over hers and stroked it. "Nothing like that." Her hand felt smooth and soft, the way her lips had felt the night before. He would never be able to get this woman out of his heart.

"I think...I think we may have gotten a little..."

They turned at the sound of a car pulling up to the bungalow. They got up and looked. There were actually two cars. Father Garrett stepped out of the town and country. Behind him, a man in a dark suit emerged from the black Cadillac sedan Matt had seen at the abbey.

Chapter Twenty-Eight

FATHER GARRETT CAME to the door first and, on entering, offered his apologies. "Sorry to barge in like this, Miss Gannon…Kate. I left you a note in your door the other evening." He gestured toward the man coming up the path. "This gentleman has been trying to get in touch with you."

"Hello, Miss Gannon." The man looked to be about fifty, and as well-groomed as she remembered from her brief days long ago in midtown Manhattan corporate life. "I'm Kyle Tillis."

"Oh, my goodness," Kate said, shaking his hand. "I am so honored to meet you." She turned to Matt. "This is Mr. Tillis from the publishing house where Abigail and I sent the book. Mr. Tillis, this is my very good friend, Matt Reagan. He and Father Garrett know each other quite well." She led them into the living room and offered them a cold drink. A few minutes later, she returned with a serving tray.

"Haven't had lemonade in a long time, Miss Gannon," Tillis said.

"Please call me, Kate."

"I was remarking to Father Garrett, Kate, what a beautiful place this is out here. Spiritu. I had only heard of it from Ben and Abigail, who came for many years, but I'd never been here myself, I'm sorry to say." He raised his glass to Father Garrett. "Full bookings every year. You're obviously doing something right."

"They do everything right," Kate said. "I had never even heard of Spiritu, and when I arrived that very first day, I could see that I had made the right decision." She looked at Matt. "The bungalows are so well kept and everyone is especially friendly and caring. Yet people are allowed their privacy."

"It must be true, Kate, because it's clear you've made some good friends." Tillis took a sip of lemonade. "Mmm, this is good. So, tell me, Kate, how did you meet Abigail Sweet? Matt moved in his chair. Both he and Father Garrett remained silent observers.

"It was amazing. Something I never expected. I came across her cottage one morning while I was out for one of my walks. I had never seen such a truly unbelievable garden. It encompassed nearly the entire cottage. It was breathtaking. I didn't see anyone, but I couldn't pass by without snapping a few pictures. Oh, in fact, I have to remember to pick the pictures up at Hughie's Pharmacy. Anyway, I wanted to stop by it again on my way back from church. But I couldn't find it. I ended up getting help. Crazy as it sounds, a little bird led me back there." She looked at Matt and Father Garrett. "That feisty little cardinal with the clipped wing."

"You never told me that," Matt said.

Kyle Tillis set his glass down on the side table and looked

at the others. "So, let me get this straight. A little bird led you to Abigail Sweet's cottage."

Matt leaned forward. "I think Kate's right – it probably does sound crazy, but …" He looked at Father Garrett. "…but he's a crazy little bird. Showed up in the garden one day not so long ago with a clipped wing and stayed. He was actually responsible for knocking Kate to the ground. I was there."

"I believe that's…that…could be true," Father Garrett chimed in. "Odd and wondrous things have been known to happen here."

"Yes," Kate said, "but then he flew off. And that's when I first saw Abigail on the front porch with her yellow watering can. I started to leave because I didn't want to intrude. But she waved me up and gave me a glass of lemonade. Such a friendly and caring woman. And so talented…as you already know."

"Did she mention her husband?" Tillis asked.

"Oh, yes. She kept his photo right there on a side table. A terrible loss for her. She spoke so lovingly about him. I understand you knew him quite well."

"So, tell me how you ended up doing the book? How did that happen?" He raised his hands in apology. "I hope you don't mind my curiosity. This is quite a story."

"Not at all. Abigail and I became instant friends. She can tell you herself. I need to stop by there later, by the way. With one thing and another, I just haven't gotten to see her in the last few days. She has no phone or anything."

Tillis leaned in, resting his arms on his knees, "And so she asked you to write pieces for her art? Just like that?"

Kate threw her hands up. "Just like that. And I have to admit there were moments that I thought she might be…I'm embarrassed to say…a little delusional. How could she possibly think a stranger could be just the right person, especially when she showed me the paintings? They were amazing. I couldn't believe she thought I was capable of doing what she wanted. But she insisted. Honestly, I can never thank her enough." She dipped her head, self-consciously. "Of course, a lot of that rests with what you think of the finished work, Mr. Tillis. It's your opinion that will count the most, isn't it?"

"Well, I can tell you right now, Kate—your writing is extraordinary. When Ben and Abigail and I talked about doing this book years back, we never imagined that the finished product would be this wonderful. I congratulate you."

"Thank you very much. Abigail said this would happen. She had such confidence that you would love the book. Have you been around to her place yet? I can't wait for her to hear this."

Matt took Kate's hand. "Congratulations, Kate. I knew your writing would be nothing short of extraordinary, to say the least."

Father Garrett nodded. "Yes, if you did it, Kate, it would have to be that and nothing less."

Tillis stood. "Well, then, if I'm not throwing anyone's plans off track, why don't we head over to Abigail's now."

"How about if we meet you there…in a few minutes?" Matt said. "There's something I…we…need to do first, if you don't mind, Mr. Tillis."

"And I'll just run along," Father Garrett said.

When they were gone, Matt took both of Kate's hands. "Sit with me a minute, Kate. There's something we've got to talk about before we go to Abigail's."

"Matt." She touched his face. "That look again. Something is wrong. Please, you're worrying me."

"I'm the one who's worried, Kate." He drew her to the sofa. "Something is definitely wrong. I've wanted to talk with you about this long before now. And today…all this with Tillis… puts a whole new color to it."

Kate got to her feet. "Matt, please. You're scaring me."

"There was a car accident, Kate. But it wasn't Ben Sweet who died. It was Abigail. Abigail Sweet died in a car accident more than a year ago."

Chapter Twenty-Nine

KATE GANNON STARED, wide-eyed and speechless, at the man she loved, and took a step back.

"It's true, Kate. Just as sure as I'm standing here, Abigail Sweet has been dead for more than a year. I swear I didn't know that part until this morning. But it's true."

"That's crazy. I spent half the summer with her. You never even met her, did you? Did you ever meet, Abigail? And if not, how could you possibly be so sure?"

Matt reached out and touched her arm. "Father Elway is positive, Kate. He said her funeral Mass."

She dropped her head and pushed away from him, then turned toward the kitchen. For a few moments they were silent before Kate turned back. "Wait. You said you only found out about *that part* this morning? What did you mean? Was there more? Is that what you've been acting so strange about—telling me how much you love me on the one hand, then holding back secrets? More crazy secrets like this?"

"It's not like that, Kate. Let me explain."

She headed for the front door. "I'm going around to Abigail's. Come if you want and see for yourself. Or just keep believing whatever ridiculous stories people tell you."

He went after her. "Come with me in the truck." He took her by the arm. "I'm on your side, Kate. No matter what." But she pulled away. Stiff and silent, she walked at a brisk pace toward Abigail's, barely aware that Matt followed behind her in the truck. What in God's name was he thinking? Abigail dead? You think you know people. You can actually fall in love. Then you find out they were hiding things from you, making up ridiculous stories. She had the strangest feeling. It was as if reality were slipping away. But everything would be all right once she reached Abigail's."

Kate Gannon arrived at the place she had known so well. She could see two cars parked along the grassy side of the road. One of the cars was Tillis's black Cadillac. She had no idea who the other belonged to. What did it matter?

She made her way forward, barely aware that Matt was nearby. She felt shaky, weak. What if her legs went out from under her? In the blink of an eye, Matt Reagan had become a total stranger. She approached the walkway to the cottage, then stopped, nearly falling back. She looked about, confused and frantic. This couldn't be the right place. She had gone the wrong way. She must have gone down the wrong lane? Yet, this had to be the right place. Everything about it was familiar. Everything…except…the garden. Where…what happened to the garden? Everything was dead.

Matt came up beside her. She wouldn't look at him. This wasn't possible. All she could see were great overgrown tendrils, flowerless, sprawling shrubs with sprouting spikes of untrimmed branches, the walkway nearly invisible. The flower boxes empty, the house lifeless. My God. When did this happen? How did this happen? She had been here only days before. Just days.

"Matt," she turned in a panic and grasped his arm. "Matt, I don't know what's happening. This can't be the same house."

"It's okay, Kate. I'm here." He led her up the short gravel path, helping her navigate the snares, where the overgrown shrubs had invaded the pathway, cascading here and there.

"Matt, this isn't how it was." She slowly shook her head, disbelieving. "It isn't. I'm telling you this can't be the same house."

The screen door opened slowly and a man stepped out, a man with a familiar looking face, one that she had seen every day, day upon day, all these many weeks. Ben Sweet.

Chapter Thirty

"Come in, please," he said, as Kate stood frozen, staring up. How could this be? she thought.

Please," he repeated. His tone as calming as she would have expected. Oh, Abigail, where are you? What's happening?

Kate looked at Matt. "I don't understand. Honestly, Matt. I don't know what's going on."

"It's okay," Matt said. "Let's just go in and we can all talk about it."

Matt guided her up the steps to the front porch, where everything appeared lifeless. She had the feeling of being at a wake. Or was it just a simple nightmare, the kind you wake up from before making your morning coffee or pouring a glass of orange juice? Her head was full of crazy thoughts all fighting for attention. This place had been real. Abigail had been real. They had sat right there, where the chairs had been. And hadn't Abigail used her yellow watering can to dowse the snapdragons in the window boxes? Yes, yes, she had. Of course, she had. But…

She and Matt entered the cottage. It was warm and stuffy, as she had never known it to be. Where was the soothing coolness? Where was the breeze? The airy sweetness and beauty. The walls were bare, Abigail's vibrant collection of art and pottery, everything…gone. All she could do was look about, searching for the familiar. There was nothing.

Ellen had warned her, hadn't she? She had warned her. She must have been right about everything all along. But then, who was the woman, this amazing artist—her dear friend. If it had been a scam of some kind, then how did this woman, whoever she was, manage to get access to the flower cottage, and live in it so comfortably as her own? By some incredible stretch of the imagination, if that woman were not Abigail Sweet then, somehow, she knew everything about Abigail, everything, even going so far as to tend to her flowers, the rose trellises as if they had always been her own and Ben's. She knew everything about the cottage and where things were kept. Where the paintings were stored. Even the doors that stuck. My God.

"Please have a seat, Miss Gannon. I'm Ben Sweet." Kate couldn't have imagined that she would ever hear those words. He was the one who had died, not Abigail. She tilted her head to the left to see as far as she could into the dining room where they had worked. It appeared to be nothing more than a dim, colorless square of emptiness. The only furniture in the room, or apparently anywhere in the cottage, were a few folding chairs. Kate sat on one of them, Matt beside her. Ben Sweet and Kyle Tillis sat across from them.

"I can appreciate how unsettled you must feel, Miss Gannon," Ben Sweet said. "It must be a great shock to see me."

"Yes…yes, it is." She gestured toward Matt. "This is Matt Reagan. You may…may already know him from the abbey."

"We never met," Ben said, "but I've heard about you, of course, from Leo…Father Elway. You'll be starting the work here next week."

Matt turned to look directly at Kate. "You remember I told you I was going to be working on a project in the area? How could either of us have known…"

Kate turned away.

The two men shook hands. "Nice to meet you, Ben."

Kate looked at the man whose face she had known so well from a small, framed photo, a dead man. He was even better looking than his picture, tall and fit in a blue golf shirt, a man of position and presence, she thought, and possibly as kind as…as…she wanted to say, his wife. But then who was really his wife? Her mind was a jumble. And what did Matt know, as mysterious as he had been? She couldn't trust that she knew him anymore than she knew Abigail. Who were these people? What was all this madness?

Kyle Tillis occupied the folding chair next to Ben Sweet. He hadn't smiled, the one with all the questions back at her bungalow, now quietly observing, analyzing the mayhem. "Ben and I would like to talk to you about the book, Miss Gannon." He leaned forward. "It's remarkable in more ways than one."

Ben Sweet gestured to Tillis. "I understand you explained

to Kyle how you came to work on the book, how you…we might say…gained access to the cottage and to my wife's paintings."

"Gained access," Kate repeated. "Hmm. The woman I knew to be your wife had the access, as you refer to it." She held her hands out in a wide spread. "She knew every inch of this house, the garden, the rose trellises out back there. She brought all the paintings out from that closet. She brought cold drinks for us out on the back porch."

"Iced tea." Ben said. "It was her favorite."

"I wouldn't know about that. We only had lemonade."

Ben Sweet gave Tillis a curious look, then turned his attention back to Kate. "Tell me about the project—what this woman told you? And can you describe her to us?"

Matt reached over and took Kate's hand. She stiffened. "Kate, are you okay? Would you rather do this another time? Tomorrow maybe, if that would be all right with Mr. Sweet and Mr. Tillis?"

"With all due respect," Tillis said, "we think this is a matter to deal with now. The sooner the better. I'll be going back to the city soon. Ben will have to head out for…"

"Croton-on-Hudson," Kate said.

Ben Sweet moved in his chair. "It seems you know everything, Miss Gannon?"

"The woman I knew as Abigail Sweet is the one who knew everything," Kate said. Her somber expression had not changed.

"Tell us again, if you could, how all of this transpired?"

Kate's description of the woman appeared to cause Ben Sweet to rise uncomfortably from his chair and move slowly here and there about the room, obviously pondering every detail. In a flat monotone, Kate explained how she had first discovered the flower cottage, how she had found it again, this time without mentioning the clipped-wing cardinal, how Abigail had called to her to come up to the porch, served her lemonade, her instant connection with the woman. "As impossible as it may be for any of you to believe, we worked for weeks on the book. Right here. She asked me to please not tell anyone, so I didn't. Not even Matt or anyone at the abbey. Not even my best friend who came out for a visit from Brooklyn."

"Did anyone else ever see the cottage? Ever comment on its beauty?" Tillis asked.

"Yes, I met a couple on the road one day when I was out for my morning walk. We were standing in front of the cottage and I asked if they lived there and…" Kate paused, thoughtful. "Well, when they turned to look at the house, it was momentarily obscured by the glare of the sun before it moved back behind the trees. The couple hurried off to catch the bus."

"So, they never actually saw the cottage."

"No." Kate looked around, searching out some memory that might help make sense of what had taken place. "I… wish there was some way for me to convince you."

"Do you know if anyone else met her, met Abigail?" Tillis asked.

"Abigail never went anywhere, not that I know of. I invited her to come to the abbey and to Hicksville with me…to have lunch. She said she really didn't go out much. I never did see her out anywhere except in the garden, but then you don't see that many people out and about here." She paused, collecting her thoughts. "She told me how she and her husband had met, how he always supported her efforts, and how forgiving and tolerant he was of her whims and fancies, as she put it. Oh, yes…she had a deadline."

"What do you mean a deadline?" Ben asked.

"She never elaborated. I tried to get her to be specific, but she would always become conveniently distracted, I thought." Kate paused again, as if trying to work something out. "I saw a moving van a few days ago. Did you have the furnishings that were here moved?"

"Yes, I did," Ben said. "I had everything moved back up to Croton. Some of those things I'll keep, but most will go into an estate sale or will be donated."

"Ben," Tillis said, "no need to go into any of that."

"Had you planned to do that all along?" Kate asked, ignoring Tillis.

"I don't think that's something that you need to concern yourself with," Tillis said.

Matt chimed in. "I think it would be respectful to answer Miss Gannon's questions. Isn't it obvious that she's as confused about all of this as you are?"

"It's all right, Kyle," Ben said. "Yes, the house has been sold—to a family. They'll be taking occupancy in a few weeks and I wanted everything out by the other day so we could do the necessary renovations."

Kate nodded, expressionless. "Abigail…this woman… knew that. I think that was her deadline. I'm sure of it now. The day the courier came to pick up the portfolios was the last time I saw her. She knew it would be. I think that's why she gave me her pair of white gloves…as a parting gift."

"White gloves?" Ben said.

"Yes. It was right as I was leaving with the book parcels. I have them. They're in my bungalow. And it was odd because I had left my white gloves on the subway. And I remember thinking—of all the things to give me, how perfect, since I hadn't had time to replace the ones I lost. I had to go back home to Brooklyn, but somewhere in there is when I saw the moving van." She looked from Ben to Tillis. "She had it timed perfectly. Don't you find that curious?"

"Only because you're trying to explain away something," Tillis said.

"Hey, wait a minute," Matt got to his feet.

"And speaking of being respectful," Tillis continued, "I don't think you should keep referring to this woman, whoever she was, as Abigail Sweet."

Ben Sweet put his hand up in a gesture to keep Tillis from going on. He gestured to Matt. "Please, let's continue."

Matt sat back down.

"I am curious," Ben said. "I can't imagine how this woman would know about the timing of the sale or the furniture being moved out. Some of the other things she could have read about—researched. If she had first cased the house and broken in, she could already have known where the paintings were kept. But the sale of the cottage came up quickly. It was never advertised. Even if this woman had been able to find that out, how would she have planned…gauged the timing so perfectly? We went back and forth on different dates until nearly the last minute. That part doesn't figure at all."

"I'll tell you what else doesn't figure," Kate said in a low flat tone of voice. "A woman, fitting the exact description of your wife, and having the exact level of artistry as your wife, who tends the garden as if she knew every single bloom and twig manages to spend weeks in this house with no concern at all, not a worry in the world, that she would be discovered. A woman who would have known about that door in your bedroom," Kate pointed toward the small hallway, "the door you took off the hinges a few years back, Mr. Sweet, because it stuck all the time."

Ben Sweet looked at Tillis, then back at Kate. "How could you possibly have known this?" He sat back down.

Tillis, unmoved, interrupted. "Whatever transpired here, Miss Gannon, you have to know the bottom line is that we are dealing with fraud."

"Okay, now," Matt said. "Let's not jump to any conclusions

here."

If Kate had found an ounce of energy for it, her laughter would have shaken the floorboards—*jumping to conclusions*. Again. First, it was embezzlement; now fraud. She couldn't imagine by what wondrous destiny she had been challenged to not *jump to conclusions* in the last few short weeks… having twice now been accused…or about to be…of a felony. Wondrous, indeed, Father Elway. She looked up with a smirk on her face.

"Let's all just take it easy," Ben said. "Miss Gannon, have you ever heard the name P. Farrell?"

Something about the name rang a far-off bell, but she couldn't place it. "I'm not sure. Is it a man, a woman?" She shrugged.

"It's my wife. That's the name she signed her paintings with, the name by which she was known in the art world. She was not known as Abigail Sweet. And all of the paintings that arrived with your book package were signed P. Farrell."

"And likely a pretty good forgery, at that," Tillis added.

"She signed them all at the end," Kate said, evenly. "I wasn't here with her when she signed them. But how could the paintings be forgeries in the first place? Weren't most of them copied from or based on your photographs, Mr. Sweet? Some of them only partially finished before she…she died?" Kate couldn't believe she was actually referring to Abigail Sweet as dead. It was inconceivable. For a moment, here and there, she had half-expected that Abigail would calmly stroll through door, her yellow watering can in hand, and ask if anyone wanted lemonade. They had to be wrong.

Matt stood. "This is getting crazier and more confusing by the minute. Does it make any sense at all that some anonymous woman, passing herself off as a famous artist, enlists an unknown author to create a book by which, clearly, none of them could profit?" He gestured to Tillis. "Who would sign your contract? Who would you send royalties to? Think about it?" He took Kate's hand. "In the meantime, you know where to find me and Miss Gannon. We'll be happy to continue to cooperate, but Miss Gannon has been through enough for today. And if it's a lawyer we need, let us know."

"We understand," Tillis said, stepping forward, "but there's one thing Miss Gannon needs to know before she leaves—it doesn't matter how great a job you did authoring those pieces for the art work, this book will never see publication."

Kate stopped in the doorway, then turned, hesitating. She looked at Tillis. "What if you're right, Mr. Tillis? What if it is one grand fraud? An absolute fake. All of it."

Matt coaxed her. "Let's not do this, Kate. Let's…"

"I'd like an answer." She looked from one to the other.

Tillis crossed his arms. "That's a felony, pure and simple."

Kate took a step closer. "And let me ask this," she said, looking directly at Ben Sweet. "What if *I'm* right?"

"Kate, let's go." Matt urged. "Let's get you home."

"That's ridiculous." Tillis gave a wry laugh. "Let's be real. How is that even a possibility?"

"You didn't answer my question, Mr. Sweet." Kate kept her gaze on him. "What if I'm right?"

Ben Sweet ran his hands across the top of his head, and took a few random steps as if pacing. "Okay, wait a minute here. We'd be talking about, what, a…a ghost? Is that it? That you worked half the summer with…God save us…the ghost of my dead wife? Is that what you would like me to believe?"

"Not at all, Mr. Sweet," she said, with a half turn toward the door. "But doesn't some small part of you have to wonder if that's what Abigail would like you to believe?"

Chapter Thirty-One

"I'M SO SORRY, Kate." Since she wouldn't agree to let him drive her back to her bungalow, Matt left the truck parked at the flower cottage and walked with her, although she refused even to acknowledge him. When they had reached her place, she entered and kept the door open behind her, allowing him to enter. She went directly to an armchair and sat, arms folded. Matt Reagan followed and took a seat opposite her on the couch.

"Kate, I…"

"What is it that you've been hiding from me all this time?" Her demeanor was sober.

"It's not that I've been hiding anything from you." He moved in his chair. "Not exactly…well…not that I meant to. It's just that I didn't know how to bring it up."

She kept her gaze on him without changing expression, and said nothing.

"Kate." He leaned forward, his hands animated. "I…this is so hard for me to say."

"Try a little harder. I really would like to know what other surprises you have in store for me."

"I…know about your drinking. I've known about it all

along…the priests do too… almost from the time you got here."

"My what!" It was as if she had been shocked awake by a torrent of freezing cold water. Her voice rose up in her to a level she hadn't heard since the day she chased a boy from the front of Ellen's house for throwing cap darts at her dog Tony. "My drinking? Are you crazy?" She got to her feet. "Has the entire world gone crazy? What universe have I suddenly catapulted into?"

Matt went to her. "Kate, it's okay. It's okay." He reached out, but she stepped back.

"What in God's name are you talking about?"

"Let it go, Kate. I just want to help. That's all I've ever wanted to do. I swear to you—I never wanted to hurt you or embarrass you in anyway."

"Hurt me? Embarrass me? Do you have any idea how ridiculous this is…all of it…and destructive…everything, every single thing that's happened in the space of a few hours?"

"Kate, please. Can't you see why I've been concerned? We all have been. It's escalated ever since you arrived. Stumbling around your bungalow, knocking things over, breaking lamps. Father Garrett heard you. He's been very concerned. Then when I picked you up at the Farmer's Market you smelled of beer. It was only three in the afternoon. The book of matches from Dusky's Tavern that fell out of your purse. On and on."

All she could do was stare at him wide-eyed and

disbelieving.

"Then… Father Garrett had to rescue you at some strange house, no purse, no money, no way to get back home. Not even your house key? No mention of where you'd been or why. At that hour of the night. Something terrible could have happened to you."

Here was the man she had fallen in love with, had prayed to spend the rest of her life with, picking at her life as though it were a grab-bag of puzzle pieces he could jamb into place to make whatever picture came into his head. How had this happened? How had any of it happened?

"That's what I'm talking about, Kate. And you deny it and fake it with such…such innocence…from that very first dinner we had at Angiolini's. All you drink is club soda and next thing you know there's a bag full of wine bottles outside your bungalow."

Kate slowly shook her head and walked about the room. "This is so amazing to me that I don't even know where to begin. I'm…speechless."

"Oh, Kate." He took her arm, but she pulled away.

"Don't even come near me."

"I know a little about alcoholics, Kate. I worked with one a long time ago. It destroyed his career, his family, his life. Even your best friend, Ellen, called Father Elway with concerns about your well-being."

Well, now it was complete, she thought, betrayed even by her closest friend. She went to the door. "So, for my well-being, you took me to dinner and Hicksville and Mass and dancing, and talked of love, all the while stringing together one falsehood at a time. Did you think that would snap me out of it—that by falling in love with you, I would be magically cured? And all along, you were actually just trying to muster the courage to get me to admit to your crazy… delusions." She tapped her head with her hand. "Oh, wait, let me get this right—I'm the one with the delusions."

"Kate, Kate…listen to me. My love for you is no delusion and I know you love me too. I was sure we could work it out…together. That I could be the one to help you. But this whole thing with Abigail Sweet—talking about working on a special project half the summer with…with a dead woman. It's gone too far. But I swear it's not too late."

She pulled the door open wider. "You're wrong about that too, Mr. Reagan. It is too late. But thank you anyway for your great care and concern. And please give my regards to Father Garrett." She straightened, stiff and silent, and faced straight ahead.

"Kate."

She gave the door a tug, signaling for him to go.

"I love you. That hasn't changed, Kate. Let me stay. Let me help you."

She remained looking straight ahead, without expression. "All right, then, if you insist, there's something that will help me—I never want to see you again. Not ever."

When he was gone, she began to pack up her belongings.

Chapter Thirty-Two

"CRAZIEST THING I'VE ever seen," Kyle Tillis said. They had lingered at the cottage a short while before heading back to the City. "I'm sorry you're going through this, Ben. It must be pretty disturbing." He started folding up the chairs.

Ben Sweet stood motionless, his hands in his pockets, remembering. "This had been Abigail's favorite place. Her joy, her refuge, her inspiration to re-create the beauty of nature. And she was so good at it, Kyle. The light here was perfect, she'd always said." The light. Funny—to him, she had been the light. He pinched the bridge of his nose to keep his eyes from tearing. It had been gut-wrenching to see the cottage again, full of all her odd and wonderful things. Since her death, he had returned only twice before today, at the beginning, to shut things off, lock things up, and again when the movers were packing that week. For sentimental reasons and a sense of deep respect after she had passed, he had left everything of hers intact. He rubbed the side of his head. Of all the ways that were possible to commit fraud, why this, especially since whoever did this was certain to be caught? "Strange, Kyle, how sure of everything that young woman is. Like it really happened."

"Well, something happened, all right, none of it good."

Ben walked over and stood in the opening to the dining room, where he could see what was left of the rose trellises through the window. "Did I tell you I found a freshly cut rose resting on a little side table in front of my photo?"

"A nice touch. Scam artists are crafty."

"It wasn't a red rose, the love rose, as anyone might guess. It was pink. A pink Damask Rose. A vintage hybrid. You know, Kyle, they have soft petals. They feel like velvet. And not the kind of fragrance that fills the room the way the more typical roses do." He turned and made a tight fist by way of illustration. "No. The fragrance of the Damask Rose is held within its petals. That's why it's the kind of rose that's used for attar, what they make essential oils with. Who would really know that, except Abigail?"

Kyle Tillis set the folding chair aside. "Hey, don't fall for this, Ben. That's how these things work—they rope you in with the details."

Ben turned. "And just how do you know so much about it?"

"We published a book on the subject." He laughed. "Some famous detective turned prosecutor. It sold over a million copies."

"Then explain the white gloves."

"Hey, don't do this," Tillis said.

Ben moved slowly and thoughtfully into the empty bedroom then back to the kitchen. "But didn't Matt Reagan have a point? How could anyone hope to profit? You wouldn't be expected to publish the book without a contract. Signatures. Whose would they be?" He leaned back against the wall. "You wouldn't send a contract to Abigail or to me. Or to Kate Gannon. Kate was expecting to leave Spiritu and we don't even have her address in Brooklyn. Whoever this woman was, it's clear that Kate was expecting her to be the…I don't know…the contact person? But who? And where? And exactly how? See what I mean, Kyle?"

Tillis walked over and stood in front of him. "You're starting to worry me. You're not actually starting to buy into this, are you?"

Ben Sweet didn't answer. For a moment, he looked off, silent. It was ridiculous to even give it another thought, wasn't it? Yet, it didn't appear to be a simple scam. There was nothing simple about it. And there were too many oddities that they couldn't logic away. She knew about the closet door. Whims and fancies, the very words Abigail always used. Ben looked at his good friend. "You know I had tried to trick her with the question about the iced tea. Abigail hated iced tea. And Miss Gannon got it right—lemonade. Abigail's favorite.

"Coincidence," Tillis said. "Sheer coincidence. A common summer drink."

Ben looked back toward the kitchen, remembering Abigail fixing meals and drinks, fussing to have this and that turn out just so even when she forgot to set the oven timer and the cottage filled with smoke. Didn't happen often, but they always laughed about it. *But you do make the best lemonade*, he would say to her. And she'd laugh. Her soft, breathless laugh.

"Ben." Tillis was at the front door. "You with me?"

"Yuh," he said, taking a last look around. "Just thinking."

OVERCOME with shock and disbelief, anger and…worst of all…heartbreak, Kate packed everything but the few items she would need to spend her last night in Spiritu. Her sense of loss was stunning…the wonderful woman she had come to know as friend didn't even exist. What kind of madness was she experiencing? She couldn't even comprehend it. And the man she had come to love with all her heart, both of them vanishing in an instant. Her inclination was to get the next train back to the City and never return, but there were a few things she had to take care of before leaving.

As she locked up and headed to the bus stop, she felt vandalized by the dizzying mix of thoughts screaming for attention. Abigail and Matt. One minute so real, the next a whorl of complete make believe. Every minute she had spent with Abigail—fiction. Abigail did not exist. How could that be possible? Every minute she had spent with Matt—fiction. He had seen her only as someone in need of help because of her "alcoholism." Both complete aberrations. Ben Sweet and Kyle Tillis had proof—Fact: Abigail Sweet died in a car accident over a year ago. Matt Reagan had proof—Fact: broken furniture and matchbooks and wine bottles, the smell of beer, the "friend" who called the abbey worried about her behavior.

She walked along, trudged really, no more the enchanted summer visitor. She let her mind play with images of Ben and Abigail together—he, supportive of her talent, patient with all of her whims and fancies; she, revering the man who, even under those most unsettling of circumstances today at the cottage, had remained respectful and reserved, as kind as he could…considering. Just the kind of man and woman, just the kind of loving marriage she would have envisioned for herself and Matt Reagan, mere hours before that dream tumbled into a deep black well from which she could hear the far-off tender affirmations of the woman she still wholeheartedly believed to be Abigail Sweet.

When the bus pulled up, Kate felt gratified to see her favorite driver behind the wheel. Oh, how she needed the warmth of a friendly soul. How ironic to think of those very words—*the warmth of a friendly soul.* Was that exactly what she had literally experienced these last many weeks?

Sal grinned, wide-eyed, when she boarded. "Well, if it isn't my favorite long lost passenger. Where you been keeping yourself or did you just decide to ditch me for a better driver?"

"Never," she said, aware that she could muster only a weak smile, and took a seat right up front. "So good to see you, Sal."

"Likewise," he said, as one other passenger boarded and moved toward the rear.

Kate sat back. "I'll be returning to Brooklyn tomorrow."

"Oh, I'm sorry to hear that. You were one of my bright spots." He glanced over at her. "But if you don't mind me saying, I'm not catching much brightness at the moment."

"Sorry, Sal. I guess it's just those end-of-summer-vacation blues." She would miss him. Funny how you can make a new friend so quickly and then possibly never see them again.

It was after 2:00. Kate had only been able to manage a hurried bite to eat before cleaning out the refrigerator—one of George's meatloaf sandwiches would have been wonderful, but she had to get to Hughie's. Thank goodness she had remembered—those photos would be all the proof she needed.

"Here you are," the man behind the counter said. "That'll be a dollar eighty-three."

Kate started tearing at the package even before reaching one of the sidewalk benches. She ripped the flap and removed the thick stack of glossy black and white photographs. Three rolls of film, a few days' worth in all, but right now there were only a handful that she was interested in. One after the other, hands shaking, she clumsily slid each photo off the stack—the bakery, the ice cream parlour and luncheonette, historic church and bank building, the bus stop, the gallery, Hughie's Pharmacy, tree-lined side streets, houses with white picket fences, the sky, the Five & Ten, the flowers in pots set here and there along the sidewalk, the movie theater. Not one photo of the flower cottage. She rushed through them again, dropping a few to the ground. A young man passing by helped her pick them up. "Thank you," she said, half frantic. "Thank you."

She sat for a moment to collect her thoughts. These couldn't be all of them. She stuffed the photos into the envelope and hurried back to Hughie's. "I'm sorry," she said, "I just picked up my photos, but I'm missing a number of them."

"Let me see," the man said, accepting the packet from her. "Let's take a look at the negatives." Kate checked her watch. She was running out of time and there were still a few stops she had to make.

The man held the negatives up to the light. "Oh, yes, here's why. Take a look." He handed the negatives to Kate. "Hold them up, and you'll see there are a number of blanks."

Kate gestured to the photo bin behind the man. "Are you sure you gave me all of mine? Is it possible there's another batch for me?"

"No, I'm sorry. These are the only ones with your name on them."

"Is there any way that you can try to re-do the negatives. Maybe the image would come out if you tried again."

The man gave a soft laugh, "No, Ma'am. It doesn't work that way. Whatever was on the frames…I'm sorry to say… it's lost. It does happen, probably more often than people like."

With an even stronger sense of dejection, Kate thanked

the man and walked slowly from the store just as Abigail's words came back to her: "I hope they come out," she'd said. Abigail knew they wouldn't. She knew.

Kate made her way around the corner to the art gallery. The woman she had first met there was there again and greeted her. "I'm just going to take a look around," Kate said.

The woman smiled. "I remember you. So glad you came back."

"Thank you." Kate started to walk about, then stopped. "I'm curious. Do you know of an artist named Abigail Sweet?

"Mmm…doesn't ring a bell."

"By chance, have you heard of an artist named P. Farrell?"

"Oh, yes," the woman said, obviously pleased. "But not by chance. Her work has always been well received." She came from behind the counter and led the way to a side wall, where she turned to Kate, squinting. "If I'm not mistaken, you looked at a couple of her pieces when you were in last time."

"Yes, I…I guess I did."

"But they're gone now, of course. This is actually the only piece we have left, a limited-edition original print. Numbered and signed by the artist." The woman looked closer at the piece. "This is number 20 of 50. The artist never circulated large runs."

And there it was—the woodland stream she had seen before.

"We sold the original oil. All of them in fact. But we'll get more prints, I imagine. I hope so. We've carried a number of her originals over the years. But once she passed away, that was it. Very sad. Car accident. Such talent. You know, she kept a little cottage not far from here in Spiritu. You may not have heard of the place; not many have. She would stay for most of the summer, using it as her studio. I understand the house has been closed since her death."

"Did you know her or ever meet her?"

"Oh, no." She laughed. "I don't even know if I ever saw her. She didn't make herself known to people. A very private woman."

There was a different bus driver for her trip back and this time she was glad. She needed quiet. There was so much to process, all of it exhausting. One of the details that she couldn't help contemplating was how different all of this was from the day she lost her job. She'd gone to pieces. She'd cried for days on end, stupefied. Oddly, not now. Wasn't this crazier? Literally, more unreal? This time, she was not crying her eyes out. No, she would not cry. This time, she had no intention of holding herself prisoner to the emotional chaos, the actions of others, their misguided opinions and beliefs. She knew in her heart, what had happened all summer long in that cottage. Yes, she was angry, at first, as she had been with Edward Darien. Back then, she had been swept with anxiety about her professional future, her income, her treatment by the school. Strange how almost minor all that Milston drama seemed by comparison. How different she felt now, even though she had a real nemesis in Kyle Tillis.

She thought about Abigail. By some miracle…wondrous, indeed, Father Elway might say…the woman…her friend… was real. Kate would never believe otherwise. Abigail, who had lost everything, and yet prevailed in her serenity, beauty and talent. No, Kate would not cry. She, too, would prevail. She could only hope for a good night's sleep to shut out the chaotic jumble of thoughts and feelings. But first, she had one more stop to make.

Chapter Thirty-Three

Father Garrett shook his head. "So sad. So very sad. Such a lovely young woman. To look at her, who would think that she could go so…so far…off?"

Matt sat in silence.

Father Elway faced them across the desk, somber, the afternoon sun coming through the mullioned windows behind him, cutting the room into slices of unrelenting heat. "I'm uneasy about this. All of it. And not for the reason you might think." He got up and walked over to the bookshelves, apparently with no intention of selecting a book. He ran his fingers across the covers and grew quiet.

"What is it, Leo? Try not to be so cryptic," Matt said. "I'm having a hard-enough time."

"Likely, not as hard a time as our Kate," Father Elway said.

Father Garrett moved in his chair. "I'm so glad I left before having to see her face those men. I could tell they meant business. Poor Miss Gannon."

Matt leaned forward, and put his face in his hands. "I still can't believe it, even though there were so many clues. I had thought I could stop it."

"Maybe there was really nothing to stop, Matthew," Father

Elway said without turning.

Matt looked up. "Sometimes, I just don't understand you, Leo. How much more proof do you need?"

Father Elway returned to his desk. "I'm not sure we've seen any proof at all."

Father Garrett and Matt gave each other a disbelieving look.

"You can't be serious." Matt said.

"Never more so." He looked at his watch. "But...I'll say no more about it now. It's getting late and I have an appointment."

MRS. Wick answered the door and threw her hands up at the sight of Kate Gannon. She reached out and drew Kate close, hugging her. "My poor girl," she said, near tears. "My poor girl."

"It's all right. I'm...I'm fine." Kate was touched by the woman's sentiment. She drew back and looked into her eyes. "Thank you, dear Mrs. Wick," and handed her the pastry box from Englert's. "My last. I won't be back after today."

"Oh, please, Kate," the woman implored, "don't say that. It will all work out somehow." She gestured toward the library. "Father Elway is there. He's waiting for you in his private office."

"But...I didn't say I was coming. How did he know?"

Mrs. Wick shrugged and put her finger to her mouth, as

if keeping a private word between them. "He always knows," she whispered. "Go."

Each time Kate had visited with the priest, they had met in his private office where, amid the bookshelves and amber lamplight, the deep, warm color of the timbering and rugs, along with Father Elway's benevolent presence, made for a cozy, welcoming setting. Kate liked it there. She liked the priest—the way he listened and looked at her with acceptance. The kinds of things they talked about, both simple and complex, and always thought provoking—he had shared with her that an old monk once told him that if people truly grasped the nature of the Eucharist, they would crawl on their knees to the altar. She couldn't imagine leaving Spiritu without seeing this lovely, Godly man. She was also curious about what he thought of…everything,

Father Elway rose when she entered and came around from behind his desk to sit beside her in one of the armchairs. "Kate," he said, in simple greeting.

She took his hand. "Hello, Father Elway." She looked about, as if searching out a clue. "How did you know I would be here?"

"After years of being privileged…blessed, really…to get closer to people than most, I sense things. Besides, I know you, Kate."

"But you also know what's happened. All of it?"

"All of it."

"I came, Father, not just to say goodbye, but because it's

important for me to know what you believe about everything. I also need to tell my side, to explain, at least to you, how wrong everyone is." She caught herself quickly. "Oh, I know you're probably thinking that the more guilty someone is the more they have to say and the faster they say it. That was a common tactic in the student experience—all the excuses and rationales for their unfinished projects and term papers. Is that what you think, Father?"

He leaned toward her. "Not even close, my dear."

"Then what?"

"None of it, Kate. I don't believe any of it." He stroked the side of his chin. "Oh, I admit that when you had first arrived and Father Garrett came to me with word of your stumbling around, things falling over—I immediately thought, as he did, that if you weren't sick, then what? And it did, at first blush, seem plausible that you might be someone hiding away in our little remote hamlet, seeking anonymity to cover a bad habit perhaps. I'll admit that."

She moved to the edge of her seat. "Then you did hear the rest. What they said must have made sense to you. I understand even my best friend, Ellen, called because she was…is…alarmed. She told me all along she didn't understand why I had attached myself so fully to Spiritu."

"There was no way that any of that made a difference as to how I felt about you, once we met and spent time together over tea." He stood and circled his chair, stopping to collect his thoughts. "You see, Kate, Matthew and I both call upon our skills and past experience to evaluate things. Matthew uses logic, necessary to his line of work, which I have to agree in the world of engineering is an indispensable tool. My line of work, so to speak, demands that I look beyond pure logic. People are made up of so much more than calculations and equations. We're not measuring wall board. And we are not robots, after all, wouldn't you agree?"

"Of course."

"First and foremost, I depend on the teaching of a man who lived…and died…two thousand years ago. I use the gifts he gave me—my instinct and intuition, which many people have but seldom use. It's sometimes also called sixth sense. What happened here is that some very good people took a bunch of weeds and twigs and other raw cuttings and baked them in the oven as though it were a pie. Follow?"

"I think so, Father. But how can you excuse the matchbook, which, by the way, I got from the bus driver, the smell of beer on my clothing from a man who spilled his glass, and the wine bottles from the company I had for dinner? By what precise degree of instinct could you possibly dismiss those without an explanation? How could anyone?"

"Because, Kate, there are truths and there are deceits, spoken and unspoken. Through the years, I've learned to recognize differences and make distinctions, and not I alone, whether it's in a certain speech pattern or the way people shift in their seats or perhaps it's the squint of an eye when the most meaningful word is uttered. Maybe even the precise moment one hesitates or stammers or loses eye contact, changes tone of voice, looks off in a certain direction, doing things with their hands or their feet while at it. There is a trueness of eye that speaks of the spirit. At least I believe so. One may not be able to see it in all people. But I saw it in your eyes the first day we met during Mrs. Wick's little reception after Mass. You may endure many trials, Kate, but your vibrancy prevails. God's grace has made you resilient. You have not given in to outside forces.

Kate sat back in her chair, uplifted and at the same time puzzled by the priest's words. "You amaze me, Father Elway. This isn't at all what I had expected coming here today." She pushed a curl of hair behind her ear. "But what about Abigail Sweet? Father, I swear to you—sorry, I shouldn't say swear. I would take an oath, like in a court of law, with my hand on the Bible, that I spent these past many weeks working, befriending a wonderful woman who…who…"

"Died a year ago?"

"Yes, Father. And I don't deny that she died, impossible as it was to believe when I first heard it this morning, impossible even now. But we were there together, Father, in her beautiful flower cottage, day after day. No one could have faked that. Now there's a finished book as hard evidence, which, of course, no one believes to be Abigail's. Very likely not even you."

"Now, Kate." He smiled and patted her shoulder. "You mustn't complicate matters by imagining things about me that aren't true."

Kate shifted in her chair. "You mean you believe me?"

Father Elway gestured to the surroundings with a sweep of his arm. "Look at where we are, Kate. Look at who we are? We are the believers in miracles. Because there are miracles. And I know about our little clipped-wing friend showing you the way. You may not know, dear Kate—Matthew found him in the garden behind the boxwood."

"Oh." Her heart sank. "Poor thing." She sat back and after a moment she looked directly at Father Elway. "Does it strike you as odd that our cardinal friend is also dead, just now, after all these weeks?"

"Yes, the timing is curious."

"See what I mean, Father." She gestured with her hands. "Why can't God just let me have my miracle? Why this whirligig of… of…chaos? Remember wondrous things? Isn't that what you said? How are loss and grief, wondrous? To say nothing of the most awful accusations. And don't believe for a minute that I'm not still in a state of shock over Abigail. I have no idea how to make sense of any of it. And I haven't even told you the rest of it." She went on to tell him about Jonathon Rorimer's embezzlement threat.

"Mmm…that's serious, all right. No denying it. All I can say, Kate, is that by now you must surely know how Our Lord operates? He always has his reasons and, what's more, he will never leave you out there on your own. It's all about the Mystery, isn't it, which, by the way, we can only glimpse from afar because the more we try to understand it, the less we can. And isn't that where faith comes in, after all? We are of this world, and being here is fraught with challenges, to say the least. But you can trust that Our Lord is always in the mix." He brought her to her feet. "You are stronger than you know."

Kate had a feeling it must be true. Somewhere in these last few hours, she had managed to collect herself. "But I do believe I will cry my eyes out tonight, Father."

"Matt Reagan?"

She nodded, dropping her head.

Father Elway gently lifted her chin. "He'll come around and get past this."

"Problem is—I'm not sure I will. He deceived me, Father."

"He loves you very much, Kate. This was no frivolous matter for him. He's suffered too. He's suffering now, to be sure. I will see to it that he knows the truth. Forgiveness will be required of you."

She looked away, gathering her thoughts. "You know, Father, when I was fifteen, my grandmother told me something pretty profound. Of course, it didn't mean much to me back then. What did I know about anything? She said, 'At some time in your life, everyone you love will hurt you in some way, whether they intend to or not, and it's going to be very important that you forgive them, because if you can't forgive them, you will never be able to love them again, and it may keep you from truly loving anyone.' I have never forgotten her words, Father."

Father Elway patted his heart. "I salute your grandmother. She was very wise." He looked into Kate's eyes and before giving her a blessing, he said, "Let these moments breathe, Kate. Stop in the garden before you go. And remember what Jeremiah said,

For I know the plans I have for you, declares the Lord, plans for welfare and not for evil, to give you a future and a hope.

Chapter Thirty-Four

MATT REAGAN TUGGED at a few more of the stubborn rose vine stragglers with his gloved hand, being careful not to get caught in one of the thorny snares. Most had died off during the year that the house had lain empty, leaving a backyard filled with skeletal vestiges of the trellises Ben Sweet had so handily crafted years before, structures that it seemed even a hurricane would have trouble taking out.

Once clear, he used the claw end of his hammer to yank out the screws that held the long, thin, crisscrossed strips of cedar in place. He'd worked at it steadily since before eight, eager to tear down as many as he could before the brutal midday sun of late summer crept in—hard work, he thought, to free his troubled mind, Kate Gannon foremost in his thoughts. He'd lost sleep and had pretty much been living on coffee since she left. It seemed as though he had not seen her in weeks when, in fact, it had been only two days since she returned to Brooklyn without seeing him or calling to say goodbye.

What did he expect? Father Elway had explained everything, which made Matt feel even worse about his lack of courage and trust. He had tried hard not to imagine what she was going through and what she must be feeling about the whole situation and about him. He had called her home in Brooklyn more than a dozen times without any luck.

Father Elway had been right, after all—Kate Gannon was everything she appeared to be—a beautiful, honest and open woman who had fallen victim to circumstances that had led him and Father Garrett to a profound error in judgment. Matt understood that now, although he still couldn't reconcile the whole Abigail Sweet business. Leo had recommended that he keep an open mind, that sometimes goodness and innocence are rewarded with the extraordinary.

At the same time, he had told Matt about the board member from Milston threatening to accuse Kate of embezzlement, an outrageous proposition. Matt wished she would allow him to stand by her and help her get through this.

At a little after eleven, he dropped the hammer into his tool kit and removed the handkerchief from the pocket of his chinos, beads of sweat trickling down his cheek. He would have to lay off for a while, he thought, mopping his brow and the back of his neck as he headed through the screen door and into the kitchen where he had left his cooler of water. He removed the plastic cup from the top of the cooler and was about to pour himself a drink when he noticed a glass sitting there on the counter, a flowered napkin under it. It had the enticing, frosted look of a chilled drink. He looked about, wondering where it had come from.

"Kate?" he called out, hopeful. Was it possible that she had forgiven him and decided to return? He picked up the glass. Ice cold. He took a sip. Lemonade. Odd. The refrigerator had long been turned off. "Kate?" He put the glass down and made his way through the empty rooms. "Are you here?" He opened the closet doors and found them as empty as the rest of the house. He hurried to the front door, imagining that he might find her out on the porch. There was no one. He looked up and down the lane, knowing that she could not have made it out of sight that quickly.

He ran his hand across the side of his head, confused. He returned to the kitchen and picked up the glass again, turning it in his hand to look at it. Of all things. An ice cold glass of lemonade. And no sign as to how it got there. None at all. He set the glass down and after a moment stepped back, swept by uneasiness. He looked about, his heart beating quicker, and considered what was surely, by every measure of logic or reason…the impossible.

Chapter Thirty-Five

"Edward, it's Kate. I'm wondering if there's any news."

"So glad to hear from you," Edward Darien said. "Thanks so much for calling." He sighed. "I just wish I had something promising to tell you, but the fact is we haven't heard a word from Rorimer and the auditors will be here tomorrow. Honestly, we've been trying everything we can think of. He's not answering anyone's calls. George Bennett even drove out to Rorimer's home twice, and each time his butler said he was gone and didn't know when he'd be returning." Darien took a deep breath. "I don't know what other options are available to us, Kate."

"I understand." Kate said. It was a perfunctory answer—she didn't mean it. Surely, there was something they could come up with. Other evidence. Anything. At the very least a commitment to stand by her, no matter what. That was an option that Darien had never offered. All these well-heeled, educated men who always so easily allowed their hands to be tied, but then, when did being well-heeled and educated mean you had good instincts, common sense, or wisdom. When did it mean that you had a set of values that mandated you go out on a limb for a colleague or a friend wrongly accused? Educated fools, the worst fools there were.

"I know how hard it is to reach you sometimes, Kate. So, please call me for updates. I promise. If I hear anything, anything at all, you'll be the first to know."

When they'd hung up, she sat back. There was no doubt the auditors would find the funds missing. There was no doubt that Rorimer, wicked beast that he was, would do as he'd threatened and implicate her. If the board sensed any jeopardy at all to themselves or the college, they'd cower, just as they'd always done. She'd been praying about it, but so far…

The doorbell rang and for at least the tenth time in two days, Kate ignored it. Ellen. She was sure of it. The phone had rung numerous times, as well. It was possible that Matt had also tried to reach her. She wanted no part of either Ellen or Matt.

Ellen couldn't look beyond any range of interests or possibilities that proved challenging to her own point of view. Matt Reagan couldn't look beyond the impossibility that his calculations and judgment were wrong. And it was clear that Father Garrett, good misguided priest that he was, had nowhere near the level of wisdom that Father Elway possessed. But what was the point of any of that now? Outside of a miracle, there was a very good chance that after the audit, she would be accused of a terrible crime. That thought was astounding to her. And even if Matt Reagan were at her side, even if Ellen had stood by her and not doubted and challenged her every move, every thought, what exactly could they do to help? Well, she knew one thing—she had no intention of throwing her hands up and giving in. She'd fight it with everything she had.

She had not seen Ellen since her return and, therefore, had not told her what happened those last days in Spiritu. She knew Ellen must be dying of curiosity about Kate's early return and the possibility of a failed relationship with this so-called love of her life. And if there was one thing Kate would never put herself through, it was telling Ellen about Abigail. Ellen had not found Abigail Sweet in any of the galleries or records because no one knew her by that name. If Ellen only knew that Abigail went by P. Farrell, she would quickly learn that, in fact, the woman was dead, and had been dead for more than a year. That's all Kate needed. That plus an indictment for embezzlement. "Lord, how could any of this be happening?"

Kate had hardly given a thought to the book she and Abigail had put together—that extraordinary project that had captivated her and brought her back to her passion for writing. How odd, yet understandable, that it would never see the light of day. Kyle Tillis had assured her of that. How could he or Ben Sweet, for that matter, ever comprehend what had taken place in that beautiful flower cottage? She couldn't comprehend it herself. Yet, Father Elway didn't dismiss her story out of hand. She would surely miss him. And Abigail. Sweet Abigail. How had it been possible for her to return? And where had she gone?

Chapter Thirty-Six

Jonathan Rorimer made his way up the long circular drive after a morning round of golf, and stopped in front of his two-story country club home that overlooked the seventeenth green. "Have Niles wash the Lincoln," he said to his butler, Henry, as he entered. "Tell him I want my clubs cleaned and polished by tomorrow morning." He picked up a small stack of mail from the round table situated in the entry hall beneath a lavish crystal chandelier that hung from the ceiling two stories above. After thumbing through the envelopes, he dropped them back onto the table. "Is Mrs. Rorimer in yet?" His voice echoed.

"No, Sir. And you did have a visitor. The same man as last time. From Milston. Oh, yes, and your nephew called a few times."

Without responding, Rorimer went into the library and poured himself a bourbon and soda. He heard the phone ring and a minute later, Henry came to the door and announced that it was Lonny Kagan.

He told Henry to close the door and waited for him to go out before picking up the receiver. Then he waited for the click to be sure that Henry had hung up the extension. "What is it now?'

"The audit starts tomorrow, Uncle Jonathan. Is everything still the way we planned?"

"*We* didn't plan anything. Remember that," Rorimer snapped. "You run wild and I'm left to clean up your mess."

"Well, you never liked Professor Gannon anyway. So, what's the big deal?"

"I can't stand Professor Gannon, to be exact. But I'll tell you what the big deal is, you moron—I've already lost my position on the board because of you."

"I'm sorry, Uncle Jonathan. Things got out of hand."

"No, you got out of hand. Just remember to keep your mouth shut." Rorimer slammed the phone down, then rang for Henry. "I'll take my lunch in the upstairs study."

Bourbon glass in hand, Rorimer climbed the wide, curving staircase and entered the double doors at the top. He went to his desk, baroque in style like most of the furnishings, behind which were a set of French doors. He removed a cigarette from the small silver case on the desk and lit it before opening the doors and stepping out onto the balcony where, for a few minutes, he took in the half acre of pristine lawn and flower beds, considering his risk.

No matter what the board said, the authorities could not technically tie him to the $50,000. Maybe he shouldn't have been so aggressive with Darien. But if those fools thought they were going to mess with Jonathon Rorimer, they were in for a big surprise. He'd drag Milston's name so far down into the mud, it would be years before their enrollment dug its way out. "In any case, Alea iacta est." He snickered, raising his glass. "The die is cast."

He flicked his cigarette over the edge of the balcony and went back inside, lit the Tiffany desk lamp and sat for a while, finishing his Bourbon and wondering what to do about his degenerate nephew. When you choose a wife, you get everything that comes with her, he thought. At one time, it had been worth it. There had been too much at stake, too much to lose. When you choose a wife…the right wife… you get everything that comes with her—a manufacturing fortune that went back four generations in her family. How could an underpaid history professor turn his back on that? Lonny Kagan had also benefitted from the family fortune, but it was never enough. Little by little, he'd built up to this grand larceny nightmare by pilfering bills from purses at family gatherings, stealing pieces of jewelry from his sister, aunts and house guests. A common thief, only not so common now.

Rorimer considered whether it was time to cut all ties and move on. His feelings for Madeleine had waned in recent years. When they married, she was a beauty—slim, shapely, interesting. He had worked at staying in shape, while eighteen years later, she had become matronly, a stately female who'd put on the pounds luncheon by luncheon, fundraiser by fundraiser. Back then, she had also cared about him. Now, she was more concerned about her charitable endeavors than about him. Different interests. Different bedrooms. Different needs.

He was certain she knew about the blond legal assistant at their attorney's office and the waitress at Donato's. The stewardess. She had to. In the beginning, he'd been sly enough to hide his misadventures. In recent months, however, to get a rise out of her, he'd deliberately left clues. But either she never noticed, as was true of most things that concerned him, or she simply chose to ignore them, content, for some unknown reason, with their disparate lifestyles.

If he wanted out, what would he do? He had some money of his own. He might be able to get a good chunk of that $50,000 that Lonny had stashed away, if the greedy lout hadn't spent most of it by now. He should take at least half of that as the price for saving his rotten neck, and go…where… Rio? Acapulco? He could vanish in a boating accident. He could change his name. Maybe just clean out one of his joint accounts with Madeleine, and disappear. It would be a sizable sum. She didn't need it. Their daughter didn't either. Spoiled teenager that she was, she had enough, and when the time came, she'd have still more by finding herself an even wealthier husband.

He turned around in his chair to face out, then leaned back. He'd been feeling the strain anticipating what lay ahead, losing sleep and appetite, his golf game a useful distraction. He needed these bits of quiet time, devoid of Madeleine's meaningless chatter and the incessant whines of his daughter.

He closed his eyes. The ball would start rolling tomorrow, but he likely wouldn't hear anything for another day or so or until the auditors had noticed enough to start asking questions. A few minutes rest would do him good, settle his nerves. It had been hot on the golf course, hotter than hell everywhere, but it was surprisingly cool up here today. He dozed.

"Oh, that is a lovely view. Just lovely."

Rorimer scrambled out of his chair, startled, stumbling. He nearly knocked over the desk lamp. That's when he saw a woman he'd never seen before sitting half way across the room in one of his brown leather club chairs. "Who the hell are you? How did you get in here?"

"I didn't mean to frighten you. So sorry. I have to get better at that." Her voice was soft and even.

"I asked who you are. Who let you in?"

She gestured to the door behind her. "I came in right through there."

He thought he must have dozed deeper than he realized because he'd heard nothing. And why in God's name didn't Henry call to announce her. He should never have let her in. A total stranger. That would be it for Henry, the ingrate.

Rorimer approached the woman. "How dare you enter my home, my private study. I won't ask you again. Who are you? What do you want?"

"Oh, I see that I've upset you," she said, "That wasn't my intention."

"I don't give a damn what your intention was. I'll have

you arrested for breaking and entering."

The woman giggled. "Oh, Professor Rorimer," she said, pulling off her short white cotton gloves, one finger at a time. She laid the gloves on the arm of the chair. "I feel certain that you can charge me with something far worse than that." She put her hand to her chin. "How about…let me think … embezzlement?"

Rorimer took a step back. How on earth? Who was she and how could she possibly know anything? A woman in about her mid to late-forties, fair, soft-spoken and completely unknown to him. She had a quirky quality about her, but something told him that she could mean business. She couldn't be a friend of Madeleine's. His wife had no idea what was going on between him and Lonny. "I don't know how you got in here or what you think you're doing, but I'm calling the police." He picked up the phone, hesitating, while she remained seated, cross-legged, with a smile on her face. It was clear that she was not buying his bluff. His palms began to sweat.

"I must say, Professor Rorimer, this is a beautiful place. What a fine collection of art and…well…everything. Lovely. I would have wanted to do a painting of this room, if only I had visited here before…you know…before…"

"Before what?" He snarled. "Before you had the gall to break in?"

"Before I died."

Rorimer backed up into his desk.

"Oh, I'm sorry—that's a bit of a frightening thought," she said, "But what can you do? People die." She rose from the chair and took a few steps toward him. "But you know what?" She spoke in a loud whisper, as if sharing a confidence. "Sometimes they can come back. Yes, when someone needs their help, they can actually come back." She laughed. "How else would I be here?"

Rorimer had not moved, his thoughts at high speed, heart quickened. This woman was clearly insane, yet she seemed to know something. But how? She couldn't have been related to Gannon. Darien had once told him she had no close relatives, that's why they could pile the extra work on her.

Darien had laughed. "What else has she got to do with her time?" he'd said. Then who was this? Where did she get her information, and how in God's name was he going to deal with her? She could ruin everything.

There was a light knock on the door and Henry entered with a silver lunch tray, oblivious. "Would you like this on your desk, Sir?"

Rorimer approached him. "How dare you let anyone into my home, my private rooms without my permission. Consider this your last day."

"But, Sir, I let no one in. No one at all."

"Then tell me, you idiot." Rorimer pointed toward the woman. "How did she get in here?"

Henry looked about. "Who, sir?"

"That woman. Are you blind?"

Henry turned around to see the entire room. "There's no one here." He set the tray on the desk. "Are you all right, Sir?"

"A crazy woman has gained entry to my home," Rorimer shouted, "and you can't see her? Right there in front of you? Have you gone crazy too?"

Henry began backing away. "Let me see if I can reach Mrs. Rorimer...or maybe Doctor Shelton. I'm sure he can give you something to settle your nerves."

Frustrated and frantic, Rorimer turned in one direction then another. "There's nothing wrong with my nerves. You're all morons." He continued to shout. "Collect your pay and get out." Then he took one long pass at the desk with the swing of his arm and swept the luncheon tray onto the floor, the lamp with it. Dishes, food and silverware, along with broken Tiffany glass in every shape and color, scattered amid the Damask in a wild mess halfway across the room.

Henry turned and hurried out.

The woman hadn't moved. "Mmm, I see that I must get on with this," she said, just as calm as at first. "You are too upset for me to keep you much longer."

Rorimer walked toward her with a menacing gait, but just as he reached her, he could move no farther. "What's happening? I can't walk," he cried out. "Who are you and what is it that you are trying to do to me?"

"All I want is for you to think twice before you do something very foolish."

"Whoever you are, whatever you are, you'll make no

threat to me, if you know what's good for you."

"Ah, belligerent. Yes, that's your style. I see." She walked back to the club chair and sat. "Well, then, let me get on with it." As if to start counting on her fingers, she said, "Lonny's account…let me see…what's that number?"

"What are you talking about?" Rorimer returned to lean against his desk, fearful.

"You know the one. Oh, no you don't. I forgot. You don't know about the secret account where the money is hidden. All that money. Nearly $50,000. Can you imagine? Did you know that it's in a United Federal safe deposit box up near Lake Skaneateles?" She looked off. "I love that name—Skaneateles—and it's such a beautiful lake. The water is so pure. All those Indian names, my favorites—Iroquois, Cayuga, Onondaga. If I were a poet, I would use those names in a poem."

Rorimer stared at her, disbelieving. "You're mad. That's what you are and no one is going to listen to a mad woman, least of all me. What's more, you have broken into my home. They would understand that I had every right to kill you." He went around behind his desk, opened a side drawer and removed a gun.

"Oh, Professor," she said, with a dismissive wave of her hand, "don't be silly. You'd shoot right through me and damage that lovely painting on the wall behind me." She gave a slight turn. "A Caravaggio? Not an original, of course, but an excellent print. I believe it is. Madeleine would be very upset with you. So, put the gun away. It will do you no good."

"All right then." Rorimer spun around and hurled the gun out through the French doors. "There! The gun is gone. Now I want you gone too."

"Where were we? Oh, yes, Lonny's account number. Let me see. Sometimes I forget. Your mind really can play tricks, even when you've passed on." Then she laughed and tapped her forehead. "4181829191. Of course, it's under a made-up name, Eric Weatherly. He picks quite nice names, your nephew. Don't you think?"

"You're crazy," Rorimer shouted. "And whatever it is you think you know, be assured you'll never get away with it."

"But I'm not the one here who has to worry about getting away with anything. After all, if I was able to locate the account number, how hard will it be for the police?"

Rorimer froze. The phone rang. He ignored it.

"Lonny Kagan will go to prison," she said, putting her gloves back on. "You will have the fight of your life not to join him. But I can tell you, Professor Rorimer, your nephew will pull you in just like a fisherman landing a whale. Oh, yes." She rose from the chair and walked slowly toward him. "Now, there is only one thing…one…that's all…that I care about. So, before I go," she said, drilling him with her gaze, "please tell me the one name that will never be mentioned in any way in connection with this or any other scheme of yours or your nephew's." She waited.

He hadn't moved.

"Professor!"

"Gannon." He stammered. "Kate Gannon. Professor Gannon."

The door opened slowly. Madeleine Rorimer peeked in and entered with caution, behind her a man in a dark suit carrying a black leather case. Then Henry.

"Jonathan darling, Doctor Shelton is here," she said. "Henry tells us you've been a little on edge." As the doctor entered, Mrs. Rorimer stayed back, surveying the condition of the room, a look of shock on her face.

"Jonathan," the doctor said. "Talk to me about what's happening."

"Why ask me?" Rorimer shouted, pointing across the room at the woman no one else could see. "She's the one who started it with her…her little white gloves and all that Indian poem stuff. Who in God's name cares anything about the Iroquois or Skaneateles, for that matter? She'd paint this room if she wasn't dead. I'd like to see that. I'd hang her and the painting on the wall and shoot them both." He walked erratically about, arms flailing. "What gall. What nerve—finding out numbers behind my back. Well, maybe dead people have trouble remembering things, but not me. I'll remember this, all right. Prison, she says. Ha. Let's just see her try it." He moved toward Henry. "And you, you treacherous beast," he yelled, taking a swipe at the butler, and missing, "you let her in here. You couldn't see her, oh, no, but you let her in anyway, didn't you, into my private study, no less?

You'll pay for this."

Doctor Shelton, clearly concerned, gave a subtle nod to Madeleine, who had remained near the door. Now, however, with her husband continuing to rant incoherently in the background, she discreetly backed away and hurried to the phone.

Chapter Thirty-Seven

AFTER MASS ON Sunday morning, Kate walked at a leisurely pace along Carroll Street, stopping at D'Amato's bakery for a Charlotte Russe. She hadn't had one in years, and the sweet cream and cake taste immediately brought her back to childhood. She'd thought a lot about her grandparents lately, wondering what they would have made of all this. They would have liked Father Elway. And Matt. Her grandfather knew Ellen. She had moved in next door years before he passed away. He appreciated her honesty, but always agreed with Kate that she could be just too pushy at times.

Kate still hadn't spoken to her honest, pushy neighbor. She would in time, of course, and with one big change—from now on their relationship would have to be on Kate's terms, not Ellen's. She'd had enough. As for Matt…well, hard as it was to admit to herself, maybe she'd been too hasty judging him. True, he had judged her, but given the circumstances, had he really been wrong to assume what he had about her? She understood that it was Father Garrett who got things rolling. But both he and Matt had meant well. Maybe it was the way she had learned about it and the fact that they had linked what they thought they knew about her with the idea that she was having delusions regarding Abigail Sweet. That would be the hardest thing to convince Matt about. How would she be able to even try?

She stopped at the corner park and sat on one of the swings, the same one she remembered sitting on months back when she had searched for firm ground underfoot following her dismissal. Was she any better off now? Even with the crazy summer and all the shocking developments that had ended her stay in Spiritu, she truly did feel better off. Centered. Strong. Scared, of course—the audit had been scheduled to start on Thursday. Maybe it was too soon for them to find anything.

"I was hoping I'd catch up with you somewhere around here."

Kate's heart leaped at the sound of Matt Reagan's voice. "How on earth…?" He had come up behind her, and when she turned she saw his blue truck parked up at the next corner.

"I had to find you. We've got to work all this out, Kate." He stood looking down at her, holding onto the swing chain. "We love each other too much to let go."

"But how did you know where I was?"

"Luckily, you told Father Elway what church you go to." He laughed. "I've already been to two Masses this morning at St. Agnes. I finally saw you at the 11, but I was all the way at the back and lost you in the crowd on the way out. I figured you couldn't go too far on your way home?"

Oh, how she had missed him. "Why didn't you just come by the house?"

"I figured since you weren't answering the phone, you probably weren't answering the door either. You're one tough lady to get hold of, Kate Gannon." He looked about. "Can we go somewhere? Maybe get a bite to eat? There are things we need to talk about, and I've got to tell you something that only you would believe."

When she stood, they looked into each other's eyes for a long moment, appreciative yet hesitant. Then, with perfect timing, they reached for each other and held on tight.

"Kate, I've missed you, like the heart in me was gone. I'm so sorry about everything."

"I know. I know," she said. "Me, too."

LENNY'S Luncheonette was open till two on Sundays, all the time they needed to enjoy a leisurely lunch and a much-needed conversation. Their explanations cleared the air, but there was one last thing…

"A few days ago," Matt said, "I was working in the backyard at the Sweet's cottage. I had to remove all the trellises."

Abigail's beautiful trellises. The very idea stuck Kate like a thorn. But none of it was any fault of Matt's.

"The house is completely empty," he said. "You saw it. But when I came in to get a drink of water from the cooler I'd brought, there was an ice cold glass of lemonade sitting on the counter."

Kate threw her hand to her mouth. "Matt."

"I was as surprised as you are right now. I thought it was you. I thought you'd come back. I searched the house. Went out to the porch. There was no one, anywhere."

Their eyes locked on each other in clear understanding.

Kate pressed his hand. "You believe me now."

"I have to be honest, Kate. That whole Abigail thing you talked about really threw me. I couldn't reconcile what you were telling us. You have to know—I was planning to come find you anyway because I love you no matter what. But you have to agree it's incredible."

"Yes. I know. I agree."

Matt ran his hand across his chin and chuckled. "When I told Father Elway about it, he shrugged. 'Why not?' was all he said."

They spent the rest of the day together, leaving the truck and taking the Brighton Beach subway line to Coney Island for a parachute ride and hot dogs at Nathan's. Back at Kate's into the evening, they sat on the living room sofa, her head on his shoulder.

"Marry me, Kate. I don't ever want us to be apart again."

Chapter Thirty-Eight

ON MONDAY MORNING, Kate went next door to Ellen's, hoping to reach her before she left for her office. There were things she needed to get off her chest and felt strongly about setting Ellen straight.

"It's about time," Ellen said. "First you have me worried. Then, you have me even more worried. What can I do with you?"

They sat over coffee in the kitchen, making awkward small talk until Kate decided to let Ellen know where she stood. "I'm not happy about you calling the abbey."

Ellen got up from the table and busied herself, apparently uncomfortable that Kate knew. "You left me no choice, Kate. Some of the things you told me seemed…I don't know…too good to be true or something. So out of the ordinary."

"These people became my friends, Ellen. You put ideas in their heads that made me look bad and made them wonder about me…and not in a favorable way. And the worst part is, I know you're not even sorry. You think bossing me around is perfectly okay. Hounding me about my choices. Can you see that this is a problem between us? A problem for our friendship?"

Ellen stood, tinkering at the sink, with her back to Kate. "It's what a friend does when they're concerned. True friends are supposed to look out for each other." She ran a damp dish cloth mindlessly over the countertop.

"Ellen, you nagged me, you tried to discourage me at every turn, challenged me on everything I shared with you. What kind of a friend does that? You've made me not want to be around you."

There was a long silence as Kate waited. Finally, Ellen turned and leaned against the sink. "That won't be a problem much longer. I'm selling the brownstone."

She might as well have pulled the chair right out from under Kate.

"What? That's crazy. You're kidding me."

"It's true." Ellen's voice was quiet, flat, lacking the vitality Kate had always seen in her. She sat back down at the table and fidgeted with a napkin.

"Ellen, what happened? Please tell me what's going on."

Ellen didn't look up. "Nothing more than what's been building up for months." She continued to mindlessly pick at the corners of the napkin. "I've lost the business."

"Oh, Ellen." Kate couldn't believe what she was hearing. She reached over and touched Ellen's hand. "I'm so sorry. But how could this have happened to you of all people? You're one of the smartest business people I know."

"The business was on the downturn for a while. It became harder and harder to make a go of it and taking on more and more debt to make things work out." She looked about. "Selling the brownstone will help me get out from under. I was just out of options."

Kate looked at her friend and for the first time saw a vulnerable woman she'd never seen before. Why didn't you tell me?"

"You were busy."

It was at that moment that Kate had a terrible realization. All this time that she had been examining her life, exploring different paths, engaged in the ups and downs of new friendships and opportunities, finding love, Ellen had been struggling, despairing, her life spiraling downward. The unwelcome truth was that over these last many weeks Kate had never once asked Ellen how her life was going. She had assumed that Ellen was successful, in control. But why should Kate have known; their conversations were all about Kate. "But where will you go? What will you do? There must be something I can do to help." Kate wondered if her offer sounded as hollow to Ellen as it did to her.

"Nothing much will happen for the next month or so." She took a deep breath. "I found a job at the Williamsburg Bank in the loan department. I guess the change will do me good. I plan to take a small apartment over by Prospect Park. They're kind enough to put a hold on it for me because of the timing. The person whose job I'm filling at the bank won't be retiring for another month. And besides, I have to finalize things at my own business...or what used to be my own business."

"I can't believe it, Ellen. I feel awful. About everything and much more than you realize. I came here this morning about a…a tiff we'd had. Not an end to friendship. Your friendship has meant everything to me. I just wanted us to get back on track. And now I can see that I've been so concerned with what kind of a friend you've been to me, that I never once considered what kind of a friend I've been to you." Kate thought about how important that trip to the Berkshires must have been to Ellen, how much she had needed a vacation, how much she had needed Kate, an opportunity now long gone. "I…I can't tell you what it's going to be like around here without you. But I know everything will be okay for you, Ellen. I know it."

"Why shouldn't it? I'll be starting fresh." She pressed the napkin against her eyes again. "Although I do have to wonder at what point in life we can stop starting over." She stiffened. "Of course, in the apartment building where I'll be moving, there are no pets allowed. So, Tony will also have a new home."

Kate got up and put her arm around her friend's shoulder. "Oh, Ellen, Ellen, it's all going to work out. It will. Prospect Park is a nice area. And no matter what, I'm not letting go of you."

Kate believed what she told Ellen, but not without reservations—her friend was hurting, her life had been turned upside down. There had obviously been a lot of pain getting to this point. She'd be giving up everything, including her wonderful Tony. Kate's eyes welled. Even with the roller coaster she'd been on, she had Matt, she had hope. It might be a fresh start for Ellen, but grief and maybe loneliness would likely be steady companions for a long time to come.

"I know I've let you down, Ellen. I don't know how I can ever make it up to you, but please allow me to try. I still have some money set aside."

Ellen put her hand on top of Kate's. "Thank you. I appreciate that, but the money part will work out once I sell the brownstone. I'll have enough to pay off the mortgage and my bills with some left over. Thank God for that."

Interesting, Kate thought, that she didn't usually hear Ellen mention God. "Then, there must be some other way I can help."

"Not sure what, if anything, can help right now. You know how I am with change, and this is change, all right—bold, all caps, three exclamation points."

"Whatever it is, Ellen, I promise I'll be here for you."

FOR the next few hours, Kate moped around, hungover from the dreariness of Ellen's situation, and the realization that they had both failed at their friendship on so many levels. But Kate knew it was her own fault that she had never seen this coming. Ellen, strong and independent, her own boss for so long, now starting over with the restraints of a tight banking structure. And unfamiliar. A small apartment. No Tony. And Kate couldn't come up with a single thing that might make a difference. She felt guilty because she *was* guilty—guilty, sick and bereft.

She couldn't even tell this friend, who at times had felt more like a sister, that she was going to be married. And although she and Matt hadn't yet set a date, Kate wanted Ellen to be her maid of honor. Was that even a possibility now? Ellen would be long gone by then. How awful to not even have her as a neighbor. Who could ever take her place? Thank goodness Kate had a bit of time to try smoothing things over before losing her and, she prayed, not forever.

At around two in the afternoon, Edward Darien called. "Well, this is a surprise," he said, "—reaching you on the first try. You'd better sit down."

"Oh, Edward, please, no bad news. I'm just not up to it right now. Give me a break."

"That's exactly why I'm calling. You've gotten your break, Professor Gannon. The audit will no longer be an issue for you."

"You're kidding." Kate plopped into a chair in the living room. "Thank God. What happened?"

"Something none of us could have guessed in a hundred years." Darien was elated.

"Don't tell me the great Jonathon Rorimer actually had a change of heart? I can't imagine."

"Well, there's been a change, all right. But you couldn't possibly imagine what it is—Rorimer went off the deep end."

Kate sat up straight in her chair. "What? Wait. You mean deep end as in gone crazy? Jonathan Rorimer?"

"None other," said Darien. "A complete mental breakdown. He was admitted to Northgate Sanitarium up in Westchester County over the weekend. I found out only a few minutes ago."

Kate couldn't fathom the news. Jonathon Rorimer—so brutally on top of every scheme—in an institution? "Edward, this doesn't even make sense. Are you sure about this?"

"Sure as sunrise. His wife and family doctor had him committed after some really bizarre behavior and a lot of incoherent babbling they still can't make sense of."

Kate paced the room. "Where did it happen? Do they know what brought it on?"

"Apparently, it started when he yelled at his butler for letting some woman into his private study without his knowledge."

"That's seems reasonable," Kate said. "I mean…Rorimer had a bit of a reputation for…you know…cavorting, as they say. Did one of his women just decide to show up at the house?"

"Nothing like that. The real problem started when the butler couldn't *see* the woman Rorimer was talking about. He insisted there was a woman there, but the butler said there wasn't. Rorimer had a fit and threw a tray of food across the room."

Kate sat again, imagining the strain that dishonesty and scheming can place on a person. "How strange, Edward."

"It gets worse. Rorimer started ranting—something about Indians and this invisible woman wanting to do a painting of the room and how even dead people can be forgetful. And…"

Although Edward Darien went on, Kate hardly heard another word. She'd had a stunning thought—a dead woman who paints? Was it possible…again?

"So, the fact is, Kate Gannon, the notorious Jonathon Rorimer is going to be in no position to render support of any kind to his inept nephew. This is going to be a piece of cake for the police. Lonny Kagan will never know what hit him."

It was late into the night before Kate could get to sleep, processing the extraordinary events…all of them shocking surprises.

One of the thoughts that emerged was how simple a life she once led, a life of reliable routine. Thinking back through all her Milston years, she couldn't recall the last time she'd been really surprised by anything, good or bad. Sad as her grandfather's passing had been, it was not a surprise. Neither was her break- up with David. Not that she had ever thought of her life at Milston as being dull. Far from it—she loved her relationship with the students, the subjects she taught, the traditions of the school, and until he revealed himself to her, she had enjoyed being a colleague of Edward Darien.

Year after year, she had been content to come home after a long day and a long commute, dropping off her slingback heels at the door, putting on her furry slippers and, because lunch was always her main meal of the day, deciding between a bowl of Cheerios or a bowl of Farina for supper. Her grandfather's words came back to her, "Are you happy?" He had asked it more than once, and every time he did, she'd dismissed his concern as being overly protective, worrying about something that was not even an issue. Not an issue at all, she had always thought. Not at all. Until Spiritu. And now, here she was with much to think about and one very important call to make. First thing in the morning she would phone Ben Sweet.

Chapter Thirty-Nine

BEN SWEET HUNG up the phone in the living room and for a few puzzling minutes processed the news that Kate Gannon had shared. It was late in the afternoon and, confusing as everything continued to be, Kate had put a weighty finishing touch on a busy day of charity and arts board meetings. He was glad she had finally been able to connect with him. Regardless of Kyle Tillis's urging, Ben Sweet had been unable to consider Kate Gannon guilty of fraud. True, it was possible for him to be taken in, but something about this young woman spoke to authenticity, exactly the kind of person Abigail would have gravitated toward. As he would have.

Still, how could his opinion of Kate Gannon do anything to explain all that had transpired…the cottage, the book, the details—so many of them, and so specific. The white gloves. He had not been able to get any of it out of his mind, and now Kate's phone call about the strange visitor to one of Milston's former board members had complicated things even further. What was he to make of it? And what about this poor young woman who'd put such a grand effort into the completion of a fabulous book. Tillis himself found her writing extraordinary. So, what was all this about?

The clock on the mantle said 5:20. He'd better get a move on if he was going to make it into the City on time for the 7:30 fundraiser at the Algonquin, the first he was to attend since Abigail's death. He still had a difficult time connecting those two words—Abigail and death.

He took the framed picture of the two of them off the mantle and looked at it. Her loving ways, her beautiful smile had brightened every moment, lightened the burden of any trial, inspired the best in him. He had wanted to please her always. *Why were you taken so young, so soon, my sweet and gifted Abigail? I would have gladly gone in your place.*

He went into the bedroom and removed his clothes before heading into the bathroom to shower. The hot water was a release for him, as if to purge him of his grief. He let the water pour over him until the entire room was filled with a steamy mist into which he thought he might one day escape. But as was the case so many times this past year, the thundering water merely muffled the sound of his weeping.

After a while, he stepped out, his entire body nearly scalded from the heat, and lifted the over-sized towel off the wall hook. He rubbed his head vigorously, then dried off before wrapping the towel about his waist. Then, as the vapor gradually lifted, he stood before the mirror to run a comb through his hair. And that's when he saw it, so plain and indisputable that it took his breath away and forced him to take a step back—written on the steamy mirror, the words he spoke to her as she lay dying, the last words he would ever say to his beautiful Abigail, *Breathe with me. Breathe.*

He glanced quickly from side to side into the disappearing mist to see…what…to see…her. He whispered her name, then stepped forward and placed his open hand over the words, as if he would be able to touch not only her words but her hand as well. *Abigail.*

Chapter Forty

KATE FOLDED A few items of clothing and put them into her small suitcase. "Please think about it, Ellen."

"I don't have to think about it. You know how I feel—Spiritu is sweet and bucolic with a big dose of boredom."

"I just figured since Father Elway is hosting the abbey's first community event in the new reception area, you'd like to come out with me. It's only for the long weekend. I'd love for you to meet Father. And Matt. And the others. Think of it as a bit of a getaway from what's going on for you around here. Besides, I'm going to nag you the way you nagged me when I lost my job, and I'm not going to give up any more than you did." Ellen was sitting on the edge of the bed as Kate packed. Kate reached over and touched her hand. "Please come. I've got a one o'clock meeting in the City, so I likely won't be back till early evening. We can leave first thing in the morning."

"Hmm," was Ellen's only response.

THE uptown train came speeding past and right behind it the local that Kate needed to get to the midtown offices of

Tillis, Wilkes and Gorman. If it weren't for Ben Sweet's gentle manner when he phoned her, Kate would be terrified. As it was, she had already twisted her lace handkerchief into a tight little rope, wondering what Kyle Tillis might have in store for their meeting. Based on his demeanor at Abigail's cottage nearly two weeks earlier, it was not inconceivable that he might want to press charges of some kind. Maybe he would just tell her that they would publish Abigail's art book without Kate's writings. She would be disappointed, of course, but at least Abigail's book would be in print and Kate might be spared a lawsuit or, God forbid, jail time. Edward Darien's shocking news about Rorimer had lifted one burden; she could only hope that this afternoon's meeting would do as much.

On the twenty-seventh floor of the Chandriss building, Kate was directed to Kyle Tillis's private office suite, an elegant, art deco space in keeping with the architecture of the historic building itself. "I'm Kate Gannon," she told the tailored looking woman whose desk plate read "Miss Jannell."

"Yes," the woman said, with a slight smile, and gestured to a small area of cream-colored leather chairs with wide curved wooden arms. "Please just have a seat, Miss Gannon. Mr. Tillis will be right with you."

Three of the walls were lined with large, smartly framed images of magazine and book covers that represented the publishing house of Tillis, Wilkes and Gorman. The minimal, if stylish, geometric furnishings were not Kate's taste, but she did admire the clean lines and decorative curves of two inlaid smoky glass and brass side tables. She wished she knew what to expect. But…she would not be intimidated.

When Ben Sweet called the day before, he had simply invited her to a meeting with him and Kyle Tillis. "There's an important matter we need to discuss with you," was how he'd put it.

Miss Jannell's desk phone buzzed and when she hung up, she summoned Kate. "Mr. Tillis will see you now." Then she opened the double mahogany doors to a spacious room where the weightiness of a dark and massive desk was offset by sleek and streamlined deco trappings. Kyle Tillis's friendly greeting surprised her as both men approached.

"So glad you could come in today," Tillis said, extending his hand.

"Good to see you again," Ben Sweet said, appearing to notice that Kate was wearing the short white gloves she said Abigail had given her.

"Thank you," was all she seemed able to say for the moment, more curious than ever.

Tillis and Ben Sweet led Kate to a cluster of armchairs by a corner window, where a coffee table was set with tea and coffee service. "May I pour you a cup?" Tillis asked.

"No thank you," she said, pleased but hesitant. Ben Sweet deferred as well, as Tillis poured himself a cup from the silver pot. Kate removed her gloves and put them into her leather handbag, and for the next few minutes the three engaged in sociable small talk about the weather, the view from the twenty-seventh floor, and the fact that in only two more weeks there would be a Labor Day parade up Fifth Avenue.

"I owe you an apology, Miss Gannon," Tillis said to her at last. "My behavior the first time we met was, in the least, rude, hasty and moronic. I hope you'll forgive me."

Kate looked to Ben Sweet, whose smile served to affirm Tillis's gesture.

"I'm not sure how else you should have reacted given the circumstances," she said. "So, I do have to wonder why you are now so…so…"

"Eager to appease?" Tillis said.

"Yes."

"Things have changed." Tillis looked at Ben, who hesitated before leaning in.

"Something has happened, Kate," Ben said, "and it's only because Kyle Tillis and I have such a long and trusting relationship…friendship, really…that he has…come to understand."

Kate looked from one to the other for a hint of meaning.

Ben Sweet took a deep breath. "Abigail…has contacted me."

Kate drew back and put her hand to her mouth. "Oh, Ben. Oh, my God."

And for the next few minutes, Ben Sweet explained the incident that occurred following his shower—Abigail's message on the mirror.

"I wouldn't have believed it," Tillis chimed in, "except that I know Ben and I knew Abigail. I guess by now we all have to agree that something extraordinary has occurred."

"I also told Kyle about Matt Reagan finding the glass of lemonade on the kitchen counter and the incident with that Milston board member."

Kate sat wide-eyed, shocked and relieved. "Nothing about this has been easy to grasp, but I'm just so glad that my experience with Abigail has been validated." She looked at Kyle Tillis. "At least I hope it has."

"It has, Miss Gannon." Tillis got up, walked over to his desk and picked up a large, flat envelope, which he carried back to his chair. "One thing that I never doubted through all of this was that you are a gifted writer, and now that I know the truth about this extraordinary thing that happened, I want to take advantage of that talent."

"I don't understand."

"The book you worked on with my wife's artwork is amazing," Ben Sweet said. "I believe Abigail wanted us to find you."

Kyle Tillis leaned forward and handed Kate the envelope. "This is an offer for you to come to work for Tillis, Wilkes and Gorman as an Editor at Large."

Kate sat back and looked at Ben Sweet, then back at Tillis. "I don't know what to say. I guess this is just more of what already is so much to comprehend."

"As you may be aware, Miss Gannon...actually...I'd like

to call you Kate," Tillis said, "we have four major magazine publications. Two of them are fashion and lifestyle, one is homespun feel-good, and one is the natural world. I can see you in the two latter magazines."

"I…I…thank you," she said. "Trust me, this is the farthest thing from what I had expected. And, frankly, I don't know what I would do? What would my job be?"

"Articles, essays, captions, creative copy wherever needed," Tillis said.

Kate turned in her chair to look at Ben Sweet more directly. "I have to ask you. Maybe you're the only one who would know—do you believe this is something Abigail would want for me? Is this something she might have been leading me towards?"

Ben Sweet reached over and touched the arm of her chair. "I believe it is." He gestured to Tillis. "And just so you know— as tough as this fellow was that day at the cottage is also how generous and caring he is. Kyle Tillis is someone that Abigail had the greatest admiration for."

"All the information is in the envelope," Tillis said. "You'd start right after Labor Day, if that works for you, and you'd be assisting my Managing Editor for a few weeks as a way to bring you up to snuff on how we do things and why. I know you're going to fit right in."

ALL the way back to Brooklyn, as if in a daze, Kate felt her heart pounding to the rhythm of the train. She could hardly believe what had just happened. The end of summer was at hand and, oh, how different everything was, how different she was, from the way things were before she had ever heard of Spiritu. She couldn't wait to tell Matt, but she knew she must not mention any of this to Ellen. Not right now. Not when there was even the slightest possibility that Kate's extraordinary news would serve as too great a contrast to her friend's deep sense of loss.

The first thing she did when she got home was phone Matt, never more thankful that she was able to reach him on the first try. Then, she hurried next door to try and talk Ellen into coming with her to Spiritu for the weekend. Now, more than ever, she just couldn't see leaving her behind, all of which made it much more gratifying when she saw Ellen's travel bag packed and ready to go.

Ellen smirked. "I said to myself, 'why not?' Boredom would be an improvement in my life right now."

Chapter Forty-One

Kate's contacts at Fordham understood completely. "We hate to lose you, but we can see why a venerable Fifth Avenue publishing house might take precedence."

Edward Darien didn't understand at all. "I'm shocked by your decision to go elsewhere, Kate, after all we've been through together."

"Oh, Edward. After all we've been through together, are you really so shocked that I would go elsewhere?"

Matt was thrilled. Kate would be able to do most of her writing from home and since they had planned to build a house in Hicksville, the commute would be manageable on those days when she did go into the City.

She wouldn't tell Ellen until after the weekend. Nor did Ellen know the truth about Abigail. Kate's hope was that this could be a true getaway for her friend.

As they entered the bungalow, it occurred to Kate how different everything was from the last time she had put the key in the door. "I love this place."

"Don't get me wrong," Ellen said. "Just because Spiritu isn't my kind of vacation spot, doesn't mean I don't see its charm."

They began unpacking. Ellen would have the bedroom, same as last time. "Father Elway says that since summer's winding down, and I've got to get back to Brooklyn, you're welcome to stay on as a guest of the abbey. It would only be for a few weeks."

Ellen sat on the edge of the bed and cried. "My life is a mess. It's just a mess."

Kate pushed the suitcase away and sat beside her. "But not for long." She rubbed Ellen's shoulder. "Things will get better. You're a smart person. You're a good person. And you've always been a great friend to me. You helped me through my rough time. Let me help you through yours."

Ellen held a handkerchief to her eyes and laughed. "And you think you're helping by throwing me down the rabbit hole in this crazy little Alice-in-Wonderland place of yours?"

"Oh, you don't know the half of it, my friend."

"That's exactly what I'm afraid of."

ON Saturday afternoon, more so than ever, the abbey reception was a feast of beauty, gaiety and sanctuary, welcoming a few dozen visitors to the very first community event. With a soft background of Celtic strings, the place was alive with chatter and high spirits along with Mrs. Wick's spread of tea sandwiches and sweets.

Kate was happy to finally introduce Ellen to Matt and

Father Elway. "And this is Father Garrett…and Mrs. Wick. You couldn't have better people to look after you."

As the event was winding down, Father Elway came over to where Kate, Matt and Ellen were sitting. "Well, what do you say, Ellen? Will you be our guest for the next little bit? It's just a few weeks. And I can already tell that our hamlet could use a bright spirit like yours."

Ellen looked to Kate and Matt. "Well, it's not the Bahamas, but it's got charm—a lot of it. I think I'll give it a go, Father."

"Wonderful. That's wonderful," Father Elway said, clasping his hands together.

Matt reached over and touched Ellen's hand. "I think so too."

"Have they told you about the garden?" Father Elway asked. "It's right out through those doors. Why not take a look while there's still a bit of light to the day?"

Ellen smiled. "I think I will."

By then everyone had gone. Father Elway sat with Kate and Matt. "I can see why you and she are such good friends."

"But it hurts me, Father, to see her going through such a hard time."

Father Elway looked off. "Well, we mustn't forget that wondrous things can happen here in Spiritu."

Matt put his arm around Kate. "I'm thinking of that very first day you came to the abbey and…"

The back door flew open. They quickly stood as Ellen came rushing in straightening her skirt. "You didn't tell me about that crazy little bird with the clipped wing. He nearly knocked me off my feet."

For a long moment there was only stunned silence as the others looked at each other, wide-eyed.

Father Elway rubbed his chin. "Wondrous things," he whispered.

WONDER

No Small

WONDER

(PREVIEW)

A Novel

— MARY FLYNN —

Chapter One

"WHAT HAVE I done?" Ellen stood on the porch outside her bungalow, staring at the woods and wondering how on earth she had agreed to stay for two weeks. Two weeks. She watched the trees stir. No other movement, except the occasional squirrel. She listened. Nothing, except the cheep and chitter of the birds. Without that, she would probably be able to hear the blood moving through her arteries. "My God."

"Just give it a try," Kate had said—wonderful, optimistic Kate. "You'll see how fast the place can grow on you." Now Kate had gone back to Brooklyn to start her new job, and here was Ellen, a good two hours from the City…or any place like it. It would grow on her, all right, like mold on a wet carpet.

"Wondrous things can happen in Spiritu," Father Elway had said, that first evening she'd arrived at the abbey. But was it a wondrous thing that a clipped-wing bird had flown up out of the boxwood hedge while she was visiting the prayer garden, nearly knocking her to the ground? Father Elway didn't seem at all surprised. "Looks like our little friend has returned. I do hope you're all right, Miss Castle."

It was Kate who had discovered this remote hamlet earlier that summer through a tiny classified ad in the paper, then promptly ditched their plans to go to a resort in the Berkshires. Ellen had grumbled about it and worried too, fearful that her friend was going into hermit mode following a couple of disastrous events in her life. Ellen had wanted no part of it. Now here she was herself, unable to believe she had let Kate Gannon talk her into using the last two weeks the bungalow was available before the official end of the rental season.

Ellen turned to go inside. It had to be time for lunch, but the kitchen clock said 10:30. This was going to be another long, long day, just like the one before. She would have to find a way to tell the people at the abbey that she would not be staying—tell them something terrible had happened, someone back home had come down with something… deathbed stuff, her house in Brooklyn had caught fire. That's it—her bungalow caught fire. Hmm. She made a cheese sandwich and thought it over.

Kate had asked her what there was to complain about. And to a point, her friend was right. The cottage was neat and quaint, with deep comfy chairs covered in floral chintz, thick rugs throughout, a pristine kitchen with yellow gingham curtains, and a cozy bedroom with maple furniture. There was a yard, front and back, along with a porch shaded by a huge tree, sycamore or maple, she hadn't looked that closely. Mrs. Wick, the housekeeper at the abbey, which owned the rentals as a source of income, had left a generous picnic basket of cheeses, bread, eggs, milk and sweets, along with a pound package of coffee. What was there not to like?

Plenty.

She hadn't seen a single person. Of course, she hadn't gone anywhere except for a stroll up and down a few of the narrow lanes. Lanes flanked by woods that mostly hid whatever small houses there were. To top it off, she had no car. She was from Brooklyn, for heaven's sake—buses, trolleys, cabs, subways. She'd had a car for her real estate business, but not anymore, a fact she didn't even want to think about. Otherwise, who needed a car, except someone out on Long Island in a tiny village called Spiritu, a hundred miles from home? She took her sandwich out onto the porch.

In fairness, there was a bus you could catch about a ten-minute walk from the bungalow. It could take you to town. Hicksville. She'd been there once, weeks earlier, when she had taken the train out from Brooklyn to visit Kate. It was okay—quaint and historic. She took a bite of her sandwich, feeling guilty to think so poorly of the place, when the accommodations were otherwise pretty nice, and the people she'd met at the abbey so friendly. But wondrous? Ha. There was no way she was staying. That's all there was to it.

A car turned into the lane. A moment later, the town-and-country pulled alongside the grass and a man dressed in black stepped out. Father Garrett, tall, lean, with a pleasing smile. "Good morning, Miss Castle. Just thought I'd stop by with the newspaper."

"Thank you, Father. Good to see you again. Would you like to come up for a cup of coffee?" Ellen wasn't thrilled passing the time of day with a priest, but hard times demanded hard choices. She had to keep from chuckling out loud.

"Oh, I can't stay, Miss Castle, but thank you. Also, I'm just wondering how you've been sleeping. I know Miss Gannon… Kate…had a particularly challenging time getting used to our nights out here. The quiet, you know. But it all worked out."

She didn't have the heart to tell him that it didn't matter because she wasn't staying. "Actually, Father, I've slept pretty well. The accommodations are wonderful." Besides, she was typically not afraid of things.

"Good to hear. Oh, and one more thing," he said, still standing at the foot of the porch steps, "hope you don't mind." He looked away and then back, lowering his voice. "Kate happened to mention that you have had some recent… difficulties. Please know that you are welcome to come and talk with any of us at the abbey…myself, Father Elway, any of the priests. We've been told that we are exceptionally good listeners."

Her back stiffened. Just how much of her private troubles had Kate told them? Ellen Castle had no intention of discussing anything with them or anyone else. "That's kind of you, Father." She picked up her sandwich plate. "Well, I guess I'd better get a move on, if I'm going to catch the bus into town." She was catching the bus, all right...to get the train back home.

"See you next time, Miss Castle." When he had driven away, she went inside to pack. She hadn't the heart to tell him there would be no next time. She was done with this place. It might have been a godsend for Kate, but Ellen did not need a shoulder to cry on, priest or otherwise. She carried her plate into the kitchen and dumped the rest of her sandwich into the trash. Who said she needed a good listener? Besides, she knew what the priest really meant—prayer. They would pray about it. Well, no thanks. She would be just fine working things out on her own. She caught sight of her reflection in the kitchen window and cringed at the hardness of her face, the fixed downward slope of her lips. She couldn't remember the last time she had smiled. She put the dish in the sink and, a moment later, covered her face with her hands. The sobs were so deep she hardly recognized her own voice. The tears poured without stopping, tears she'd been holding in for weeks. No, she didn't need a good listener or a prayer or a shoulder to cry on; she needed a miracle, but it had been many years since she'd held out for a miracle. Those days were gone. And at this moment, Ellen Castle believed that her hope was gone, as well.

# *About the Author*

MARY FLYNN IS an award-winning author of poetry, fiction and nonfiction. Her writing is an imaginative mix of humor, pathos and irony that explores the human experience, often with a surprising twist. She is also an expert on leadership and service delivery, having taught and spoken for Disney Institute for nearly fifteen years before three-quarters of a million professionals including CEOs of major corporations.

As a full-time staff writer for Hallmark Cards in Kansas City, Mary wrote for every category of Hallmark greetings as well as Hallmark's special poetry collections. Since then, Mary's observational humor has appeared in the *Sunday New York Times*, *Newsday* and other dailies and magazines. She was a poetry prizewinner in the *Writer's Digest* Writing Competition, a double finalist in the Royal Palm Literary Awards, and her short story, "Jeremiah's Orchard," is published in *The Saturday Evening Post Anthology of Great American Fiction.*

Mary recently retired from her international speaking role with Disney to write full-time.

She continues to inspire organizational change and inform professional development with her groundbreaking program, "The Million Dollar Question."

On the lighter side, "Confessions of a Hallmark Greeting Card Writer" is Mary's fun opportunity to present an engaging program that delights her audiences with the how-to as well as the mishaps behind the scene at Hallmark. Her debut novel, *Margaret Ferry*, which has a five-star rating on Amazon, won the Gold Medal in fiction, the Silver Medal in Religious writing and the Silver Medal in Christian writing. Her Silver award-winner, *"Disney's Secret Sauce—the-little-known factor behind the business world's most legendary leadership,"* is enjoying five stars on Amazon.

To find out more about
Mary's books and talks please visit »

www.MaryFlynnWrites.com